HOUSE OF LIES

Merryn Allingham

House of Lies

First published in Great Britain 2018 by The Verrall Press

Cover art: Berni Stevens Book Cover Design

ISBN 978-1-9997824-3-6

Chapter One

London, October, 1849.

Through the window, a new world awaited. If she craned her head around the lifted sash, she could see the brougham at the very end of the street, the horse standing silent in the dawn mist. The time had come to leave. She opened the closet door and pulled from its depths the valise that for several days she had been packing in secret, then gathered up the very last item – the heart-shaped trinket box of Bristol blue glass that her mother had given her as a small girl. She laid it reverently between the few dresses she possessed and glanced around the room; there was nothing more to do but fasten the valise.

But now the moment was here, she was beset with panic. She had made a decision that would change her life for ever; after this, there was no going back. If only her parents had not insisted she renounce him. She loved them dearly, but she loved him more.

She pulled her woollen cape from the peg behind the bedroom door and slipped it on. The carriage would be draughty and there would be many hours of travel before they reached the south coast. Very carefully she inched the door open. Not a sound. But why would there be? She had betrayed nothing of what she intended, and in the room across the landing her mother and father slept untroubled. She was about to creep downstairs when she remembered, and went swiftly back into the room. Scrabbling under the bed, she tugged clear a square-shaped parcel, packaged in brown paper and string. Then, parcel in one hand and valise in the other, she made her way down the staircase, step by step, avoiding the last from the bottom. Its creak would surely have woken her sleeping parents.

She left the valise and the parcel in the hall while she stole into the parlour. From her pocket she drew a letter and propped it against the gilt mirror that sat above the mantelpiece. Seeing it there, its black and white characters dancing before her eyes, her heart swelled with tears. If only she could have made them understand that when they commanded her to give him up, they were asking her to give up life itself.

She stood for too long, caught between the letter on the mantelpiece and the valise that waited in the hall, but a glimpse of her mother's fine Chinoiserie clock brought her to her senses. Its ornamental hands showed half past four and she knew she must go. She reached for the large iron key and the front door opened noiselessly to her touch. Thank goodness her father was meticulous in the oiling of locks and bolts. A lump formed in her throat when she thought of him, but then she was out in the chill of an autumn dawn and her lover was walking towards her.

Chapter Two

Hastings, April, present day

I'd been wrong to come. The conviction had grown on me as I'd walked from the station, and now standing outside the cottage, I knew it for truth. I shouldn't be here. I fumbled for the key that Deepna's uncle had given me, but my hands were so cold from the freezing rain that it slipped from my grasp and fell with a jangle onto slippery stone. There was more fumbling before I could fit key to lock and push open the heavy wooden door, then gingerly back down the front steps awash with water to collect my small case. The small case said it all. I must have known I wouldn't be staying.

But it was a relief to find shelter, even though the hallway was dark and narrow and there was an unpleasantly fusty smell of a house still deep in its winter sleep. *Uncle Das has no bookings until June*, Deepna had said, *and he's happy for you to have the house on a low rent.* Hopefully June would prove more clement for Uncle Das's visitors: I'd walked through sheets of almost horizontal rain to get here.

I abandoned the case in the hall and turned into what was an attractive room. It was lighter here, but the overcast sky and driving rain still cast a gloom. An ornamented cast iron stove took up a large part of one wall, the blackened bricks on either side testifying to its age. I guessed it must be the cottage's sole form of heating and felt lucky it wasn't the middle of winter. I walked over to the bow window. It looked out on a line of black railings that climbed the entire length of the narrow street, seeming to guard the cluster of timber-framed houses. The buildings' white plastered walls and sloping ceilings, unchanged for centuries, made me feel I had entered another world.

I sank wearily into a chair. I must go back tomorrow – catch an early train and be in Hampstead well before midday. I'd leave the key at Mr Patil's as I passed, telling him there was some kind of emergency in London and I'd had to return.

Deepna would be a more difficult proposition. She had been so certain and so persuasive that I needed time away from the shop, away from the flat. *Somewhere completely different*, she'd said. Somewhere, she meant, with no link to Dan. *It will be new for you, peaceful and quiet. You can talk to people or be alone, and I'll make sure the shop runs smoothly. I'll have Julia around for anything difficult.* She was a dear girl, an irreplaceable assistant, but she had never lost someone she loved as suddenly and as brutally as I'd lost Dan. He had been torn from my life and she didn't understand, couldn't understand, the limbo in which I'd been left.

I would have done better to stay in London and keep myself busy at Palette and Paint. I'd made mistakes lately, I knew, silly mistakes. Ordering too many easels, delivering a canvas to the wrong address, forgetting to send Zac Martin his supply of Venetian Red. It was why Deepna had offered to run the shop single-handed while I sorted myself out. She didn't actually say those words, but that's what she meant. I wasn't going to sort myself out, though, sitting in a musty cottage in the middle of a strange town.

I wasn't going to sort myself out anywhere, since nothing was likely to erase that night from my memory. Dan had left shortly after five – I remembered looking at the clock – and after a scratch meal I'd watched some television, half asleep. Then washed up the last dishes, changed the water in the cat's bowl and taken myself to bed as I'd done a thousand times before. But the phone call in the middle of the night hadn't happened a thousand times before. Nor the waiting police car, its blue light chopping at the darkness. Nor the morgue and Dan's body covered with a sheet – there had been internal bleeding they told me – covered except for his feet and the manila coloured label attached to one toe.

The image haunted me still and I got up quickly and walked to the back of the house. It felt far less welcoming, the passageway dark and oppressive. It seemed as though it should lead somewhere but instead ended in a completely blank wall. At one time, I could see, there had been a doorway on the right, perhaps to an unused cellar. A tingle of unease made itself felt and I wheeled sharply to the left and into the small kitchen. An old ascot boiler clung to the wall, but an attempt had been made to give life to what was a dreary space, the worktop glowing bright blue and the cupboards painted a startling yellow.

The refrigerator had been stocked with butter and milk and a small pack of supermarket cheese. A bottle of white wine had been added, too. Thoughtful, but nothing I could make a meal of. I bent to look through the small window at the little courtyard beyond. A blue painted table and slatted chairs had survived the rigours of winter, and when the sun shone would make a pleasant place to sit. But not today, though the rain had almost stopped and the sky was marginally less grey.

Reluctantly, I picked up my handbag again; I would have to go in search of food and I'd seen a pizza shop on the seafront. It was the best I could do. There was a time when I'd looked forward to the evening meal, but now eating had become purely a means to stay alive. Dan enjoyed cooking and I enjoyed eating what he cooked. It was a civilised oasis, that moment in each day when we shared our lives over chopped vegetables and a bottle of wine. A moment to feel warm and secure.

I was checking my purse for money as the door knocker sounded. Deepna's uncle? When I'd collected the key, he had apologised profusely that he couldn't accompany me. But by now he would have closed his antiques shop and be here to discover what I thought of his cottage. When I opened the front door, though, it was a young girl who stood on the threshold.

'Hello, I'm Lucy.' Her voice brimmed with life. 'Well, actually, Lucia Martinez, but that's too much of a mouthful.' A smile spread across her face. 'I work with Das, Mr Patil.' Both her hands were gripping a swathe of tea towels. Whatever was underneath looked heavy.

'Come in – please – and put that down.'

'Phew, thanks. I was hoping I'd find you in. I didn't fancy toting this round Hastings for too long. I'll put it in the kitchen, shall I? All you need do is heat it up when you're ready to eat.'

'How nice of you.' For a moment I was taken aback by this simple act of kindness arriving so unexpectedly. It made me feel guilty I'd already decided to abandon ship.

'Think nothing of it. Look, if you're hungry, I can light the stove for you. It can be a bit temperamental. There's a knack to it, but you'll get the hang soon enough.'

'I am hungry.' And for once, it was true. It must be the sea air. 'I was going in search of a pizza.'

Lucy pulled her mouth down. 'I hope you'll think this is better. Gil says the only pizza worth eating is in Italy. He's my brother, by the way.'

'And Gil is Italian? And you, too, of course – your name…'

'Spanish. Kind of. Argentinian really and then only half. Mum is English, but our father's family come from Buenos Aires. We lived in Spain for years before we moved to England. Then Dad inherited a ranch in Argentina. Can you believe it? Neither of us fancied life on the pampas, so we stayed.'

'In Hastings?' I was curious. Lucy's background seemed altogether too exotic for this small town.

'London first. I moved here when Gil got a job in the art gallery. He's the chief curator.'

'Hastings has an art gallery?'

'It has two! Gil's is small but perfectly formed. Das said you're in that line, too. That you sell artists' supplies.'

'I do. I've a shop in Hampstead. Deepna is my assistant.'

'That must be exciting, working in such a smart area.'

If nothing exciting ever happened to me again, it would be too soon. My face must have shown what I was thinking because she said, 'Deepna told me a little of what happened. I'm so sorry – such a dreadful thing.'

'Thank you. It is dreadful but I'm coping.' I wasn't, but Lucy didn't need to know that.

She'd opened the oven door and was kneeling on the floor in order to wave a match at the stove. As if by magic,

9

it took light. 'There, give it half an hour and it should be piping.'

'It's very kind of you.' I felt obliged to keep thanking her.

'That's okay, Megan. It's all right to call you Megan? Deepna said you needed feeding up.' She stopped, aware she had betrayed a confidence.

'I know Deepna has my best interests at heart,' I was quick to say. I didn't want this bright, bubbly girl to feel bad.

'She really does. She thought you would love Hastings – it's a haven for artists, you know.'

'Is it?' I was surprised.

'There's an art school here and the town is full of students. And a lot of established artists come to paint as well. It's the quality of light – and the seascape.'

When we walked back into the sitting room, the air had cleared sufficiently to glimpse a small wedge of sea from one side of the bow window. The water was no longer an angry froth of metallic grey, and there was beauty in the way a shaft of light played across the tips of the waves.

'I can see the attraction.' And I could now. The water and the hills and the old town itself were natural subjects.

'There are masses of great views. East Beach is at the bottom of your street and, if you turn left before you get there, that's the way up to East Hill. Or you can take the funicular railway. Do you paint yourself?'

Instinctively, I covered my hand. 'No, not any more. But I enjoy walking and I'm sure I'll find plenty to interest me.' Why was I saying this when I had no intention of staying?

'You'll love Gil's gallery, too. Just say the word, and Das will let me off for an hour and I'll walk you round.'

I smiled faintly. This was getting way too difficult, but Lucy seemed to sense my reluctance and made for the door.

'Don't forget – come and visit me at the shop.'

When she'd gone, I wandered back to the kitchen and rooted through the cupboards to find plates and cutlery. A cruet of salt and pepper had survived the damp of winter, and a bottle opener was placed handily on a lower shelf. Mr Patil rose in my estimation. The chicken casserole turned out to be delicious and I savoured each mouthful. So delicious I allowed myself a glass of wine. It was the first time I'd drunk wine since... I'd thought the crash might have been due to Dan drinking, and that had put a stop to any desire for alcohol. He had been drinking a lot more than usual in the few months before he died, but the police had assured me there was no evidence to suggest alcohol had been to blame. It was plainly an accident, they said, an accident on an unlit country road. He'd swerved to avoid a deer, they thought, the tyres spinning in the mud, and then the vehicle hitting a submerged rock at the side of the road. It was as simple and as devastating as that. But why he'd been on that road, I had no idea. It wasn't the most straightforward route to Winchester.

But I must shut my mind down – its constant harrying was exhausting. I would have an early night and be up and away soon after dawn. I climbed the steep, narrow stairway, plastered white like the rest of the house, and chose the bedroom directly above the sitting room. It was the larger and brighter of the two with a solid oak beam running across the ceiling and a small, rough-hewn fireplace that stood bare and empty. I dropped my case onto the bed and rummaged for pyjamas. Lucy had been so friendly I couldn't face telling her I wouldn't be staying. Before the shop opened tomorrow, I'd post the key through the door with a note. Then back to the busyness of Hampstead, though in my heart I knew it would make little difference. There would still be a dreadful emptiness filling every minute, every hour, every day.

Losing Dan had been devastating, more so for the sense I had of something not completed. In the weeks before the accident, we'd had several disagreements – low level affairs – my mother's operatic nature had taught me to run scared of massive rows and he was too easy going to get deeply embroiled. But the disagreements were a cover for what was beneath, the feeling we were slowly growing apart. I'd wondered if he were unhappy, but I wasn't brave enough to ask. I'd meant to talk to him but I hadn't had the conversation. It seemed to me now that if I had, it might have stopped him from dashing to that conference on the spur of the moment. Stopped him from being on that country road, miles from help, alone and dying.

Chapter Three

Since the accident, I'd hardly slept and tonight was destined to be no different. If anything, my sleep was more fitful. The small hours saw me in a tangle of rumpled sheets, throwing myself from one side of the bed to the other desperate to find rest, the image of a mangled car, a mangled body, as always colonising my mind. But there was something else, too, something new. Voices. Whispers really. Unfamiliar noises I couldn't get out of my head. I was in a strange bed, I reasoned, in a strange room, and had lived through a difficult day – it wasn't surprising I was disturbed.

Whatever the reason, by the time my travel clock showed six in the morning, I'd had enough. A bright sun was washing the room and when I pulled back the thin curtains, I saw a sea transformed. Today it was laced with diamonds and the colour of indigo. I had an urge to walk out and discover. It was unlikely I'd get a train for several hours; meanwhile I could stretch aching limbs, pick up some breakfast on the way, and still be in time to collect my case and get to the station by nine o'clock.

Once out of the front door, I remembered Lucy's words and turned left, down the hill for several yards and then another sharp left until I reached the bottom of a long flight of steps. The sandstone cliff – East Hill, I think, was the name she'd given it – towered over me. This was going to be a long climb. The gradient turned out to be as steep as it looked and I was soon breathing hard. If the funicular had been running this early, I would have been tempted. Half way up the twisting set of steps, I stopped to take in the view.

The drop from the cliff to sea level appeared almost vertical and immediately below me, at the mouth of the valley, a wide shingle beach stretched itself to the sun. It was dotted with fishing boats, and several more arrived into harbour as I watched. Despite the early hour, a fish market was in process, already heaving with activity, the daily catch being bought and sold at a spanking pace.

The seascape was magnificent, and newly enthused I began to climb again. It was worth every step since at the very top, I found a vast grass-covered space and the most stunning vista of hills and open downland to my right and below, the grand sweep of the English Channel. I don't know how long I stood looking, but I felt my heart lighten. There was a buzz in my head, an itch to my fingers. The possibilities were endless: the Old Town, the beach, the hills, the cliffs eroded by storm into magical shapes.

But I had a train to catch and forced myself to turn back. I was half way down the hill when a voice, coming out of nowhere, startled me. 'It's a great view, isn't it?'

I'd thought myself alone, but then a man emerged around one of the turns in the steps, a few feet below me. It was a solitary spot at this time of the morning and instinctively I shrank back..

'Have you seen the fish market? It's in full swing.' The man arrived at my side and pointed to where the beach had again come into view.

'I noticed it on my way up. It's something quite new to me.' He didn't appear threatening – average height, hair a soft brown and a face that was pleasant enough. It seemed safe to talk.

'New to most people who don't know the town, but the Stade has been used for over a thousand years.'

'The Stade?'

'The beach directly below us.'

'A thousand years is quite a history. Are you a fisherman yourself?'

He gave a small laugh. 'Sometimes I wish I were.'

'But you live in Hastings?'

'I'm no native, though I've been here three years. How about you? Is this a holiday?'

'Yes. No. I'm here for the summer.' Why had I said that when I'd already decided to leave?

'You'll love it, I guarantee. Where are you from?'

'London.'

'Where else?' He smiled at me and for the first time I noticed his eyes. They were grey with a hint of green, or was that blue? They were smiling, but they held a discernment, a shrewdness, that surprised me. I doubted you'd ever be able to lie to them.

'I ought to be going,' I said rather too quickly. There was something about those eyes that made me feel a fraud.

'Then be sure to come again. And early. It's the best time of the day and the view is worth the climb. Be careful going down. The steps get steeper towards the bottom and they're still wet from yesterday's storm.'

'Thanks. I'll be careful.'

I started back down the steps, travelling as fast as I could but on my guard for slippery stone. I'd been far longer than

I'd intended; my watch was already showing eight o'clock. Somehow, though, once I reached the road, I found myself slowing, legs lagging, feet dragging. There was no real rush, was there? Nothing to make me hurry back to Hampstead. My assistant was expecting to run the shop for weeks and I knew she'd do it every bit as well as me. I might stay – a few days. Deepna would be delighted if I did. Julia, too.

When Hastings was first suggested, I'd been worried she would think I was running away, refusing to accept the truth of my new life. Julia was strong and would face loss, if it came to her, far more robustly than I had. The night of the accident I'd phoned her, hoping, longing, she would go to the morgue in my stead. That's how feeble I was. She was at a party with friends I didn't know and had been drinking heavily. It was too far away, she said, to call a cab. She'd have to stay over, but promised she'd be with me in the morning. And she was. She always kept her promises, and in the days that followed she'd been my strength. Along with Deepna, she'd encouraged me to pack my case. *Give Hastings a try,* she'd urged. *I'll call every day and see how things are going.*

She hadn't phoned last night, but I could guess why. She'd had to travel down to Bath the day before I left and she must still be there. She'd been hoping to stay only one night, but Nicky was her son, after all, and deserved to see his mother on his birthday. I knew she wouldn't want to speak to me in front of others – right now, I could be unpredictable – but she'd call as soon as she got back to London.

The first thing that hit me as I neared the cottage, was the large box sitting on the doorstep. My first thought was that a carrier had made a wrong delivery, but the parcel seemed familiar, and then it came to me. These were my artists' materials. I'd packed them up and sent them ahead days ago and, now I'd decided not to stay, I'd have to make arrangements to send them back.

I heaved the box inside – how much had I packed! – and left it in the sitting room, meaning to make a cup of tea. I was parched after the walk and in my rummagings last night had found an old box of teabags left by last summer's visitors. But when I got to the sitting room door, an intense desire to unpack my paints and brushes and easel took a grip. I wanted to get those colours down. The sea and the hill. But first the street outside – the red brick, the white plastered walls, the dark wood beams, the black iron railings. It was all there. On the spur of the moment, I tore off the packaging and ripped open the box, unfolding the easel and setting it up in the bow window.

'So you do paint?' It was Lucy. In my struggle with the box, I'd left the front door open.

'Only a little. Nothing I'd want to admit to.'

'Far better than I'd ever manage, I'm sure. I hope you slept okay? I thought you might like some breakfast. The café down the road does a good scrambled egg unless you prefer something posher.'

'No, I was…' I trailed off. How could I tell this engaging girl that I had no time for breakfast, in fact I'd have to run if I were to catch the train I intended? It wouldn't be kind. And it would be illogical. I'd set up an easel – why would I be catching a train?

'That's a great idea,' I heard myself say. 'Thanks for stopping by.'

The cafe was a five minute walk along the seafront and already busy. With practised ease, Lucy got our order in before a gaggle of office workers arrived for their take-away coffees. She sat me down at a small table overlooking the beach and smiled out at the sparkling scene a few yards distant.

'Brilliant on a day like this, isn't it?'

I had to agree and told her of my hike up the East Hill, and how wonderful the air had been and how exciting the view of sea and sky.

'Hastings is going to keep you busy,' she teased. 'You'll never leave your easel.'

I didn't want to disappoint her so I nodded and reached for my coffee cup. I saw her eyes fix on my scarred hand.

'An accident years ago,' I explained. 'It means I'll never be able to paint professionally.'

Her young face filled with concern. 'What a dreadful thing to happen.'

Another dreadful thing. Perhaps there are people who are destined to take on the dreadful things of the world and so protect everyone else.

'It was bad at the time,' I agreed, 'but I've been lucky. My fingers have regained enough movement over the years to be able at least to hold a paint brush.'

'So were you going to be an artist?' she ventured.

'Instead of running a shop for artists?'

'Yes. I mean… We all change our minds, don't we?' She was trying rather awkwardly to be kind. 'I still don't know what I want to do. My job with Das is only temporary.'

'*I* knew what I wanted.' My voice carried conviction. I'd known since I was a young child, but the accident had put paid to any career in art. A saucepan of boiling water tends to do that. 'But I had to drop out of college. The scar tissue tightens, you see, and you lose dexterity.'

She made sympathetic murmurings and we drank our coffee in silence. I didn't mention that my mother had hurled enough water to send me to a burns ward for weeks.

The scrambled egg arrived and Lucy set to with a will. 'I suppose you couldn't paint with your left hand?' she asked in a muffled voice.

'My tutors suggested I try, but it was just too difficult and I gave up. Now I use my hands to sell instead – it's easier.'

'And more lucrative, I imagine.' She threw back her head and laughed. 'Have you had your shop long?'

The scrambled egg was as good as she'd promised, soft and buttery, and sitting on nicely crunchy toast, and I took my time to reply. 'Five years now. And it's worked well. At first I was a bit dubious I'd enjoy dealing with artists when *I* couldn't paint, but I like them and it helps me feel I've kept a little of my old self.'

And a little of my old self-esteem. It had taken a long time to get to that point. For months after the accident, I'd been drained of confidence and filled with mistrust for everyone and everything. I'd been lost and rootless in what had become a dangerous world.

'It sounds like the shop idea was a success.' She gulped down a mouthful of coffee.

'It was. It is. Palette and Paint is probably the best thing I've ever done. It was a step in the dark at first – a gamble moneywise – but we've made it work. I guess the shop opened in the right place at the right time.'

'You share it with someone else then?'

The 'we' had slipped out automatically. Julia was as much a part of Palette and Paint as I was. 'Julia is my partner. Julia Fallon. She's been with me since the beginning. She's my financial guru, a whizz at the books. She's also my best friend.'

'I hope I can meet her.' Lucy stabbed the last piece of

toast with her fork and chewed vigorously. 'She'll be down to visit you, I expect.' She said it with certainty.

'If she does, we must have a meal together – my treat after that wonderful chicken last night.'

'I'm glad you liked it.' Her cheeks flushed with pleasure. 'To be honest, it's the only thing I can make. Gil is a much better cook than me.'

'One dish is all you need. I could eat that casserole every evening.'

'Oh lord!' She jumped up suddenly, clasping her watch and banging her knee on the underside of the table. 'I should be at the shop. You must give us a look-in when you have a minute. Some of the stuff is tat but don't tell Das I said so. Some of it's genuine, though. Antiques, you know.'

'Some time this week, perhaps?'

'That's great. I'll look forward to it. I can take you along to the gallery afterwards.'

She lunged to the floor and retrieved a small backpack, then with a wave of her hand she was out of the door and heading in the opposite direction from the way we'd come. Had I just made a false promise? I thought of her bright, friendly face. Thought of the easel I'd set up in the sitting room. I wouldn't be false, I decided. I'd stay, but not for long, certainly not as long as Deepna envisaged. But long enough. And I would paint every day I was here.

My heels had a gentle spring in them and, retracing my steps along the seafront, my shoulders felt looser and lighter. I reached the cottage in record time and spent a good half hour unpacking my box of goodies, disentangling every item from layers of bubble wrap and arranging them as best I could on the small table that sat beneath the window. The light had retained its earlier purity, but grown warmer as the clock moved on to midday and the street was bathed in sunlight. That's what I would paint – the view from this window. Yesterday, I'd seen the possibilities and today I'd make a start. I looked around the room. The walls were bare except for one small picture hanging in the furthest corner. I could paint a canvas for this room, a present for Uncle Das for allowing me to stay at a peppercorn rent.

A street scene, though, might not complement the sole image Mr Patil had thought to hang. I'd taken only vague notice of it before, but now I went up and looked closely. I was surprised. It wasn't a painting at all, but an embroidery. The image of a child, a young girl, embroidered in fine stitches and subtle hues. The girl wore a figured blue gown, its motifs picked out in a deeper blue silk, and its voluminous sleeves boasting small frilled cuffs. A bodice, white and tiny, was decorated with a brooch in the shape of a silver butterfly. It was exquisitely sewn. The girl's hair was a rich auburn and flowed loosely down to her shoulders, her complexion clear and creamy, with the slightest tinge of pink, an echo of the pink lilies half hidden in a background of dark green leaves.

How wonderful to be the mother of such a child! The thought hit me without warning, and a longing, as strange as it was powerful, swept through me. There had been a time when I'd dared to suggest a baby to Dan, but he had looked so horrified I never mentioned it again.

I gave myself a shake. This was getting me nowhere. But when I turned to go, something drew me back to the picture. It was the child's eyes that made me prisoner. Eyes of dreamy blue, eyes that were innocent yet searching. They pulled me in, making me look ever deeper, as though I were walking into the picture itself, as though I were walking through it. The eyes sought something from me and I struggled to understand.

And struggling, I lost all focus. The air became dense and the embroidery seemed to swirl in a mist and vanish from view. I tried to fix my gaze on the wall where it had been, but the wall was bare. And the room itself was changing – fading into sepia, returning and fading again. I was ill, I must be. For some reason, the picture had stirred hurtful memories of Dan and I was suffering the breakdown I'd feared. I must keep it at bay. I'd escape the room, go upstairs and rest, and the madness would subside. But then I heard the noise. Whispers, the whispers of the night, but this time louder. Sounds coming nearer. A man's voice close by, then a woman's low laugh and the door opening.

Chapter Four

'**P**ut me down Spencer, this minute!' Sophia was laughing, but she could feel him stagger a little as he pushed open the sitting room door.

'Not until I have carried you over every threshold in the cottage.'

'You will drop me well before you've finished.'

'Probably. You must have eaten another dinner when I wasn't looking.'

She laid back in his arms and smiled up at him. 'We have been married an hour and already you are insulting me.' She tapped him on the nose. 'Might it be that you lack the strength?'

'I will make sure you know differently – and soon!'

He bent his mouth to hers and for several minutes she allowed herself to cling to him. Then she broke free and smoothed a lock of hair back from his forehead. 'You had better put me down.'

At that, he straightened his back and walked across the room to lay her gently on the couch. 'There, my lady. Welcome to your new home.' He pulled a white linen handkerchief from his trouser pocket and dabbed at his forehead. 'The weather has gone mad, I believe. The dawn was chilly enough, but now… who would have thought it this hot in October?'

'The sun has shone especially for us.' She felt a bubble of joy within. 'It has been the most wonderful day.'

He came to sit beside her and took hold of her hand. 'It has, Sophia, the very best day of my life. And we have even better to come.'

She leaned against his shoulder. So far their happiness had been hard won, but they were here and they were married and a new life was beginning. 'I think St Clements the nicest of churches. I'm so glad we waited to marry until we arrived. London churches are too large and much too fusty.'

'The vicar was fusty enough, though the church itself was splendid. He didn't like the special licence, did he? Suspicious chappie – looked at me as if I had abducted you.'

The vicar had not been far from the truth, but if it were an abduction, it was the most glorious ever. And so, too, this cottage, a home of their own at last. 'I want to explore. You told me there was a dear little courtyard through the kitchen door.'

'You can explore all you want, my darling, but first I should retrieve our valises. I left them on the pavement, remember? Any miscreant could make off with everything we own.'

'Our whole world packed into two suitcases! How frightening that is.'

'Then I had better rescue them,' he said cheerfully.

She had few clothes, but even so it had been a scramble to pack sufficient for the coming winter in one valise, and do so secretly. Distressing, too. And distressing to leave her parents with only a short note of apology. Deep beneath the joy, there was a heaviness she could not lose.

Two loud bangs sounded from the narrow hall. Spencer had hefted the heavy bags up the front steps and thumped them down, one after another, on the stone floor. He was out of breath when he reappeared.

'All done. It must be time to find the bedroom.' He was eager and shining, but when he saw her face he came over to the couch and knelt beside her. 'You are not to worry. Your parents will relent. They have always liked me, and how could they not be happy that you have found your true love?'

'They were happy,' she conceded. 'At first. And they do like you, Spencer, but they hate that your parents so clearly oppose our marriage. It was the minute my father learned of Mr Wayland's anger that he forbade me to see you.'

And worse still, had issued an ultimatum that if she did not relinquish Spencer, she must leave the family home. There had been no alternative then to the special licence and the waiting brougham early this morning.

'He will come about.' Spencer exuded assurance. 'After all, it is an advantageous marriage for a clerk's daughter. Once your father sees that my family's disapproval means nothing, he will welcome us into his home.'

Sophia frowned, worry eating at her. 'But *does* your family's disapproval mean nothing? Your parents have withdrawn their support, and with it all offer of help.'

'Papa must learn to accept I am determined on a different life from the one he has decreed. Once he realises my desire to paint is not a passing phase, his attitude will change.'

Spencer was used to getting his own way, she had learned that very quickly. She wondered sometimes if his insistence they marry was as much a rejection of his parents' wishes as love for her. One thing was certain, he did not brook refusal. He had been treated with indulgence, granted the freedom to play with paint – until it was time for him to take his place at Barnes and Wayland as his father's successor.

Mr Wayland must have hoped that allowing his son to attend art school would purge him of 'all that nonsense' Instead, it had simply confirmed to Spencer that he was an artist and not a stockbroker. He had no head for figures or for money, only how to spend it. Sophia could applaud her new husband's courage, but it did nothing to stem her fear.

'We will manage,' he was insisting. She tried to look confident, but evidently failed because he reached out for her hands and gripped them tightly. 'Hastings is an inexpensive town and we have enough money to pay rent for the next six months. The inheritance from my godfather will see us through. And by the time that has gone, I will have sold some pictures. Come, let's unpack. I want to set up my easel immediately. Well, almost immediately.' He stroked the soft white flesh of her inner wrist and she felt the familiar melt at his touch.

'I'm not doubting for a moment that you will sell your pictures.' Her belief in him was total and she wanted him to know it. 'But we will need money for furniture. There is very little here.'

Twin glances around the room confirmed her words. Apart from the couch and a table, a wooden settle filled the space beneath the bay window, and to the side of the cast iron stove, a small cane chair sat forlorn, its back badly in need of repair.

'The rent is dear enough for such a dilapidated place, I grant you.' He got to his feet. 'But we have a table and chairs and there is a bed in the room upstairs. I saw it when I paid the advance. What more could we want?'

For the moment, her dark brown eyes had lost their sparkle. 'It is only I worry that if we should fall into debt, we have no one to turn to. We cannot go back.'

'No indeed. Nothing would induce me to speak to my father again – until he is willing to listen. But I have plans, exciting plans. Only a few weeks ago, I met Rossetti. He has formed a group of artists, a secret society almost, and I'm convinced he and his fellows will prove the greatest challenge to British painting. I intend to be with them, Sophia.'

Spencer had mentioned these rebel artists to her several times. His enthusiasm for their new style of painting was boundless, but a harder life had taught her the unkind distinction between dream and reality. He might talk of challenge and successful rebellion, but these things did not always materialise and she must support him in every way possible.

'I can bring in a little money, too.' She looked around the room. 'The light here is good and sewing will be no problem. I have been trained by one of the best couturiers in London – I shouldn't find it difficult to attract customers.'

He frowned. 'I have no wish that you sew for other women. That is finished. Your life is with me now and I shall provide whatever we need.'

She would say no more for the moment, but she was adept with a needle and could foresee that the time might come when she would need her skills again. Her family's watchword had been security, Rowena Fairchild saving every penny she could from her wages as a jobbing dress-maker to pay for her daughter's apprenticeship. It was a different world from Spencer's. His mother could afford the clothes fashioned at Delauney's, otherwise how would she ever have met him?

The moment she had been called to the shop floor by Madame Vionnet was still vivid in her memory. She was to model a dress for a customer, an older woman, very thin and very fashionable. Mrs Wayland had been escorted by her son that day and he'd appeared mesmerised by the young girl walking the length of soft blue carpet.

His mother had not. She had dismissed the dress after only a few minutes, saying in a bored voice, *I don't think so*, and then swept up her handbag and left for the town house in Green Street. It hadn't been that way for her son. That evening when Sophia had finished work, he had been waiting in the alley outside Delauney's and persuaded her to eat her evening meal with him. She had felt daring doing so, and uncomfortable when she arrived home two hours late and was compelled to lie to her parents. Her father, ever the solicitor's clerk, had looked at her over his spectacles; she had felt the force of his gaze and quaked inwardly.

She did not want to think now of her father and jumped up from the couch. 'At least you must allow me to do my embroidery. See here. I have brought a present for our new home.' She picked up the brown paper parcel and tore off the wrapping. 'It's fortunate we have a picture rail and I can hang it straight away.'

She carried the embroidery to the wall. It had taken many months of intricate sewing, but she felt immense pride in the work. She'd had the canvas framed last month, pretending to her mother it would grace the family sitting room, but secretly hoarding it for the home she hoped to have with Spencer.

'There.'

She stood back to view the picture and was delighted. It

was a blaze of colour in an otherwise dreary room. She had chosen exactly the right shade of blue for the figured cotton the girl was wearing, and how wonderfully dreamy she had managed to make the child's eyes. A cherub of a child, the child Spencer and she would one day have. 'It brightens the room, do you not think?'

'It looks well enough,' he said a trifle grudgingly, 'but you need to forget sewing and learn to paint. You have an artist's eye for line and colour, but what you lack is technical knowledge. And I will be the one to teach you – you will be my best pupil.'

'Thank you, kind sir. I would like that.' She twirled a circle in the middle of the room, her skirt of pink silk echoing the lively movement.

'Enough! There are other things to learn, my darling girl, and I suggest we make a start.' He stopped her mid-pirouette and wrapped her in his arms. Then very gently stroked the dark ringlets to one side and brushed his lips against her cheek. Then his mouth found hers and he kissed her long and deep.

Chapter Five

A loud ringing and I started up, trying to dislodge from my head a vision that had been so sharp it had seemed real. I glanced wildly around. The noise was coming from one of the easy chairs where I'd flung my bag when I came in. The phone, it was my phone.

'Hallo.' My breath was coming short. I could hear my heartbeat thump in my ears.

'Megan? Are you okay?'

Julia. Thank God. 'Yes, yes fine,' I said as normally as I could. There was no way I could tell her what I'd just seen, what I'd just heard. It was too crazy. I was crazy. I'd be in the hands of a psychiatrist if I weren't careful.

'Yes, I'm fine,' I repeated more slowly. 'A bit breathless, that's all. I ran from the kitchen when I heard the phone.' In the circumstances, a white lie was excusable.

'How are you doing by the seaside? What's the place like? Deepna said it was pretty basic.'

'It is, but it has charm. It's very old and quirky. I think you'd love it. And there's a beautiful small garden outside the kitchen door – a real sun trap.'

'Brilliant.' I could hear the relief in her voice. 'And Hastings – how have you found it?'

'Not great when I first arrived. There was a howling south-westerly and torrential rain. But today the sun is shining and it's magic.' I was keen to talk up the town's attractions. I wanted Julia here, more now than ever. Something to anchor me, something to prevent me tipping over the edge. 'How was Bath?'

'Much the same. It doesn't change.'

As always, she was tight-lipped when talking of her son. He was barely a presence in Julia's life and to all intents and purposes she was childless, which suited her fine. She'd had him at eighteen, her first year at university, putting her life on hold, which was something she'd told me would never happen again. There'd not been a question of marriage. Nicky's father was an older man, long divorced and with no wish for a permanent partner, and that suited her fine, too. It was a bonus that Mark had been delighted at becoming a father so unexpectedly, and willing and financially able to care for his son.

'And Nicky?'

'A year older.'

Sometimes Julia's flintiness upset me, she seemed to have so little feeling for the boy. But I shouldn't be surprised since family life was foreign to her. She had never known her own father and I don't think her mother had either, but it bothered neither of them.

'So, will you come down? There's a nice spare bedroom.' I didn't want to appear needy, but if Julia had walked through the door at that moment, I would have hugged her tight.

'I promised, didn't I? I can't make this weekend, but perhaps next.'

That sank my spirits. When I'd decided to stay another three or four days, I'd been hoping Julia would share them.

'Next weekend will be fine,' I said airily. 'I'll look forward to it.'

Another lie. I would have left Hastings long before then, but I couldn't say so or I'd get a lecture on how much good the change of scene was doing me. Then Deepna would be phoning, reiterating the health properties of a stay by the sea. It was easier to say nothing and simply pack up and leave when I was ready.

'I've got to go, Meg, I've a hundred and one things to sort out. Going away has put me all behind.'

I had never found it difficult to talk to Julia. We usually chatted ten to the dozen – we had ever since we'd met at her mother's gallery – but today the conversation was sticky. I wondered if she was blaming my absence for her workload. I scolded myself – she wasn't thinking that at all.

'I'll ring again,' she said, and her voice was warm and friendly.

'Thanks. When you've more time it will be good to talk, Jules.'

I threw the phone back into the chair. Good to talk, perhaps, after I'd worked out what was going on. I could do the psychoanalysis bit as well as anyone. I was disturbed and it was playing hell with my mind. If I were honest, it wasn't the first time I'd had this kind of vision; each time it had been in the aftermath of a shocking event, but nowhere near as vividly.

As a small child, my father had walked away to live in Venice. I'd made sense of it at the time by believing it was the kind of thing famous artists did, but a few weeks after he'd left, I'd seen a vision of him with my mother in the same city. At least, I thought it must be Venice. At five years old, I knew little of the world, but my father had shown me a painting of the city – a Canaletto, it had to be. The pair of them were walking hand in hand over one of the small canal bridges and my mother looked very young and very happy, which in itself was unusual. Years later, I could see it was a child's way of dealing with the misery of abandonment.

I was in my late teens before it happened again. It was after my mother had snatched a saucepan full of boiling water from the hob and changed my life. I saw her with an older woman who looked very like her. It was her own mother. My grandmother, whom I'd never known. And she'd been hurling what looked like a large china dish across a kitchen and narrowly missing the small child rooted to the floor in fear. I suppose I was trying to understand my mother's volatile temper, another attempt on my part to rationalise the hurt I'd suffered.

Was this morning's experience the same? It was odd the people I'd seen so distinctly had no connection to me, while the visions of my father and my mother were deeply personal. If it were the same mechanism at work, then surely I should have seen Dan in my attempt to come to terms with his death? But I hadn't. I'd seen complete strangers and judging from their dress, strangers from at least a hundred and fifty years ago. And I'd heard every word they said. That was new. Previously, the soundtrack to these visions had been indistinct, mere murmurings. But this time I'd heard the scene as though I'd been standing alongside, and it had been played out, not in an unknown kitchen or a European city, but in this very room. A little bleaker, a little barer, but in essence a replica, even down to the same picture.

It was the picture that had started the trouble. In studying it so intently, I must have sent a badly shocked mind into freefall. Why, I couldn't imagine, except I must be more distressed than I realised. In future I'd make sure to pass without a second glance. Right now, though, I needed some comforting.

I delved into the depths of my handbag for a photograph of Dan. He'd been my fiercest supporter, admiring the way I ran the business, insisting my damaged hand was unimportant, a single chapter in a story that was bound for success. When I was with him, I forgot my life would always be the second best I could have had. I'd look at his photograph now and remember these things. Remember him as he was, not as the crumpled body that haunted my sleep.

The old Dan smiled out from the image, a little twist to his mouth, as though he were telling me he was there for me. I'd met him a few years ago when he'd come to Palette and Paint to buy supplies. He was a teacher at a local comprehensive, but in his spare time painted furiously, always hoping for the break that would enable him to relinquish teaching and paint full-time. Not that he disliked his work, he was amazing with his students, but simply that to be a fully fledged artist was his dream.

I looked again at the enigmatic smile and knew I should have talked to him. There was a trace there of something I'd not noticed before, a hint of catch-me-if-you-can. And it was true I had never caught him. I met him when he'd called at the shop for paints – he'd won a rare commission – but then he'd asked me out for a coffee and told me he'd like to get to know me. He'd been cautious. I was protective of myself, he said later, hiding behind a barrier. He reckoned that bad things had happened to me and he hadn't wanted to rush me.

Whether or not that were true, a year later he moved in. The tenancy of his flat was up and the owner wanted to sell.

It seemed more sensible for him to share the apartment above Palette and Paint than find another place to rent. It was a sizeable flat and if I were honest, I wanted him with me. I'd grown to hope it would be permanent, and in a sense it was. Marriage and children hadn't figured, but that hadn't seemed important.

It was when I'd gazed at the child in the picture that I'd been made to question my indifference. Had the woman embroidered the portrait of her own child, I wondered? Sophia, the man had called her. She couldn't have, of course, they had only just married. They were at the beginning of their lives together and a child would come later; children, if it were a typical Victorian family. I pulled myself up on the thought. I was making these people real, assuming they had an existence beyond the turbulence of my mind. It was something I must stop.

All desire to paint had gone and I decided to spend the last hour of sunshine in the small garden. I hurried through the dark end of the hall – it hadn't felt oppressive in my fantasy, I noticed – and into the kitchen. I made a cup of tea and took it out to the painted table where the old brick paving dozed in the warmth. I was soon dozing alongside. It was a passing shadow, a coolness, that jerked me awake. I looked up at the sky and saw that cloud had temporarily blotted the sun from view. It brought with it a sudden thought, unbidden and unwelcome. She had spoken of this, hadn't she, Sophia? She had spoken of the small courtyard; her husband had spoken of the bedroom above. The surface of my skin prickled painfully. Their conversation seemed to give them an existence beyond the one scene I'd witnessed, the one room, as though they had actually walked upstairs, walked out here. As though, in fact, they *were* real.

Chapter Six

It was odd that I slept well. After yesterday's outlandish experience, I should have been pacing the floorboards, but within minutes of my head hitting the pillow, I'd fallen into a deep sleep. The night remained peaceful without a whisper to disturb me and I didn't stir until the clock showed seven in the morning. Over an early cup of tea, I tried to take stock. Had I really seen this cottage a hundred odd years ago and overheard the people who lived here? I couldn't believe it. The whole thing had to have sprung from a mind still reeling from shock. It was the only plausible explanation.

It was another bright, sunny day, the light perfect for painting. My easel was ready, my oils arranged neatly in rows across the small wooden table, so what was stopping me? I worked solidly for two hours, my mind focussed so tightly on the canvas in front of me it had little time to wander dangerous pathways. My painting was awkward. It always would be with a hand skewed out of shape by contracted scars, but despite the hindrance I was pleased with what I'd managed. The outline of a street scene was taking shape – impressionistic and colourful. Colourful enough to satisfy Rossetti himself, or any of his Pre-Raphaelite chums.

Awkward or not, painting worked its magic, and by the time I'd spent the afternoon on a long walk up the West Hill to enjoy yet another glorious view, my mind had cleared completely. I was ready to confront any number of phantom figures, if they chanced by again. The good feeling didn't desert me the next day, and for the first time in weeks, I tumbled out of bed energised and ready to work.

Breakfast was sparse – a slice of toast and a cup of tea – but it didn't matter. I was engrossed, so much so that the toast went half eaten and I let my tea go cold. I had just wiped my brush and decided to make another drink, when the front door knocker, an old brass lion's head, sounded loudly through the cottage. I thought it might be Lucy – no open door this morning – but it was the postman who stood on the threshold with a packet to sign for. I recognised Deepna's writing straightaway.

She'd parcelled up several cards of condolence that had arrived since I left and several letters addressed to me personally she hadn't wanted to open. In the event, they turned out not to be personal, but merely orders from the one or two artists who seemed to feel it was creatively necessary to deal only with me. I would have to phone the shop later and pass on the orders – Zac Martin wouldn't want to wait until I was back in Hampstead for his monthly supplies. There was another smaller envelope within the package and Deepna had stuck a post-it to it. The envelope apparently contained items returned by the police and she hadn't known whether or not to send it on, but thought I might want what was inside. *If you don't feel up to opening it, don't,* was her advice.

It would be Dan's possessions, retrieved on the night of the accident. At the thought, my new energy began to seep away. I'd asked the hospital to dump his bloodstained clothes, but the police had taken charge of any valuable items and here they were: a leather portfolio case, his phone now slightly battered, the Tissot watch he'd been so proud of, but no sign of the gold signet ring I'd given him last Christmas. I'd had it made to order, our two initials entwined on its upper face. I rummaged in the envelope again, but came out empty-handed. Perhaps under the violent impact, it had come loose and fallen into the ditch. I picked up the phone and turned it screen upwards. A picture of the two of us on a Norfolk beach last August, laughing, waving ice creams, looked out at me. The tears welled and I blew my nose hard.

I was glad I'd opened the parcel, it would only have tormented me if I hadn't, but being plunged back into the life I had known wasn't easy. Be practical, I urged myself. Check Dan's phone for people who might still not have heard he'd died. I thought I had reached everyone, but I'd been in such a state, I couldn't be certain. Deepna had been brilliant, but she didn't know many of Dan's personal contacts. I picked up the phone again and scrolled through the list. I was relieved to see I'd covered them all. All except one number which I didn't recognise. I would have to ring and leave a brief message.

I'd do it now, get it over with. But when I rang the number, a recorded message told me this was the Thornton Manor Hotel. I didn't recognise the name, but when I looked at the call log I could see Dan had phoned the place regularly over the past six months. I googled the hotel name and saw it was on a minor road, the road Dan had been travelling when he'd crashed the car.

I was puzzled. He'd been on his way to attend an art therapy course in Winchester, but maybe he'd told me wrongly – it was very much a last minute arrangement. It didn't explain the previous calls, but then Thornton Manor could be the venue for any of the job related meetings he attended. Dan was always being co-opted on to one committee or another and its members might prefer to meet away from school. But I'd better make sure there was no one at this number unaware of what had happened.

When I got through, the receptionist knew Dan's name immediately. I had been right to ring. The manager was probably an acquaintance I hadn't known about. I took a deep breath and started to explain. I still found it difficult to talk about the accident though I was getting better.

'I'm so sorry to hear that, Mrs Travis.' The woman at the other end of the phone sounded genuinely sorrowful. 'But thank you so much for letting us know. We haven't seen you both for a while, and were wondering whether to continue to reserve the room for Mr Travis.'

I stood in total silence, the phone clamped to my ear as though of its own volition.

'Hallo? Mrs Travis?'

They hadn't seen us for a while. They'd been in the habit of reserving a room for us.

'Mrs Travis?'

I dropped the phone with a loud thud on to the table, the receptionist's words still ringing in my ears. Dan had been to the hotel regularly, but I hadn't. The man I loved had been there many times, but not for any meeting with colleagues. I gripped the table with both hands, my fingers landing in a pool of titanium white. I stood immobile, unaware of the mess I'd created, hardly able to breathe while my brain contorted itself into a thousand twisted circles. He had been there to meet Mrs Travis, whoever she was. She wasn't me, that's all I knew. Not me. Instead, I was the walking cliché, trapping my lover from his phone log. I was a joke without the humour. I was the simpleton, who knew nothing of a sordid liaison with a woman I'd no idea existed.

I almost crawled to the couch. Was this really happening? If I doubted, I had only to look at the package squatting toad-like on the table to be assured that yes, it really was. How could I have missed the signs? He had been seeing this woman for months, yet I'd suspected nothing, and months suggested a steady relationship – not so sordid after all.

Before I met him, I knew Dan had drifted in and out of several affairs without any real commitment. Had this been different? Something wormed its way into my mind that was treacherous and unwelcome. Is that why his ring was missing? Had he taken it off so he could pretend to himself he was a single man? So the woman could pretend it, too? Perhaps the affair had been serious. Deep down, I'd known things weren't right between us. I had sensed him drawing away, but why hadn't he told me the truth? Hadn't I deserved it? Or was he expecting to continue his double life: on the one hand, free accommodation and painting materials and on the other, an exciting new lover. That was unnecessarily bitter of me, but I felt unnecessarily bitter. I felt a fool, a stupid grieving fool.

I almost flung the tea cup into the sink and on impulse grabbed my jacket and bag and marched out of the house. I needed time to grapple with news that changed everything. Whatever Dan had done, I would still grieve for him, but my sorrow now was layered with jealousy and cut through with doubt – about him, about me. I needed distraction, but I'd nowhere to go except take up Lucy's invitation to visit Mr Patil's shop. Anything to keep my mind from dwelling on this new disaster.

And there was no dwelling with Das Patil. I had thought that the day I'd arrived, and he was no different today. Effervescent, that was the best word to describe him. As soon as I walked through his door, he was eager to know how I was faring in the cottage, overwhelming me with question after question and before I'd had time to answer any of them, literally bouncing me around every corner of his shop, oozing pride as he went. Lucy had spoken truly when she'd dismissed some of the shop's contents as tat. Dog-eared books vied for place with kitchenware last seen in the 1950s and ornaments that wouldn't have been out of place on a fairground stall. But equally he owned some beautiful Georgian furniture: satinwood card tables, a pair of George III hall chairs, oak and mahogany corner cupboards, and my particular favourite, an early Regency walnut bureau, the wood's shining swirls lighting the space around it.

'How long have you owned the shop, Mr Patil?' He was an unusual man and I was genuinely interested.

'Das, please. You must call me Das. Let me see...' He paused while he made the mental calculation. 'Twenty-two years. Yes, it was twenty-two years ago I moved from Bethnal Green.'

It seemed freakish for an Indian from the East End to be running a bric-a- brac cum antique shop in a faded seaside town, but then everything about my life was freakish.

'And why Hastings?'

'I came on a visit, just for a day you understand, but I knew straightaway this was the place I would live. As soon as I could afford to. Then my uncle died and left me enough money to buy this shop. It was my dream and it came true.'

'You have some beautiful items here.'

'Thank you, Miss Lacey. You are kind. I am a good businessman, I hope.'

That much was clear. I wondered if he was as good an historian. 'Mr Patil, Das, you've been here a long time. Do you know much of the history of Hastings? What it was like in the nineteenth century perhaps?' It was safer to focus on my mystery visitors than think of Dan. But in retrospect, it was a silly question and I got the laugh I deserved.

'My goodness, at that time my family had not ventured further than Lahore. But Lucy will know. Lucy knows everything.'

As if on cue, she emerged from the back of the shop, looking dusty and with a stray cobweb decorating her dark brown hair. 'Know what?'

'The history of this wonderful town. Your friend is most interested.'

'I know a little. It was once *the* place to visit – lots of quite famous people came. Keats and Byron… I think? And Rossetti. He lived a few doors away from you in High Street.'

'Dante Gabriel?'

'The very same. With Lizzie Siddal. They were married at St Clements, just round the corner.'

'Do you know if Rossetti had friends living in my cottage?' I hoped she wouldn't notice how odd that sounded.

She wrinkled her forehead. 'I don't, but it's more than likely. There wouldn't be that many places to live. Hastings isn't large now and it must have been even smaller then. The town was cheap, too, the perfect base for struggling artists. Why do you ask?'

'I had a thought I might be following in their footsteps.' It was a limp reason, but I said it as confidently as I could.

Lucy smiled, unfazed by my idiocy. 'How are you fixed

this morning? I could go a doughnut and coffee if you fancied it.'

It would mean another half hour of distraction and I grabbed at the offer. 'I'd like that, if Das can spare you.'

'Mr P can always spare me.'

Das leaned over and ruffled her hair. 'This one is a trial to me.'

* * *

'It's good of you to spare the time,' I said, once we were walking side by side.

'I could do with a break from stocktaking. You wouldn't believe it, but Das has as much out back as he has in the shop. And this morning, I thought you looked a little, what's the word – *distraida* in Spanish. A pick-me-up is what you need.'

'Whatever the word is, a doughnut should do the trick.'

We had walked only fifty yards before she turned into a side street leading away from the sea. 'It's up here, tucked away, but a hidden gem. Like the Driftwood – that's Gil's gallery. He's in London for a few days, but I'll introduce you when he gets back.'

A few paces more and she'd pushed open the door of a boldly painted café, flinging an order for doughnuts and coffee at the young man behind the counter, and leading the way to a small garden at its rear.

'I think it's warm enough to eat outside, and a good deal quieter. We can hear ourselves talk here.'

Talking was the last thing I wanted, but if I asked enough questions, I could keep Lucy busy. 'How long have you worked for Das?'

'Around two years.' She sounded vague. 'I'm not sure exactly. He's a sweetie and I've been lucky. It was the only job I could find in Hastings with a remote connection to what I'd studied at uni. Conservation,' she added, when she saw the question in my face.

I thought 'remote' was underplaying it. Das's shop was delightful, but there was little relation to Lucy's future career.

'I think you said you moved to London from Spain?'

'That's right. It was when Gil – his real name is Gilberto by the way, even worse than Lucia. It was when he began his degree. He won a bursary from UCL, so it made sense for us to move. But my father never really settled in London and when the ranch in Argentina came along, he was keen to go.'

'I take it the rest of the family weren't so keen?'

She shook her head and her face was without its usual smile. 'Mum was happy being back in her own country and didn't want to leave, Gil had a job promised once he'd finished his Master's and I wanted to train in conservation. Moving to Argentina wasn't really an option. So we stayed, and Dad went.' Her voice tailed off.

'And you came to Hastings – might it have been better to stay in London?'

'It's where the jobs are, certainly.'

The man who had taken her order appeared at the open doorway with a laden tray. He sidled his way through a bank of ferns and climbed the shallow steps to where we sat. Two doughnuts and two mugs of coffee appeared on the table. She turned to beam at him, then inspected the plate he'd brought. 'Thanks, Mikey. They look particularly jammy this morning.'

'For you, Lucy, the jammiest.'

I couldn't help smiling. When he'd gone, I said, 'How do you manage to stay so slim?'

'It's in the genes – a family bonus. Though Gil is very good about cooking healthy meals. I'm useless in the kitchen, except for the chicken casserole.'

'You live with your brother then?'

'We share a house in the newer part of town. It's nowhere near as interesting as your cottage.'

But far less worrisome, I thought. 'And your mother?' I wondered whether in the end Mrs Martinez had decided that Argentina was an option.

'She's a few miles along the coast. She had to sell the house in London when Dad left and bought the place down here.' Her voice told me the subject was still raw.

'It must have been a difficult time.'

'It was. I try not to mind, but I do miss Dad. And I didn't want to lose the rest of my family, so I came here.'

'You don't think your father will come back, when he's had enough of playing rancher?'

She shook her head again, her eyes downcast. 'No chance. He met someone else there and married again.'

I felt bad. Getting Lucy to talk had been a way of deflecting attention from my own troubles, and it hadn't been kind. I went to apologise but she stopped me. 'Sometimes it's good to talk. Gil has shrugged it off, I think, but he was older when it happened, more independent. Dad's going didn't seem to affect him as badly.'

'You never know. People respond differently to the bad things in life. And maybe in time you'll want to go back to London and look for that job in conservation.'

'I'm leaving it a bit late,' she said ruefully. 'Talking of which, I better not stretch Das's patience too far.' She whisked a napkin round a sugary mouth and brushed her hands.

'Thanks for showing me the café,' I said. 'Whenever I want a sugar fix, I'll know where to come.'

'Great. And don't forget the gallery. It's only a few doors up and you'll like Gil.'

Once outside, she bounded off in the direction of Das's shop and I walked slowly back along the seafront, hearing the children's shouts of delight and watching the carousel turn for its umpteenth time that day. The amusements had petered out by the time I began a reluctant climb up All Saints Street. Home meant confronting what I'd discovered this morning. But it also meant an easel and paints and a picture that yesterday had proved therapeutic.

Chapter Seven

I phoned Deepna the next day to pass on the orders she'd sent by mistake, and hearing her calm, sensible tones did me a power of good. I was keen to hear news of Julia – our last talk had been brief and disjointed – but Deepna had seen little of her. I imagined she was working from home; she often did. Her absence seemed not to have been a problem since Deepna was full of confidence and bursting with fresh ideas of how best to make our retail space work. I offered an occasional murmur of agreement, though my side of the discussion was decidedly minimal. I found it difficult to think of anything other than Dan's phone and its shattering contents, but I'd no wish to burden her and I had the idiotic thought that if I didn't speak about it, it might fade from my mind so completely I'd assume it hadn't happened.

When she'd rung off, I wandered over to the window and looked out. The street was unusually deserted and my solitariness suddenly hit, the weekend stretching long and lonely before me. I had been hoping Julia would text to say she was on her way down to Hastings after all, but my phone remained stubbornly silent. On reflection, it was better it did. My first thought had been to pour out my unhappiness and hope that, as always, she would make sense of the situation; my second was very different. I didn't want to mar her memory of Dan and decided I'd keep his infidelity locked away as my own personal demon. But that would take some practice.

As if echoing my mood, the weather took a turn for the worst and, when I braved a blustery walk into town, what visitors there were had taken refuge from the blast and were huddled deep in the seafront shelters. When I wasn't out walking, I tried picking up my brushes, but my fingers felt stiff and inflexible. It could have been the colder air tightening the fibrous tissues; more likely, it was that my heart wasn't in it. It was a relief when Monday morning finally arrived.

I was up shortly after dawn and tried once more to get to grips with the painting. This time I managed several hours before my hand grew less elastic and I grew more hungry. I broke off in search of food, but kitchen cupboards and refrigerator told the same story. No breakfast. So far, I'd been existing on small items bought here and there and what I really needed was a serious shopping expedition. Painting would have to wait. The supermarket lay south of the station and it shouldn't take long to walk there, cram a trolley full of food, and take a taxi back.

There was still a stiff breeze blowing, but the sky had begun to clear and a spread of blue appear between fast moving clouds. I strode along the seafront, the tang of salt air making me feel better than I had for several days, and was about to turn inland when I glimpsed a woman a few yards ahead, sitting at an easel. The sight transfixed me. Why hadn't I thought of that?

There was a good light in the sitting room and I'd chosen All Saints Street as my first subject, so painting in the cottage made sense. But after a while its rooms always felt a little suffocating, particularly the hall and the dead end that rose abruptly out of nowhere. It was something I couldn't explain, but I was beginning to dread that part of the house, and to be out in the fresh air painting seemed suddenly the most desirable thing in the world. I itched to take a look at the canvas on which the woman was working so assiduously. If I kept a respectful distance, I wouldn't disturb her.

I'd gone only a few steps when the breeze that had been blowing strongly whipped itself into a small whirlwind and bowled several sheets of paper along the promenade towards me. I rescued them before they could fly beachwards and saw straightaway they were initial sketches, no doubt for the painting on the easel. Returning them would be a good excuse to see the work close up.

The woman seemed a little flustered by my presence, but when I held out the errant sheets, she thanked me with genuine pleasure. I said something anodyne about the brilliant view and she mentioned travelling from Sevenoaks that morning purely to get sight of a squally sea. She put down her brushes while we chatted, and it gave me an opportunity to look properly at the painting. I was impressed. It reminded me of a picture Dan and I had seen in a Suffolk gallery. I'd suggested buying it to hang in our bedroom, but for one reason or another we'd left for home without it. This painting, though, was clearly an amateur work, but to my eyes, a carefully executed one. I thought she had caught the curling froth of waves extremely well, though the sky, I saw, needed further work.

And then, quite suddenly, it didn't. In an instant, the streaks of cloud hazing the blue were at just the right height, an elegant gull dipping in and out of their fat whiteness. And lingering on the horizon, the pale pink of a dawn that had not yet disappeared. The sea was now flat and glassy and a boat with bright red sails floated towards the centre of the painting. I couldn't recall seeing such a distinctive colour before There was a soft murmur in my ears that I half recognised, and realisation spluttered into life. I was no longer looking at the same scene, nor the same painting. No longer looking at the same woman.

* * *

'Clever girl!'

A man in a thick wool cape had crept up on the artist and put his mouth to her ear. Abruptly, Sophia twisted around and then with a cry of joy, jumped up from her seat, in danger of sending easel and palette flying.

'Careful, my darling.' With a smile, he gathered her into his arms. 'Yours is truly a welcome to warm a man's heart. I must always have it so.'

'You will, Spencer, you will.' She was filled with a deep joy. 'You cannot know how pleased I am to see you. I thought you were never coming back.'

'Silly wife.' He stroked the soft curls that had escaped her braiding. 'I have been gone three days only, and have been as swift as I can.' He bent to look at the half-finished canvas. 'But what great strides you have made since I've been away.'

'Painting is all I have had to do.' Her tone was one of resignation, but inside she fizzed with happiness. His praise was a small compensation for the dreary days since he had left.

'Now I am home, we must remedy that,' he said in a low voice.

Knowing his meaning, she felt herself blush, and uncaring of who might see, reached up and planted a kiss on his cheek. 'Tell me about London.'

He sat himself down on the sea wall opposite. 'It was busy, but exciting – very exciting. I cannot wait until we are both part of it. I met with Rossetti again. He is an interesting fellow, hugely creative and most knowledgeable on literature. Remember, I told you we were students together at the Academy and he left in disgust at the kind of pap the school produces? He is treading his own path now and he is not alone – Millais has already broken away and they have been joined by several other like-minded fellows – Holman Hunt, Stephenson, Collinson. Their work is revolutionary.' He took a deep breath and turned his head to gaze out to sea. 'And I must be part of it.'

'Revolutionary? You mean in colour?' She hesitated over the question. She was still learning, but had listened intently to her husband, and taking his advice had begun to experiment with intense colour painted over a wet, white ground. Spencer had said that by doing this she would mimic the brilliance of early Renaissance art.

'Colour certainly, but simplicity, too. A truth to nature. Their work is utterly different, Sophia – there is a sharpness to it, a rejection of what has gone before. Paintings are built through planes that lie parallel to the surface, and the effect is sensational.'

She nodded, hoping she understood. 'And Mr Rossetti was helpful?'

'Indeed he was. He assures me that if I produce the right canvas, I can submit to the Free Exhibition at Hyde Park Corner. He sent *The Girlhood of Mary Virgin* earlier this year, though Millais and Hunt exhibited at the Academy. *Girlhood* attracted much admiration. And a great deal of interest – the Brotherhood sign their work as PRB and that has people talking. The next Free Exhibition is only months away, and once London society sees my work, the commissions will roll in.' He was almost punching the air with eagerness and she loved him for it.

'This is what I want to do, Sophia. How I want to paint.'

'And you will.'

His face clouded. 'But will I ever be good enough to emulate them?'

She leant across and clasped his hand. 'You will, dearest. You are committed to your art and when your painting is shown, the world will see how good you are.'

His smile did not quite reach his eyes and that worried her. Could he truly be doubting his abilities? 'The Exhibition is in March and that is still some way off,' he said despondently, 'though this year it seems winter will never come. Here we are in December and you are painting in the open air. Should you not protect yourself more?'

'I have been working in the studio all week, but I've found the sea difficult to get just the way I want. I had to see it close up – though I'm still not sure I've captured it aright.'

'Let me see.' He rose from the wall and walked around to look over her shoulder. 'Perhaps a touch more cobalt here – and here.' He flicked a finger towards two small spots on the canvas. 'But the slightest touch only or you will unbalance the composition. You have conjured a fascinating image: a winter day, one can see that from the cold pink dawn, but an unusually flat, almost lifeless, sea. I feel when I look at your painting I could walk out on that sea, as though it were a sheet of cold blue ice.'

'Do you? Do you really?'

'You are becoming an artist, there is no doubt.'

'I would love that to be true – eventually. And if it happens, it will be entirely due to you. You have taught me so much.' She took hold of the edge of his cape. 'Dearest, painting gives me great pleasure, you know that, but I would so much like to return to my embroidery. With the house to manage as well, it's difficult to give time to both.' Then she added shyly, 'I hope, too, that very soon there will be a little one to care for.'

She could not see his face, but felt his figure tense beside her. 'You must know, Sophia, we are in no position to think of a child. That must be for the future.'

He spoke the truth, of course. Their finances were shaky and another mouth to feed could tip them over the edge. But she longed for a baby and had hoped Spencer would welcome fatherhood. Over the months she had grown less sure. Sometimes he seemed almost a child himself, happy and exuberant when things were going his way but irritable, even ill-tempered, when faced with difficulties. Her mother had said as much. Rowena Fairchild had liked Spencer, but it hadn't prevented her from warning: *Your sweetheart has been indulged his whole short life and he'll expect to be indulged for the rest of it.*

She was thinking wistfully of the parents that were lost to her, when Spencer reached out for her hands and held them tightly in his. 'Embroidery is all very well, my dear, but the world needs art. Real art. And this is how you must spend your time. When you've progressed a little more, it may be that we can sell our paintings together.'

She laughed at that. She was little more than a dauber and no one would ever buy her work. 'That can only be a dream. Your skill far surpasses mine, and always will.'

'Exactly as it should be.' His voice radiated contentment. 'But I have not told you the best news yet. Gabriel himself will be with us very soon. '

'Mr Rossetti? Here? In Hastings?' She was astonished.

'He has promised to visit and select one of my works for the Exhibition.'

'That is wonderful news, Spencer. I am so pleased for you.'

'For us both. Come here, my darling.' He put his hands beneath her elbows and raised her from her seat. Then clasping her close, he bent his head and pressed his lips to hers. She felt the the firmness of his mouth, the warmth of his caress, and whatever doubts there had been floated away to join the sea mist.

* * *

'Thank you for rescuing my drawings.' The woman seated at the easel had turned her head and was looking wary. 'Thank you,' she repeated.

I don't know how long I'd been staring at her picture, but it was evident she had started to think I might be a problem.

'Sorry, I'm in a daydream,' I stuttered. She gave a faint smile, but looked relieved when I turned to go.

I was thoroughly shaken. I thought I had beaten whatever madness I'd suffered before, that I'd sent the phantoms packing. Not so. My mind must still be dreadfully disturbed. I found myself running, setting a frantic pace back along the seafront, back to the cottage, which in the absence of any other was the sole haven I knew. I was running from myself, I suppose. Head down, I charged blindly ahead until I ran full tilt into a man coming from the opposite direction. The collision winded me badly and I ended sprawled across paving slabs, my bag shedding its contents far and wide.

'Here, let me help you.'

A hand reached down and I grasped it. 'Thank you. I'm sorry – I wasn't looking where I was going.'

'To put it mildly.' Once he'd seen me upright, he fixed me with a steady gaze. 'And have we met?'

I'd recognised him instantly. The man on East Hill. The man who had looked at me in the same way he was doing now, his grey green eyes worryingly thoughtful.

'East Hill!' he said suddenly. 'I hope you've been back there.'

'Yes. No.' Why could I never give him a straight answer? 'I mean to,' I lied, hoping he wouldn't fix me with that gaze again. But he was collecting my belongings: purse and comb, tissues and phone, and odd pieces of paper that had sat at the bottom of my bag for ever.

'Let me do that.' I was fearful of what else I'd stored there. 'And sorry again.'

'No need to apologise.' It was the same warm smile. '*You* came off the worst. But if you're okay, I'll get going.'

'I'm fine,' I said as brightly as I could, though I was anything but.

Chapter Eight

I stumbled through the front door and staggered into the sitting room. Then felt very stupid. I'd panicked as though chased by the fiends of hell, but who was coming after me? The answer, of course, was no one. It was sheer terror that my mind was foundering, that Dan's adultery had been one stress too many and I'd ceased to cope. I collapsed onto the hard sofa and tried to think logically – ambitious considering my life at the moment was wholly illogical. But, sitting there, I forced myself to replay the scenes I found so frightening.

Both times I had been studying a picture intently when something about them had reminded me of Dan. That seemed to confirm the people I had seen were a chimera, conjured from a mind badly out of joint. Yet doubt had niggled at me earlier and was niggling again. I couldn't be entirely sure that I was the one who had created these people. There was a small part of me that suspected they might have an independent existence. For one thing, my 'ghosts' were no longer confined to the cottage, but able to roam the town at will. And when they had spoken today, their conversation had flowed naturally from what I'd heard before. On both occasions, it felt as though I had been watching the opening scenes of a play, hearing the beginning of a story. But what that story was and why I was involved, I had no idea. All I knew was that it was terrifying.

Terrifying to slip out of time, seemingly to walk through a picture and find an unknown place, a world I could hear and see and that appeared as real as this one. I wondered if I should search the internet to discover how common this might be, or more likely, if it had ever occurred to anyone other than me. But I stopped myself. It would make things worse; it would be like checking a minor health problem and finding I had any number of serious diseases.

I must have sat there for almost an hour before I felt calm enough to realise I was still hungry. In something of a trance, I drifted into the kitchen. I had no food. Naturally, I had no food. The supermarket was where I had been heading when I'd taken a detour to another century. I needed to get a grip, refuse to allow my life to be disrupted in this way. Accept what had happened, no matter how, and move on. There was one benefit at least from the shock I'd had today: Dan's infidelity seemed almost trivial. That was the way I should see it. Not let his betrayal matter so much, then my unconscious mind would relax and stop its wandering, and today's experience would be the last of its kind.

The most practical thing I could do was to start for the supermarket again, but this time walk a different way, keeping one or two streets back from the seafront. Shopping for mundane items of food steadied me further and by the time I'd taken a taxi home and unpacked my goods, I was feeling cheerful enough to make toast and poach a couple of eggs.

And cheerful enough the next morning to push yester-day's unnerving experience out of my head and spend the entire day painting. I'd already begun detailed work on the background and was cheered when I saw the sky I had fashioned becoming more or less what I wanted. But I was unused to concentrating so intensely for such a long period and by four o'clock my hand was aching badly. The scar tissue had long ago healed, but it always told me when I'd done enough. I made a final cup of tea and took the drink out into the small garden. The sky had clouded over a little but it was still warm. Humid even. Looking around at the neglected flower beds, I wondered if I should buy plants to brighten them. The garden was such an inviting small space that it cried out for colour. If not plants, then pots of flowers maybe. I stopped myself there. I wasn't staying, was I? I'd given myself three or four days at most and I had already been here nearly a week.

It began to spatter with rain as I sat there, small warm drops trickling to earth as though they lacked the energy to escape the sky. I let myself sit and get wet. The feeling wasn't unpleasant, a cool balm to soothe my head and my hand. But when I felt the chair squelch beneath me, I judged it time to leave. The evening stretched ahead with nowhere to go and little to do. I'd found a small radio tucked away in one of the wardrobes and that would be my company tonight. In the event, I was tired enough to climb between the sheets before the clock struck ten. The feather bed was bliss, moulding itself around me, while the soft pattering of rain on glass lulled me to sleep.

* * *

It must have been around two in the morning when an enormous crash overhead woke me. I sat bolt upright, my heart jumping. The room was ablaze with light and for a moment I thought the curtains were on fire. Then I realised it was lightning I was looking at. Huge jagged stripes of pure energy tearing the sky apart. The rain was no longer gentle, but falling in torrents. I could hear its thunder as it rushed headlong down the gutters of the narrow street towards the sea. There was another loud crack, seeming as though it would break open the roof, then more strobes of brilliant light illuminating the entire room.

Until the storm passed I knew I'd get no sleep, and I cast around on the floor for the book I had been reading. I had a momentary doubt whether it was sensible to use the bedside lamp in such a powerful electrical storm, but shrugged it off. I had to have some distraction. But when I fumbled my way to the switch, nothing happened. The bulb must have gone. I climbed out of bed, fished around for my slippers and felt my way to the door. The switch to the ceiling light was on the left, I remembered, but that, too, failed to respond.

The same with the light on the landing. The lightning must have knocked out the electricity supply, though with luck only temporarily. Nothing to do then but hide under the duvet until morning, but half way back to the bed, I heard it. The sound of water. I shuffled forward along the lower end of the mattress and then something swished beneath my feet. I bent down and in the darkness felt around with my fingers. Wet. I looked up and a large drop of water hit me in the eye, then another, then another. I had a leak. A small one at the moment, but I'd have to get a tray or a basin or whatever the kitchen could offer to prevent it doing serious damage.

Getting down the stairs was tricky. They were steep and narrow with a tortuous right hand bend at the half way mark, but somehow I shuffled and crawled to the bottom. The staircase ended a few yards from the front door and luckily a small amount of light seeped through the glass transom. Not from the street lights, they had gone out, too, but from a sky made vivid by the storm. The muted light allowed me to walk a little more confidently towards the darkness at the end of the hall. I would have to turn sharp left into the kitchen to avoid walking into the blank wall, but hopefully I'd find a candle there to light me back.

I had reached the end of the hall when quite suddenly I was swamped by the most terrible sensation, a feeling that swept across me, over me, into me. Dank and cold. Grave cold. This part of the house was never warm, but this was cold of a whole different dimension. It was a shroud that smothered and held me fast. The kitchen was only a yard ahead, yet I couldn't move. The wall of ice had me in its grasp, sucking the life from me. I felt my breath tangle, the gorge rise in my throat. With a superhuman effort, I lunged forward and hurled myself through the open doorway. For an age, I stood gripping the kitchen table, waiting for my pulse to quieten, my heart to stop its noisy pounding. How could a scrap of cold affect me so badly? Except that it hadn't been a scrap, but an insidious force that scared me witless.

It took a long time before I felt able to begin a search of the kitchen cabinets. The darkness at this end of the house was almost complete and the search wasn't easy. By dint of opening every cupboard and drawer and feeling around every inch of their interiors, my numb fingers managed at last to find a basin I thought large enough. At some point, too, I came across a candle – half a stub of candle rather, and left over from goodness knows when. There were no matches, but a sudden brainwave had me scrabbling for the gas hob. The burner fired up beautifully, its flame sufficient to light the candle. It could keep me company for what looked like being a long night. Somehow, though, I had to get back to the bedroom, and it would take every ounce of my courage.

I breathed deeply and plunged into the hall, expecting the dreadful suffocation to encircle me at any moment. But it didn't. The candle fluttered and bent, but it held fast. With a rush, I leapt through that dreadful space and up the stairs, and was beneath the covers in seconds.

* * *

The storm must have continued to rage most of the night, but at some stage I managed to fall asleep, leaving the candle still burning. I was lucky it blew itself out without mishap. The morning brought calm, patches of blue sky showing through a chink in the drawn curtains. The rain must have petered out a few hours previously – the basin was almost full but I had been saved a major emergency. I would need to see Das, though. It was still only May and there would be more summer storms to come, though I wouldn't be here to see them. I knew I couldn't cope with another such night. Julia was coming this weekend and I'd had every intention of travelling back with her.

The thought of returning wasn't entirely welcome and that surprised me. By any reckoning, I should be packing my bag, and this morning if the cottage had not returned to what passed as normal, I would have left without a backward glance. But when I crept down the stairs and along the hall, I passed through the kitchen doorway unmolested. The hall outside felt prickly and uncomfortable, but then it always did. The ghastly coldness that had held me in its grip had vanished. I wondered if I had imagined it. Dreamed it, perhaps. But the remains of the candle told me I hadn't.

I was at Patil's shortly before ten o'clock. The electricity supply had been restored, but the till had stopped working and Lucy was bent over it, pressing tabs wildly and getting progressively more exasperated.

'It's gone on strike,' she said in greeting. 'I could, too. What a night, I didn't get a wink. How about you?'

'Pretty bad. It's why I'm here.' I wouldn't mention my dreadful experience, but keep to the repair that was needed. 'I'm sorry to give you more trouble, but the bedroom ceiling has sprung a leak. I think maybe a roof tile has gone missing. I managed to catch most of the water and I've mopped up what I didn't, but I think it's something that needs looking at – before the next thunderstorm.'

'There will be no more storms,' Lucy said grumpily. 'I've decreed it.'

'She is not a happy person,' Das put in.

'No, she is not.' She did another round of tab pressing. 'I'm supposed to work out how to get this thing going again. Das hasn't a clue.'

'Not a clue.' He didn't sound too concerned. 'But I will telephone a builder this morning. We can't have the ceiling falling on Miss Lacey.'

'Megan. I'd rather it didn't.'

'I'll get on to the till people before you phone,' Lucy said, 'I could be banging buttons all day and not make the slightest difference.'

She marched off to the small office situated at the back of the shop, her voice on the phone sounding unusually sharp. Das pulled a face. 'Poor Lucy. She has been trying for two hours to get this monster working but no luck.'

'I'm sure she'll get it sorted. And thanks for finding a builder for me.'

I had turned to go and was almost at the door, when he dashed after me. 'I am glad you came this morning, Megan. There's something I want to talk to you about.'

Before I could start wondering what on earth that could be, he'd rushed back to the counter and whipped a magazine from beneath.

'See here.' He waved it at me. 'This is Lucy's – *Conservation and Restoration*. She takes it every month and I know she reads every page.'

I wasn't sure what he was getting at and shook my head slightly. 'Look!' A box had been drawn on the open page and appeared to highlight an advertisement. 'A job!' He was almost dancing with excitement. 'A job for a conservation assistant – and not in London this time. In Surrey. A very nice part of the world.'

I was beginning to catch on. 'The job is for Lucy?'

'It would be perfect.' His smile was as wide as the shop.

'But does she think so?'

He waggled his head back and forth. 'We have to make her think so.' I didn't like the sound of the 'we'.

'It was you who drew the box around the advert?' And when he nodded, I said, 'I don't think you can push her into something she doesn't want. She's happy here with you.'

He clasped the magazine to his chest. 'I would love to keep her for ever, but there is no future here. 'This,' and he jabbed his finger at the page, 'this is where her future is. You must talk to her. Maybe she will listen to you more.' And maybe not, I thought, but instead put me down as an interfering busybody.

I was spared answering him because she came back at that moment, the familiar grin in place. 'They're coming. Not until after lunch. But they are coming.'

'I will call the builder now,' Das said, giving me a knowing nod. 'You are at home for the rest of the day, Megan?'

'I am and thank you.'

He trotted off to the office and I was left looking at Lucy and wondering where to begin. She pre-empted me. 'If it's about the job, I've already seen the advert.'

'Das asked me –' I broke off.

'I know. He means well, but I'll decide for myself.'

'Still…' I'd read the advert by now and Das had been right when he said it was a great opportunity. 'You might want to apply. You've nothing to lose.'

'I'll think about it.' I wasn't sure if her promise was genuine or made to keep me quiet. 'I hope Das doesn't mention it to Mum. He sometimes phones her – when he comes across a piece of porcelain she might like. If he does, I'll never hear the last of it.'

'Would she want you to go for the job?'

'Wouldn't she just! She's always nagging me about the need 'to get a career'. And Gil, too. He's back, by the way. *He* slept through the night, he is the most annoying man.'

'Then it's a worth a try, surely?'

'I'm beginning to think you're in their pay. How many doughnuts have they promised you?'

'None, I swear. But your mother is right behind you. That's priceless.'

'Wasn't yours then?'

I blinked. I hadn't expected the question. 'She never stopped me painting.' That was true at least. 'But other than that, there was no encouragement.'

'How strange.'

'Not for my mother.' The words were fierce.

She stared at me, surprised by my vehemence. 'Are you angry with her?'

'If I am, it's not for that.'

'For what then?'

'Oh, a hundred things,' I said obscurely. 'It's all too complicated.'

'Life is. Mothers are. They can be tricky.'

Lucy had spoken lovingly of Mrs Martinez and I couldn't imagine her mother presenting any problem. But when it came to my own history, 'tricky' was an understatement. I found myself wondering about Sophia, whether she felt *her* mother to be friend or enemy. There had been a wistfulness when she had spoken of her parents, and I guessed that despite the great love she had for her husband, there were times when she must feel very alone.

The thought had me frowning until Lucy punched me lightly on the arm. 'Don't look so worried, Megan. I'll talk to Mum about the job, promise!'

Chapter Nine

Das Patil was as good as his word and a builder turned up mid-afternoon. I'd been right to think a roof tile had become dislodged.

'Though it's funny,' the man said, 'I'd have thought you'd have had more water through.' I was thankful I hadn't and thankful, too, when after hanging at a crazy angle from a very long ladder, he managed to fix the tile back into position.

When he'd gone, the cottage seemed very empty. I wondered if I should ring Julia to finalise arrangements for the weekend. She had given up the idea of calling me every day and the once or twice she had phoned, our exchanges had been brief and concerned only with work. I was longing to confide in her, if only to have her laugh and rubbish my fears. Since my encounter on the seafront, I'd lost the certainty my Victorian intruders were the result of shock and nothing more. Something more troublesome was happening and somehow last night's shocking experience was part of it.

But Julia was busy, too busy to talk for long, and I had to be content with her promise that she'd be with me this Friday or Saturday. I would tell her about the Waylands then and tell her, too, that I was returning to London. I'd fulfilled my side of the bargain. I couldn't see how staying any longer was going to help me. Quite the contrary. Last night's terror had shattered any peace I'd found. Try as I might, I couldn't get that icy grip out of my head.

I had cooked supper and was washing the few dishes when the phone pinged. A text message from Julia. She was sorry, but she wasn't going to make it this weekend. Perhaps next? I thumped the phone back on to the worktop. I felt like grabbing my suitcase and leaving right away. I hadn't realised how much I had been counting on her coming, how much I needed to share fears that were beginning to control me.

* * *

The next morning, I had my case ready, though paints and easel would have to be despatched separately. When I wandered into the sitting room, the picture that had so enthused me looked suddenly forlorn. I would pack it with care and take it with me, I decided. That way, I wouldn't be deserting Hastings altogether, though I felt guilty at leaving Lucy so abruptly. My imminent departure gave me the courage to brave the seafront again, and I'd covered a fair stretch of it walking at a smart pace, when I saw a familiar figure turning out of the side street opposite. It was Lucy carrying two full beakers.

'Megan, hi! Fancy a coffee?' She thrust the cardboard tray towards me. 'Das won't mind.'

'Thanks, but no. I must be getting back. The fresh air has done its job and I'm wide awake now.'

'Ready to begin the great work again?'

I agreed. There was no point in stirring a hornet's nest.

I would write to her once I was safely back in Hampstead.

'If you won't have a coffee, how about a ticket? There's a fundraiser at the Driftwood tonight and I've several spare. Here.' She fished awkwardly in her satchel while balancing the coffees in the other hand. 'Don't worry, you won't have to contribute money – just your company. And it's a good opportunity for you to meet some of the locals.'

The world appeared to be conspiring against my ever leaving Hastings. I wanted to refuse, tell Lucy I was catching a train this morning, but I found myself taking the ticket and asking her the reason for the fundraising.

'It's to buy a Jepson for the gallery.'

'Ambitious.'

Jason Jepson was the latest young British painter to catch the eye of the art loving public and his work had begun to attract a lot of money. Not yet stratospheric prices, but it was easy to see it wouldn't be long before Sotheby's was auctioning his work on the world market.

'Gil *is* ambitious,' Lucy said. 'He's been negotiating with the owner of the Jepson for an age. He's almost got his sticky little hands on the picture, but not quite. The fundraiser might clinch it for the Driftwood.'

'I'd better come then.' I'd not made the promised visit to her brother's gallery and it seemed the least I could do before I left Hastings for good.

'That's great. But I must go – this coffee will be stone cold if I don't. See you outside the shop at seven.'

* * *

When I saw her that evening, it was clear she had scurried home after closing time and changed her dungarees for something more appropriate. At least I imagine that was her calculation. Skin-tight leggings and a crop top didn't seem that appropriate for an evening of great art, but perhaps she was hoping it would loosen a few purses. She was probably right; she looked fresh and young and fun. She saw me in the distance and came rushing towards me, tucking her hand in my arm and propelling me along the seafront and into the street in which we'd eaten doughnuts. A few doors beyond the café, she guided me through the revolving glass door of the Driftwood Gallery.

'Not far, you see. It's smart isn't it?'

The gallery may have been small, but it was stylishly modern with marble floors and glass stairways. A plan of the layout was on the wall by the entrance desk and I saw the collection was spread over three floors.

The woman behind the ticket counter smiled at Lucy. 'Your brother's in his office, but the party's going full swing downstairs.'

'I want Megan to meet him first. Is it okay to go up?'

'Sure, he's taking a last call but he won't be long.'

I followed Lucy up two flights of the glass-sided stairway and along a wide avenue of white wall until we reached a small office at the end. The door was open and a man, dressed in jacket and jeans and casual shirt, was walking backwards and forwards across dark blue carpet tiles, a phone to one ear, a sheaf of papers in his hand. There was a familiarity about him, and as he turned and began to pace back towards the door, I saw why I knew him.

He was the man I had cannoned into on the seafront. The man from East Hill. Hastings wasn't a large town, but even so it seemed an extraordinary coincidence. *Not a coincidence*, my inner voice told me. There was a pattern to this, I could sense it dimly, a pattern to everything that had happened these last few weeks, a deliberate working out – but of what, I struggled to say.

He saw Lucy on the threshold and mouthed, *a few minutes?* She gave him the thumbs up. 'He'll be out in a tick. We could have a mooch around the gallery in the meantime or join the party downstairs,'

'You must have seen the paintings a hundred times.'

'And been lectured on them.' She grimaced.

'Then let's take ourselves to the ball.'

'If you're sure.'

'I'm sure.' More than sure, I thought. For some reason, I felt reluctant to meet Gil Martinez and a busy event would be the best place to hide, especially if Lucy forgot the introduction. And once she started enjoying herself, I thought she might.

The party had spilled out across a large basement room, complete with potted palms and tastefully subdued lighting. A soft cream carpet cushioned the hubbub of a substantial crowd, though the chatter had already reached an uncomfortable level. Panelled walls led my gaze upwards to a surprising find: a frieze, three foot deep, and painted in brilliant oils. I tipped my head back and allowed my gaze to wander from wall to wall, recognising many of the Hastings landmarks, though not the scenes of Sussex countryside.

I was about to ask Lucy if she knew them when a waiter appeared at my shoulder with flutes of champagne. Several of his fellows followed close behind carrying trays that groaned with food. I took a glass and helped myself to a canapé. It looked uncommonly like a miniature pillar box, a slightly tipsy one at that, but turned out to be a vertical roll of smoked salmon sitting on cream cheese.

'Yummy,' Lucy murmured, looking round for the waiter

and his tray. 'Let's get another.'

But it wasn't the waiter who bore down on her but a bouncing ball of a man, as wide as he was tall. He scooped her into a crushing embrace mouthing *Dahling* above the din of a hundred raised voices. 'Such fun, my dear. And all for a Jepson. Personally I wouldn't give a hundred for one, but don't tell Gil I said so.'

'I won't. I don't think Gill would be interested if I did. He trusts his own judgement and he's right to. I'm sorry – you'll have to excuse us for a moment, Trevor, but thanks for coming.'

When we'd turned away, she hissed, 'Loathsome man. He's only here to make mischief. He's convinced he knows all there is to know about art, but he's clueless. He's bought some real turkeys in the past – more money than sense.'

'Hopefully some of it will go to the fund.'

'I wouldn't bet on it. Gil has crossed swords with him a number of times and there's no love lost. He'll eat and drink as much as he can, you'll see, and avoid paying a cent.'

'I hope he's an exception then.'

'Really, they're not a bad crowd. Trevor is by far the worst, but you have to pick and choose. As long as they keep supporting Gil, I'm happy… you know, you and I should make an evening to go out together. It would be a lot more fun.'

She cast a knowledgeable eye around the seething crowd. 'The Orlov brothers are over there, to the left of the podium. They're an interesting pair, into icons – they sell zillions. But there's such a jam of people, I don't think we can reach them.'

I wasn't too bothered. Icon dealers weren't exactly at the top of my list of people to meet, but it was evident Lucy was keen to get me circulating. 'Who can I introduce you to?' She wrinkled her forehead. 'Someone we can actually get to… how about Maud Sutcliffe? She's the one under the potted palm. She paints landscapes, like you.'

Mine was a townscape but I didn't quibble, and I tried to look interested when Maud raised her bored eyes to me and said, 'How long have you been in Hastings? I don't recall hearing your name.'

'Why would you? I've only been here a few weeks and my name is nothing special.' Lucy had melted away and my heart sank at the thought of too many minutes with Maud, but rescue came from an unexpected quarter.

'I disagree.' It was Gil Martinez. 'Lacey is a very special name. Robert Lacey, a painter of the seventies and eighties, don't you recall?' Maud sniffed and turned to talk to her neighbour.

'You know Robert Lacey's work?' I asked.

'Who doesn't? He was as famous as Jepson in his day. More famous. By the way, I'm Gil Martinez and I think we've met before.'

'Kind of,' I conceded. 'Megan Lacey.'

'That's what I mean. A special name.' He leaned a little closer and said, 'He's no relation of yours, I suppose?'

I had a choice. I could lie or I could tell the truth. And beneath the gaze of those thoughtful eyes, I went for the latter. 'He was my father.'

'No wonder you're into all things artistic. Lucy told me. He was a brilliant painter.'

'*Was* being the operative word. He didn't sustain the brilliance.'

'Neverthless his work was hung at the Royal Academy and that's some accolade. He died a few years ago, I believe?' Gil's voice was gentle. 'It's good you're keeping the flame alive.'

'I wouldn't say that exactly.' I badly needed to change the subject. 'How close are you to making your target?'

'Within an inch, I'd say. I'm hoping this evening will mark the final stretch.'

'And does Jepson have a particular significance for the town?'

He scratched his head and gave me a half smile. 'Actually no. The collection here comes mainly from earlier centuries – primarily eighteenth and nineteenth – but I'm desperate to bring in modern works. The more modern the better. I want to attract a new, younger audience.'

'Is there one in Hastings?' I hoped I didn't sound rude.

'We'll find out when I buy the Jepson! But it's important to spread the word.'

'Is that why you moved from London – to spread the word?'

'Not entirely, but the job offered huge scope. I'd been working in a gallery where nobody even knew my name. I was one of a team of assistants. Then I heard on the grapevine that a new place was opening in Hastings and it seemed too good an opportunity to miss.'

'No regrets at leaving London then?'

'I liked the city, I enjoyed working there, but I don't think I ever really understood it. Probably because I'd spent most of my life in a small Spanish town – Calaspara. It was bang in the middle of the country and miles from water. The beach was a once-a-year treat, so the idea of living by the sea was very attractive. I wanted to wake up and hear the waves.'

'The Sussex coast is a little different from Spain's.'

'True, but I've learned to value it. It has a charm of its own.'

I had to agree, but I was intrigued by the move he'd made. 'It must have been quite a jump, going from an assistant role to chief curator.'

'Let's say the interview panel had their doubts, but my personality won the day.' He gave me a broad smile this time, and I thought how attractive he was, his pleasant face transformed.

'I imagine your academic qualifications had something to say to it, too.'

'Everyone has them,' he said indifferently. As someone who didn't, it was good of him to make light of his learning. 'I hope you'll take a look around the gallery some time. We've several paintings here that *are* significant for Hastings. The Wayland, for instance.'

I gaped at him. I couldn't help it. Then I tried to cover my embarrassment with a cough, only it wasn't necessary, thank goodness. A tall, distinguished looking man wearing a dark suit had edged up to us and was tapping Gil on the arm.

'Time for your speech, old chap. Give it to them.'

And he did. At least I think he did. The only word in my head was Wayland. I knew I wouldn't be going anywhere until I had seen that painting for myself.

Chapter Ten

The gallery opened at ten and the next day I was outside its glass doors on the dot. There was no sign of Gil Martinez and I was glad of it. I had liked him but I hadn't wanted to, which sounds perverse but I had no space in my life, in my heart, for a friendship that might demand too much. And I had an inkling that this one could. I paid for my ticket and started a slow drift around the gallery. The collection was laid out chronologically and that's how I tackled it, starting on the ground floor with the seventeenth century. Right now, there was really only one era that interested me, but I made myself look at everything, almost as though I were scared of what I might find.

And I was right to be scared. As soon as I wandered into the nineteenth century, I saw it. A painting by S Wayland. Spencer Wayland! This was confirmation, if I'd needed it, that the man I had seen and heard a few days ago had actually lived. And quite possibly lived and painted in my cottage. If there had been a chair handy, I'd have fallen into it.

I took a deep breath and looked at the painting again. Spencer was a skilful artist, I had to concede. I was glad his contact with Rossetti had paid off and he had been granted the public recognition he deserved. I knew the view he'd painted, a view of All Saints Street. I was painting it myself, but his perspective was subtly different. By my reckoning, he was working from a vantage point considerably higher than the sitting room, higher even than my bedroom. Had there been an attic, I wondered? There was no trace of one, but it would be the perfect space for an artist.

I kept looking at the picture trying to work out where the painter would be standing. Then I remembered the blocked-off doorway at the end of my dark, narrow hall. That was what was behind the blank wall. A stairway that made its way up to an attic, not down to a cellar, as I'd presumed. It explained why there was a step down to my bedroom: its floor had been lowered to allow for a studio above, and explained, too, why my room had not been completely flooded three nights ago. The studio's floorboards must have soaked up much of the water.

But how perfect to paint there. If I'd been staying, I might have tried to persuade Das to unblock the doorway, always assuming the stairs were safe and the attic floorboards would hold. If I'd been staying, I would have the same view as Spencer – undulating hills in the distance, the trees a cluster of bright green on their lower slopes, and was that a waterfall? Then I realised I'd see none of this, no matter how much unblocking went on. The skylight which must have existed in the 1850s had long ago been tiled over.

I bent down to look more closely at the painting, trying to imagine how the upper floor had been arranged, where the stairway would have entered, how much space the room would have offered. But then my focus started to go, my vision to blur. Abruptly, I straightened up, only to find the air around me growing cloudy. I felt a choking in my chest and in my ears, voices. Voices growing ever louder. It was happening again. It couldn't be, but it was.

* * *

Sophia stood, hands clasped, the wide skylight at her back, waiting for her visitor. The young man emerging from the stairway, Spencer at his shoulder, was clean-shaven but wore his dark waving hair shoulder length. Despite the winter chill, he had no overcoat but instead a light coloured jacket, loose and unstructured. The bow tie that fastened the narrow collar of his shirt was to her mind a decisive element, marking him out as an artist.

'Mrs Wayland.' He strode across the studio, the floor-boards squeaking beneath his tread. 'It is good to meet you at last. Your husband is a constant singer of your praises.'

'Then I must hope I can live up to them.'

What he lacked in stature, he made up for in charm, and she wasn't impervious to it. She kept her glance lowered, but his slim form was in front of her now and he was taking her hand and raising it to his lips. She had learned from Spencer that the man's family was Italian and perhaps this was how it was done in Italy. She blushed nevertheless. And blushed again when she saw the look of appreciation in his large hazel eyes.

'I'm afraid you have had bad weather for your journey.' She smoothed the skirt of her gown trying to gain confidence. It was her very best dress. She had made it herself from the blue plaid cotton Madame had given her as a leaving present, and decorated it with extravagant bows of blue satin and a lace hem.

'Bad maybe,' Rossetti said, 'but not desperate. No snow at least with which to contend. And it is always a great pleasure to visit Hastings. I am quite often here, you know.' That surprised her. This flamboyant personage hardly seemed to fit the staid town she had encountered. 'I first came as a child. I was suffering from bronchitis and my parents took a house in High Street. They thought the sea air would do me good.'

'And did it?'

'Absolutely. Hastings is a splendid town.' He turned to Spencer. 'I'm hoping very soon to introduce Millais to its delights. Hunt, too. They will love the light. There is something very special about the light here. To see the sun rise over the sea is the most wonderful of earthly sights. And then there is a stay at the Cutter – it makes one's visit perfect.'

'The Cutter?' She half recognised the name, though she was not yet completely familiar with the town.

'The inn, Mrs Wayland. I always stay there.'

She saw Spencer's head incline meaningfully towards her and took the hint. 'May I offer you some refreshment, Mr Rossetti?'

'No, I thank you. I have called only to select a picture and then I am to dinner at the inn and will catch a late train back to London. How lucky we are to have the new railway. A mere four hours' travelling.'

She hoped this charismatic young man would find the journey worth his while and leave with one of Spencer's works beneath his arm. But that was by no means certain, and she had a frantic urge to grab him by the sleeve and thrust a picture at him. By springtime, their need of a sale would be desperate. But she kept her poise and he filled the silence for her.

'I am looking forward to seeing your husband's work. I

intend to enter next year's Free Exhibition myself so he will be in good company! This time, I have decided to submit an Annunciation. I've called it *Ecce Ancilla Domini*. My sister, Christina, sat for me and I am tempted to believe that the work is better even than my last entry. Though, to be honest, *The Girlhood of Mary Virgin* did remarkably well.'

Her polite murmur of approval was lost in a forest of words. 'My comrades have decided differently. Millais is showing at the Academy again, I imagine because his *Isabella* did well last year. Yes, very well.' He paused for a moment to think about it, and she wasn't entirely sure he had been pleased by his colleague's success.

'It received good reviews. The critics liked the detail. The mediaeval costumes in particular. Detail, Mrs Wayland, is one of the Brotherhood's hallmarks. But this year, he is showing something rather different – *Christ in the House of his Parents*. I have some doubts how the painting will be received. Not that it isn't brilliant, it is. But a red-headed Christ child from a labouring family could be a step too far, the Academy is so fixed in its views. And now the Brotherhood is more widely known, we have gained a reputation as revolutionaries out to destroy every artistic value.'

'You feel judgement will be fairer at the Free Exhibition?' It was the first time Spencer had spoken and she noticed how tentative he was.

Rossetti nodded energetically, his luxuriant hair bouncing on his shoulders. 'It is a personal view, of course, but I think it preferable to show at Hyde Park. No jury is involved as there is at the RA, and a painter can rely directly on his audience for appraisal. And it is an informed audience, make no mistake.' He looked around the studio, his eyes expectant. 'So where are you hiding these masterpieces.

Shall we take a look?'

Her attentive ear had noted the hint of sarcasm and it worried her. But Spencer had thrust himself forward and was guiding his visitor to a stack of canvases piled in one corner of the studio. This was the crucial moment, the one they had been counting on. Her hands grasped the large bow tucked beneath her bust and twisted its satin mercilessly. They had sufficient money to pay the rent for a few months hence, but their small pile was dwindling by the day and it was of the utmost importance that Spencer began to sell his work.

For her part, she had put aside painting and begun another embroidery, this time of the town. It was a delicate rendering of East and West hills and the tumble of houses that filled each slope. She had high hopes of selling it, since unknown to her husband she had found a small shop tucked away in one of the lanes off High Street, whose proprietor had expressed an interest. But embroidery was a painstaking art and she fretted her work was taking too long. If only Spencer would allow her to take in dressmaking. That would give them a small but regular income.

He was standing to one side of his mentor, his breathing too shallow. She knew he was as nervous as she, both of them watching Rossetti flick through the stack of canvases. A minute, two minutes. Then their visitor began to shuffle backwards through the paintings he had already seen. Did that mean there was nothing worthy of his interest? She exchanged an anguished glance with her husband. Back once more through the stack and at length Rossetti drew from the pile a landscape, modest in size, but one that appeared to give him satisfaction.

'This is the one. By far the most professional. It will

compete comfortably with others in the show.' He drew out an oil of Old Roar, the local waterfall.

'But –' She was about to step forward when her husband stopped her with a raised hand and a fierce glare. 'I am glad you think so,' he said to Rossetti. She couldn't understand how his voice was so untroubled.

'It does you justice, my friend. You should be pleased.'

The bow on her dress was now mangled into an unrecognisable shape. Why was Spencer doing this? Why did he not speak? But Rossetti was talking again and addressing her. 'If you could have it packed for me, Mrs Wayland, I would be much obliged.'

'Sophia will do it herself.' Her husband glared at her once more. 'I believe we have some materials in the kitchen.'

'Good. Have it sent to the Cutter. Now, I think we should be off. We are meeting several of the town's worthies and should not be late.'

She swallowed hard, but said nothing. Rossetti paused in the doorway of the attic and spoke to her across the room. 'Your husband has done you proud, Mrs Wayland. To be honest, I doubted I would leave with anything, but of late he has made such great strides in his work we must ensure the wider world sees it.'

She kept silent and Spencer said quickly, 'That is most kind of you. If you will allow me a minute to find the packing for my wife, I will meet you in the street.'

'Do not be long then. It is far too cold to wait around.' He nodded a farewell and was half way down the stairs by the time she reached Spencer's side.

'Why did you not tell him?' she said beneath her breath.

'I couldn't.'

'But it is deceit.'

'If we sell the picture, it's money. A small deceit is worth it.'

'No deceit is worth it. And it is my picture so surely I should have a say.'

He put his arms around her and for a moment she allowed herself to relax into his warm clasp. Then she remembered what he had done. 'I won't allow it, Spencer. You must tell him the truth.'

'You're not jealous, are you, my little one? You shouldn't be. Rossetti is my friend and happens to like what you have painted. Don't forget, it was I who taught you. So in a way, the picture is a shared venture. When it goes into the exhibition, it will attract notice and likely sell. That will give me the audience I need.'

'But it is a falsehood.'

'The painting says quite clearly S Wayland. What is false about that?'

She flung away from him and walked jerkily towards the window. 'I don't like it. We will be discovered.'

'How can that be? It is only we two who are privy to the secret, and it is common knowledge that women cannot earn money from public exhibition. Now I must go, my clever little wife. Pack up the painting and get a boy to deliver it to the inn. This is the start of good fortune for us, you will see.'

She ran towards him, hoping to stop him from leaving. She must argue him out of this deception for both their sakes. But he was already on the stairs when she reached the doorway and clattering noisily towards the street.

Chapter Eleven

The footsteps should be fading, but they weren't. Instead, they were drawing nearer. They were on top of me now and I felt the ground sway.

'Megan?' The shrewd eyes scanned my face. 'Are you okay?

'Yes, fine,' I said hastily, and tried to wrench my mind into shape. Gil Martinez was looking worried and no wonder.

'Are you sure you're all right?'

'Yes, yes…' Despite a huge effort, my speech was stumbling. I tried again to pull myself together. 'Sorry. I was concentrating on the picture. Too hard. It made me dizzy, I think.'

'Ah yes, it's a great painting, isn't it? The artist is a local man. I mentioned him last night. One of the few heroes Hastings can lay claim to – Spencer Wayland.'

No, I wanted to yell. Not Spencer, but Sophia. Most likely, Sophia.

'Look, I'm due a break. Why don't we go for a sandwich? You look as if you could do with a stiff coffee.' He fixed me with those unwavering eyes.

A stiff brandy might be better, but he was right that I needed something to steady my nerves. 'A sandwich and a coffee would be perfect.' I sounded amazingly sane. If I could manage a vaguely sensible conversation in the next half hour, I might redeem myself.

When we were sitting in the café, minus the doughnuts, but with a baguette between us and two steaming mugs of coffee, I tried to explain my strange behaviour in the gallery, almost impossible given the fact I'd been seeing people from a hundred and fifty years ago, but he stopped me before I'd managed more than a few words. Lucy must have told him of Dan's death, and he was busy putting my oddities down to bereavement. I should be glad of his sympathy, but in the light of what I'd discovered, it jarred. And it wasn't the real reason I was floundering. While I witnessed the scene in the attic, there had not been a thought of Dan in my mind.

Once we had made inroads into the enormous baguette piled high with cheese and salad, I asked him about the artist. If I were to be haunted by long dead painters, it would be worth learning something of them. 'Does the gallery own many Waylands?'

'Just the one, unfortunately. There are two or three works dotted around other galleries, and one, the first to be exhibited – a painting of Old Roar, our local waterfall – is in private hands, I believe. But Wayland didn't paint for long. Or at least, he didn't exhibit for long.' Or Sophia didn't, I added to myself.

'Yet you called him a local hero.'

'That was by virtue of being hung in the Royal Academy. Hastings can't boast too many artists with those credentials, even one with only a handful of paintings to his name.' His smile was infectious and made me want to smile back.

'I guess some of his fame derives from being a Pre-Raphaelite?' The painting had been very much in their style.

'He wasn't, in fact.' Gil's reply was surprising. 'I get the impression he hung around the edges of the group, but never became a full member. And, of course, the Brotherhood itself didn't last long. 1850 was the year they burst upon an unsuspecting public, but by 1853 they'd dissolved as a functional group.'

'But the Pre-Raphaelite style didn't disappear.'

'Sure, the characteristics that made them different remained – flattened perspective, sharp outlines, brilliant colours. But once the group dissolved, each artist developed his own distinctive style.'

'I have to admit my knowledge is shaky. I managed only a year of my degree and the Pre-Raphs weren't on the curriculum.'

He munched the rest of his baguette before he answered. 'They were special, the first avant-garde group. Literally a breath of fresh air blowing through the gloomy corridors of the Academy.'

'I can just about recall a lecture on the art of the period. It was pretty stultifying, if I remember rightly.'

'It was. The RA maintained a rigid structure for training its students. The poor devils had to suffer three years drawing casts of Greek and Roman sculpture before they were allowed anywhere near life drawing – not to mention painting. It tended to produce chocolate box art. Rossetti thought so at least. He saw the pictures coming out of the RA as bland and inconsequential.'

From what I'd seen of Rossetti, that wasn't unexpected. Gil pushed his empty plate to one side, and attempted without much success to smooth his tangle of soft brown hair into some kind of order. I imagined he must have an appointment to go to, but he made no immediate effort to move.

'Tell me why you left college after a year. Were you on the wrong course?'

'The course was fine. I left for personal reasons.'

'Lucy mentioned you had some kind of accident. Was that it?'

I laid my right hand as flat as it would go on the table, palm upwards, so the thick, raised scars were plainly visible. 'Boiling water.'

He winced at the thought, or maybe it was the sight of my puckered skin, but to my relief he asked no more. 'So tell me how you came to set up shop.'

Lucy had been busy. It seemed she had recounted every detail she'd learned of Das's new tenant.

'I'm not sure exactly how it happened.' I would keep it vague; he'd no need to know of my depression and the long miserable months that followed the accident. 'I was at a loose end and then fortunate enough to inherit some money. A friend, Julia Fallon, persuaded me to use it for a new business. She was convinced Hampstead needed to be sold artists' supplies. There was a small shop there already, but ours was going to be bigger and better.'

'It seems she was right.'

'Eventually,' I conceded. 'There were some hairy moments at the start, but Julia was on top of the finance. She'd worked as the financial director of an art gallery her mother ran, so she knew the ins and outs of staying solvent. And she forwent her salary for the whole of the first year.'

He laid back and stretched his legs to one side of the table. 'She sounds a good friend. How did you meet?'

'By accident. I'd left college and my mother wanted me

from under her feet.' Not completely untrue, but definitely economical. Ruth Lacey's response to the accident was far too complex to distil in a few words. 'She saw an advert for volunteers at a gallery in the next borough. They needed someone to give occasional talks and guide visitors. It wasn't my kind of thing, but she nagged me to go along and I'm very glad I did. I met Julia and we became firm friends.'

'And did you volunteer?'

'No. I wasn't persuaded I'd be any good at it, but then my father died and left me money and suddenly setting up a business was a possibility.'

'What's the shop called? Lacey and Fallon?'

He had a frighteningly good memory. 'Palette and Paint. The name is a bit chintzy, I know, but it seems to attract the amateur dabbler as well as the professionals.'

'It's a great way to have used your inheritance – it must be satisfying to follow in your father's footsteps. More satisfying, of course, if you'd never had the accident. How did he take it?'

'Opening the shop?'

Gil laughed at my bemusement. 'Your father may have been looking down from heaven and blessing the enterprise, but I really meant how did he take the accident? After all, it robbed you of the chance to become a fellow artist.'

'He never knew.' I had to be honest. Once you've started on the path of truth, it's difficult to get off. 'He left my mother when I was a small child and I hardly remember him.'

'Did you never see him after he left?' Gil looked taken aback, as well he might.

'Never. He travelled to Venice and then moved in with a German countess.'

The smile was back. 'That sounds a painterly thing to do. But didn't you want to see him?'

'The subject never came up.' There had to be a limit to my honesty.

He glanced at the clock over the serving counter. 'Hey, I'm going to have to scoot. Sorry to leave you so abruptly, but I've a meeting at two.'

'That's fine. I'll treat myself to another coffee and then wander back to the cottage.'

He looked at me with a measuring glance. 'You're looking a good deal better now. You had me worried for a moment back there.'

'I've talked myself better. I'm sorry – all I've done is natter about myself.'

He was a few paces from the table, but turned back to me then. 'There's a solution to that. Why don't you come out for a drink one evening, then I can bore you to death about me.'

'Your sister has already invited me.'

'Fine. We'll make it a threesome.'

It was evident I was not a romantic possibility and I'd nothing to fear from him. I was relieved – it would be the last thing I needed – but stupid enough, too, to feel a niggling disappointment.

* * *

I strolled back to the cottage feeling relatively calm, but with a mind filled with questions. Would I continue to be plagued by flashes from the past? Would they stop if I returned to London? Did I, in fact, want them to stop? There was something compulsive about the pattern that was emerging, as though I were meant to witness a story unfolding in a parallel world.

Except that suggested a separation I was no longer sure existed. Seeing Sophia today, I'd sensed her doubts, her fear of fraud, her desperation for her husband to tell the truth. I'd sensed them not just from her words, but from her innermost feelings. Whether I liked it or not, I was no longer a mere observer. I was involved.

After the long, slow days of utter blankness that followed Dan's accident, too much seemed to be happening in a very short time. A week ago, I had been decimated when I discovered his infidelity, but in the last few days I'd not given it a thought. The Waylands hadn't just pushed Dan to the back of my mind, but for a short while completely out of it. They were not an hallucination, not a fantasy, but people who had existed and still existed in a continuum far from my own. In some way, my mind had developed an ability to disrupt the usual order of time and, at moments of intensity and without wishing it, I'd learned to walk a path back into the past.

Dan's sudden death might have been the initial trigger – shock had been responsible for those earlier, far less disquieting visions – but it was clear a damaged mind could not be blamed for what was happening now. Slowly and certainly, I was being dragged into the Waylands' story and made to feel for its protagonists.

Poor Sophia. I remember her husband telling her on their wedding day that she must give up sewing and let him teach her to paint. I could see from the picture hanging in the Driftwood that she painted in a style adopted from Spencer's beloved Pre-Raphaelites. She had done what he asked and with what result? Ironically, she had become the better artist. It was an irony I wasn't sure he'd accepted with equanimity. So far, he had dealt with it by seeing only commercial gain. Perhaps the personal implications were too painful to contemplate.

Sophia had learned to paint to please the new husband she adored, but what he was doing to her was far from adoration. He was making her a party in his deceit, in his fraud if you were going to say honestly, and she hated it. He seemed indifferent to the hurt he was causing; at bott, he'd not given it serious thought. The situation wore a familiar face. Not that anyone had claimed a painting of mine as their own, nor were they likely to. But deceit can wear numerous guises. Like Spencer Wayland, Dan had been uncaring of the hurt he caused and wounded unthinkingly.

Chapter Twelve

Whenever I walked along the dark, narrow hall of the cottage, I felt uneasy, but the uneasiness had increased from the moment I saw the Wayland picture at the Driftwood. With every passing day that uninviting space seemed colder and my skin to prickle more sharply. It was knowing there had once been an attic beyond the blocked wall, I think, a feeling that something bad lay in wait. Rotting stairs, I forced myself to believe, rotting stairs and equally rotting floorboards in the studio above. But still, the idea of something hidden, something waiting, persisted.

It was time to pack, though. Now the Wayland painting had convinced me the couple I'd seen and heard was real, there was no reason to stay. For several days, though, I was unwilling to make plans. Instead I walked. I was beginning to enjoy just walking around the town. I put it down to the open skies and the tang in the air since I never had the same enjoyment walking in London.

The promenade had become increasingly busy, with large crowds of day trippers. Plates of fish and chips and paper cones of cockles were everywhere. A sprinkling of children dug furiously on the beach, while others dared the waves, or munched sticks of rock and mounds of candy floss. Some of the fishermen on the Stade were offering trips around the adjoining bays. It was fun the old-fashioned way, but people seemed to like it. And so did I. I found it exhilarating to be chased along the seafront by a scurrying breeze, cliffs of white chalk on one side, glinting water on the other.

Julia's text came as a surprise and shook me out of the comfortable drift in which I'd settled. She would be down the coming weekend, she said. It had taken an age for her to come, but it was heartening to know she'd soon be with me. She was arriving Saturday morning and would return on Sunday – and I would be with her. She'd mount a protest and want me to stay, and I could see why. The sea air had done its job: my face was no longer pinched, but sported a light tan, my hair was bleached blonde, my eyes clear and alive. I had to admit I was looking a good deal better. But I must go before there was more time travelling, before I became too involved with the Waylands to retreat. I didn't doubt for a moment that if I stayed, I would see them again, and I'd begun to think it unwise. Far better to return to London and lose myself in running the shop.

I'd finally made a date to meet Lucy and her brother. We'd agreed to have a drink at the Cutter around six o'clock on Wednesday. Lucy was eager to show me the inn that had been Rossetti's home from home when he stayed in Hastings and I was curious too, now that I'd seen the man for myself. They had promised me a curry afterwards at the Indian restaurant they both favoured and it was sounding a good evening. I dressed in jeans – I didn't want them to think I'd made too much of an effort. I didn't want Gil to think it at least, and then I spoiled the effect by choosing a chiffon blouse that had effort written all over it.

They were already at the pub when I arrived and had

bagged one of the outside tables that faced the sea. I'd read the building had been here since the end of the eighteenth century, but over time its façade had been considerably altered. Inside, though, when Lucy and I went to order, nothing much seemed to have changed, its walls reeking history.

'One of the landlords was once valet to Lord Nelson,' she told me. 'He ran the pub during the Napoleonic Wars. I bet he got a lot of trade.' She rolled off our order, then grabbed several packets of crisps from the counter and waved them at the girl behind the bar.

'I bet he did. The history's impressive. But tell me about Rossetti staying here.'

'Let's get this lot back to the table and then I'll tell you what I know. Or Gil will. Where has he got to?'

'He was accosted by a man in fishing kit as we came in.'

'That's what comes of living in a small town. Everyone knows everyone.' But Gil was back at the table when we returned and helped unload the tray.

'Sorry, I got waylaid.'

'Your round next,' Lucy announced. 'Here, these will stave off the hunger pangs.' She threw him a bag of crisps. 'Megan wants to know about Rossetti.'

'There's not much to tell,' Gil said, 'or at least I don't know much. He came to Hastings fairly often. It was the clear air, the clear colours that drew him, I think. And he brought other members of the Brotherhood. They stayed here at the Cutter.'

'But he married in Hastings, didn't he? Lizzie Siddal?' I was remembering what Lucy had told me earlier.

'At St Clements. That was in 1860, but she'd visited a good eight years earlier. He stayed in the inn at that time, and she lodged in one of the cottages in High Street. They were living in High Street when they married.'

'It took a long time for him to walk her up the aisle.'

'Too many other distractions, I guess, despite his thinking her 'a stunner.''

That didn't surprise me. I could imagine the man I'd seen was something of a womaniser. His liveliness and Italian good looks would have attracted plenty of attention.

'But he did fall in love with her,' Lucy insisted. 'He said that as soon as he saw her, his destiny was defined. Isn't that romantic?'

'The reality wasn't quite so romantic.' Gil took a cautious sip of his wine. 'Mmm. Good choice, Luce. Lizzie was dogged by ill health and developed an addiction to laudanum. That may have been why he put off committing himself.'

'I suppose,' she agreed. 'And the marriage didn't last long either. Less than two years before poor old Lizzie took one drop of laudanum too many and popped off.'

'My sister is so sensitive.'

'Siddal seems an interesting woman,' I said. 'A model – but an artist, too, when it was unbecoming for a lady to paint professionally.'

'But she wasn't a lady, was she?' Gil dived into his crisps in workmanlike fashion. 'She was a working-class woman, as were most of the PRB's models. A milliner by trade. If she'd been a lady, she'd have had far less appeal for them. Middle-class women didn't enjoy the same freedom.'

'I wouldn't say Lizzie had that much freedom,' Lucy argued. 'She had to work.'

'True, but working-class girls weren't chaperoned. A man could go up to someone like Lizzie Siddal in the street and speak to her. That's what Deverell did. He saw this woman with amazing hair and a delicate face and decided she must be the model for his painting of *Twelfth Night*. If she'd been from a different class, he'd wouldn't have dared accost her.'

The idea of a milliner turned artist's model unsettled me. 'Do you think the Brotherhood exploited the women who modelled for them?'

'Probably. On the other hand, many of them gained from friendship with the group. Lizzie wasn't alone in being intelligent and ambitious, and the women often used their contacts to good effect. Meeting Rossetti transformed Siddal's life – it was he who encouraged her to launch an artistic career of her own.'

I found my stomach tightening. Lizzie Siddal's career had eerie parallels to Sophia's. 'My friend is coming down for the weekend,' I said brightly, trying to brush the subject from my mind.

'Hey, that's great,' Lucy enthused. 'We're both working Saturday, but we could do something together on Sunday, unless the two of you want to spend it alone. You must have a lot to catch up on.'

Lucy could be sensitive when she chose. Strangely, though, I had no strong wish to keep Julia to myself even though I'd not seen her for an age. It would be good to enjoy some time as a group. Lucy was fun and Gil was... I liked being with him, I liked looking at him, even though I didn't want to admit it. He had a solidity about him that in my frail state I found attractive.

'We could walk up to Old Roar,' he offered. The name was familiar. It was the waterfall that Sophia had painted. The picture Rossetti had extracted from the stack of canvases.

'Not that it's much of a waterfall these days,' he added. 'It should be though. The rock is perpendicular, forty or fifty feet high, and there are three or four chalybeate springs that flow from it. But it's much drier these days and we've had only one storm since you arrived, Megan.'

'It hasn't rained much, has it?' Lucy chimed in. 'I've just realised – Megan must be a good luck omen.'

I was far from being that, but I wouldn't spoil her enjoyment. She had an enviably sunny nature, inherited perhaps from her absent father. Without a second thought, it seemed, he had upped sticks and thrown himself into a whole new life.

'Do either of you ever visit Argentina?' I was following my thoughts, and spoke too quickly.

'We don't see Dad any more.' Lucy sounded awkward.

'Divorced parents, isn't that everyone's problem these days?' Gil's words were said lightly, but there was something deeper there, too.

'I'm sorry, I shouldn't have mentioned it.'

'Don't worry, it's not a big deal,' he assured me. 'The split was as amicable as these things can be. It was simple really – they were travelling in different directions. Dad hated London and had a real hang-up about English weather and Mum didn't want to move to a country thousands of miles away. So a parting was inevitable. And inevitable that Dad met someone else and remarried.'

'Lucy said your mother lives along the coast now.'

'Happy as a grig in a cottage in Rye. We get to see her pretty regularly, though she still works full time – she's a secretary in a local business. The job's way below her capabilities but she enjoys it, and she's plenty of friends for when we're not around.'

'Mum is the kind of woman who enjoys life whatever happens,' her daughter said lovingly.

I wish I could have said the same of my own mother. She hadn't remarried either, and like Mrs Martinez had taken work as a secretary, though in her case much against her will. But she certainly didn't enjoy life. From the day my father walked out of the door, she'd carried a fount of resentment. A cancer of bitterness. Or so it seemed to me, as soon as I was old enough to have any understanding.

'Come on, drink up,' Gil urged. 'At this rate, even the vindaloo will be cold.'

Lucy groaned. 'You are such a loser.'

Chapter Thirteen

I don't know how it happened, but over that curry I found myself accepting a ride in a small boat. Not that I've much experience of boats, small or otherwise, but somehow it didn't seem the kind of thing I should be doing. And particularly not with Gil. After several glasses of wine I'd agreed, thinking it might be fun, only to find that Lucy wouldn't be a fellow passenger. *Lucy loves the sea but hates boats*, Gil had said laughingly. So here I was, two days later at five o'clock in the afternoon, walking to meet him. I turned sharp left at the promenade and strolled towards the Stade. The shingle beach was dotted with fishing boats and scattered with cables and trailing chains – it didn't imbue me with confidence. I had no idea how skilful a sailor Gil was, but I was glad I could swim.

'In case you're worried,' he greeted me from the small rowing boat half way along the harbour arm, 'I take a boat out quite often and we won't venture far.' He looked tanned and relaxed in rolled up denims and a tee shirt that had seen better days.

'We've chosen a calm evening, at least.' I managed to keep my voice this side of squeaky.

'Even less to worry about! Here, let me help you down –

the steps are slippery.' I could see his point, the worn stone was green with lichen.

Getting into the boat was another matter altogether. It was held fast by a rope tied to a wooden post on the harbour arm, but was bobbing about in a worrying fashion. With one hand, Gil held the craft as firmly as he could, and with the other, steadied me as I took a hesitant step onto the side of the boat. Somehow I lost my footing and in a sudden crash, tumbled into its well. It was impossible to struggle to my feet and I had to crawl crabwise along the bottom of the boat to the seat furthest from the oars. When I got my breath back and could feel firm wood beneath me, I looked up to see Gil trying hard to suppress a laugh.

'Don't you dare! Or I'll get off this minute and you can sail into the sunset alone.'

'Seeing you getting off would be almost as good.' He untied the rope, then slipped into his seat with annoying ease, and settled himself between the oars.

For a while, as he rowed us out of the harbour and into the wider sea, we didn't speak. I had been lucky with the evening. Even when we were past the sheltering bay in which the town nestled, the sea remained calm with only small wavelets disturbing its polished surface. The day had been another one of warm sunshine and I needed only a light pashmina over my shoulders. I was glad I'd packed it, though at the time I couldn't see it would be needed. But Julia had brought the shawl back from India the previous year and I adored its brilliant colours.

The sun had begun to set in a magnificent slide to the horizon, casting a golden shaft across the sea's enamel. 'What do you think?' My companion rested his oars and we drifted softly on the tide.

'I think it's beautiful.'

He looked pleased. 'Worth the terror then?'

'I'm beginning to think so.'

'I was surprised when you said you'd come. But glad.'

'Did you put me down as a die-hard landlubber?'

'I put you down as wary.'

I was wary and plenty in life had taught me to be so. 'Sometimes it pays to be careful.'

'But not always. If you're too cautious, you can build a shell that isolates. Your painting, for instance. You paint, but you don't share your work with anyone. Why not?'

I was discomfited by the turn the conversation had taken. 'Because it's not good enough.'

'Lucy says otherwise.' I cursed his sister silently. She had called that morning with some early strawberries from a neighbour and seen my painting of All Saints Street on the easel.

'She's being kind.'

'I don't think so. I think she's right. Why don't you take a chance – let the world see what you have to offer? After all, you've the genes and I imagine you've been painting from a young age.'

I had and though my mother had given little encouragement, she hadn't stopped me. Nor prevented me taking up a place at art school.

'What did your teachers say at college?' He had almost read my mind.

'That I had talent.'

'Great talent, I imagine, but no one is ever going to know it. Why let an accident stop you?'

'You've seen my hand,' I said crudely. 'Why do you think?'

'But you're still painting.'

'The scar tissue affects the tendons. It makes painting difficult.'

'Okay, maybe you don't paint with the same dexterity, but you're managing. You were once set on being a professional artist, so why let a single moment of inattention destroy your dream?'

'It wasn't inattention.' I'd snapped back my response, and then wished I hadn't.'

'What was it then?'

'An accident. My mother's.' I didn't enjoy saying it, but I felt trapped. 'It was a pure accident,' I insisted.

'I don't doubt it.'

'She can be volatile.' I needed to explain, to excuse her. It was a compulsion to be fair, despite what she had done to me. 'She loses her temper quite suddenly, and then her actions are all over the place.'

'She must have lost her temper in a very big way to be throwing boiling water around.'

I didn't say anything. The peace of the evening was still there, but I wasn't feeling it any more. I was back in that angry scene.

'What happened, Megan?' His voice was quietly determined.

A last splash of sunlight was streaking the sea, its gold spreading and contracting with the gentle movement of the waves and gilding the polished wood of the boat. I looked across at him and saw sympathy in his face. Understanding, too.

'It's a miserable tale. Do you really want to know?'

When he nodded, I took a deep breath. 'It was after my first year at art school. We had finished our final project and several of my friends wanted to celebrate. They had a fancy to go to Italy in the summer vacation and thought it would be great to wander round the galleries and maybe hire a place for a few weeks and paint. I suggested to my mother I travelled with them and she went crazy. She accused me of being underhand, of deceiving her. I wasn't really going to paint, she said, I was going to see my father.'

'And would that have been so very bad?'

'It would for her. She saw it as a betrayal.'

'That doesn't sound too reasonable.' His face was receding into the darkening air, but his voice came to me strong and thoughtful.

'She isn't reasonable, not when she's in a temper. She was bitter – she's still bitter – at being abandoned, and my mentioning Italy was enough to enrage her. It signalled every grievance she'd nursed for fourteen years. If I went there, it must mean I was hell-bent on seeing my father.'

'It would hardly have been the end of the world if you had. Did you never try to see him? Once you weren't a child?'

'No, and I wasn't about to. He'd never been interested in me, and I was hardly going to turn up on the steps of his palazzo unannounced.'

Gil picked up the oars and began a slow row back towards the harbour. I could just make out the outline of his face in the gathering dusk.

'Was he genuinely uninterested in his daughter?'

'No, not really,' I said in a small voice. 'But I only found that out after he died. He left a letter with his will, addressed to me. In it he said he'd always loved me and it had broken his heart to leave, but he couldn't cope with my mother's moods any longer. He thought she would settle once he had gone and that I'd be better off without him.'

'And did you believe that?'

'I wanted to. If I were harsh, I'd say it was his way of justifying what he did. But in his favour, it seems he tried to keep in touch. He'd sent presents, cards, that sort of thing. It was my mother who'd seen off every attempt. He'd left this letter with his will, he said, because if he had sent it, he knew I would never get it.'

'Was he right?'

'I'd never received anything he had sent, so I guess so.'

'It must have been tough for you, knowing he'd tried to keep in touch when it was too late to do anything about it.'

I had wanted to shout and scream when I'd learned how often my father had tried to contact me, wanted to beat the wall with clenched fists at a life of lost opportunities. Wanted, I'm ashamed to confess, to beat my mother. But Julia had been by my side, her sensible voice persuading me to channel my anger positively.

After the will was read, my mother had erupted into a full-blown tempest, bristling with fury that her daughter had inherited every penny of Robert Lacey's estate. What better, Julia had said, than to use the money, all the money, for myself: *Buy your own shop, Meg, one that deals in art, and make sure it's a success.*

'It was tough, and I've never stopped blaming myself.' As I spoke the words, I realised for the first time they were true. I did blame myself, and the guilt I felt was corroding the already damaged relationship I had with my mother.

Quite suddenly out of the gloom, a speedboat cut across our bow, jolting me from my thoughts. It left a vee-shaped furrow boiling in its wake and Gil stopped rowing immediately. But it didn't prevent our boat from swinging violently, first to one side then to the other. A placid sea became a patchwork of glittering pinpricks.

'Are you okay?' He sounded anxious.

'More or less.' I'd grabbed the side of the boat as the sea had swelled beneath me.

'They're a menace.' He jerked his head towards the offender, now almost out of sight, but then picked up the conversation where he'd left it. 'You shouldn't blame your self for your father. You were a child. How could you know what was happening? It's not where the blame lies. But did you never talk of him to your mother?'

'That was a lesson I learned early – to keep a still tongue on the subject. I knew he was in Italy, I knew he was in Venice, though I can't remember how, but I'd no intention of seeing him. That summer, I just wanted to go to Italy. Instead, I was weeks in hospital.'

'You poor love.'

'I wasn't the only one damaged – after the accident my mother tried everything to make amends.' I was determined to be fair to her. 'But there was nothing she could do, nothing either of us could do, except wait for the hand to heal as best it could.'

'And when it healed, you never went back to college?' My silence was his answer. 'So what did you do?'

We were on the move again, the oars dipping effortlessly in and out of the still waters. The first glimmerings of moonlight were turning the gold of the sea into silver.

'Nothing. Stayed in my bedroom, let myself go.'

'And fell into a depression?'

'Sort of. I'm not proud of it.'

'I think I might have ranted instead.'

'What would be the point? My mother hadn't intended to harm me. And she tried all the tricks she could think of to get me out of that bedroom, but I was stubborn and refused. I couldn't paint so life was futile. That's how it felt at the time.'

'But you did get out of the bedroom. You did get interested in life again.'

I pulled a face. 'And that was my mother's doing, too. She was the one who saw the advert for volunteers. She even wrote a letter to the gallery's curator – Julia's mother. It was how I met Julia, I think I told you. My mother always liked to keep me to herself, even after I started college, and Julia was the first real friend I had. She shook me up and made me see sense. She's so full of confidence, so full of energy, no one languishes in her company for long.'

'I'm looking forward to meeting this whirlwind. Are you still up for the waterfall on Sunday?'

I murmured agreement though I felt a traitor. I didn't know how I was going to tell him that our trip to Old Roar would be the last time I would see him. I didn't know how I was going to tell myself. His quiet strength suited me, and every time I met him I found myself wanting more of his company.

He was such a contrast to Dan. On the surface, Dan had been the most casual of creatures, but beneath he'd been a fizz of tension. That's what had first attracted me, I guess – like Julia, he seemed to have boundless optimism. When I'd met him, he'd been living in a crummy bedsit in Hoxton and coming to Palette and Paint to buy whatever he could afford each week. He'd been fun to be with but he'd had deeper tones, too. He'd recognised my vulnerability – until, that is, he'd stopped recognising it. Uninvited, the image of Thornton Manor swam into my mind.

'Give me your hand.'

While I had been daydreaming, we'd arrived back at the

jetty and Gil was leaning over to hoist me onto dry land. Once I was safely on the slipway, he anchored the boat with some seriously impressive knots.

'I never asked you, is the boat yours?'

'I hire it from Jim Lister, but I'm thinking of buying one. If I stay.'

I was taken aback. He seemed to fit the town so well, I hadn't imagined he wouldn't stay. 'Are you likely to move then?'

'You never know. Probably not. I've been here three years and my roots are growing.'

'Do your roots tell you what those towers are?' I looked across the beach at the cluster of wooden structures, gaunt and black-tarred, that I'd seen from the steps up to East Hill. From this angle, they looked even taller and a good deal blacker.

'They're net huts. They were used for drying fishing nets to prevent them from rotting. Nowadays, the nets are made of nylon and can be left outside, so the huts are primarily for storage. They can be two or three storeys high and some even have a cellar. Interesting, aren't they? Unique to Hastings, too. In Victorian times, the sea was closer and they were built tall because of the limited space at the head of the beach. That's the official version anyway. Myself, I think it was to avoid paying excess ground tax.'

'I'm impressed. Such a fount of knowledge – Pre-Raphaelites to fishing nets. There's no stopping you.'

'Oh, I don't know. I reckon I could be stopped.' And before I realised what he was doing, he'd bent down and brushed my lips with his.

Chapter Fourteen

I tried not to think about the kiss – there was really nothing to think of. It had been a small token of friendship, that was all. Gil and I had spent several hours together cooped up in a small boat, peculiarly intimate hours in which I'd spilled out the unhappiness of my family life and the truth behind my damaged hand. I had never told that to anyone, not even Julia, yet last evening I hadn't hesitated. No wonder he'd felt it right to offer me a brief kiss. But I knew that wasn't the whole story. If his kiss were such a small matter, why was my reaction so complicated? Why did I feel so bad? As though I were betraying Dan's memory. I'd been betrayed by him, but it didn't make it right to follow the same path.

I was relieved when Saturday morning came and I knew that in an hour or so I'd be meeting Julia. There would be plenty for us to talk about other than Gil Martinez. She had offered to take a cab from the station to All Saints Street, but I'd suggested we walk. It meant she would see something of Hastings before we reached the cottage.

Her train wasn't due until shortly before midday, but I left the cottage early to dawdle along the promenade. A stiff breeze blew off the Channel, but the sun was shining and I took my time. I had reached the point where I'd have to turn inland towards the station when, on impulse, I made a detour into the small uphill road that led to the Driftwood Gallery. I had no clear plan in mind, only that after the boat ride I felt I'd met someone I could trust.

I had saved my secret for the moment when I'd meet Julia again, but now the moment had come, I was uncertain. My first instinct had been right. I should keep silent, otherwise she would think me mad, or at best laugh at me. Yet more and more I felt the need to confide. It was my voice alone that was telling me I was sane, and I was desperate for someone else to tell me, too. Someone who would listen to the unbelievable and not dismiss it instantly.

I was lucky to find Gil on the second floor, supervising the rehanging of a painting that had recently been restored. 'Megan! I didn't expect to see you this morning. But how nice.'

I found myself remembering the kiss and blushed, then felt ridiculous. 'Can you spare me a moment?'

'Of course, come on up to the office.' He gave a few murmured instructions to the men, then led the way to the third floor. 'Can I get you a coffee?'

I refused, too nervous to think of drinking. And by the time he had cleared a space for me amid the overflow of papers and boxes, my hands were visibly shaking. It had been a stupid idea to come.

'Something's happened. What is it?' He had seen the shaking hands.

I forced them into a tight grip, then cleared my throat. 'This is going to sound crazy.'

'Try me.'

So I did, relating in a deadpan voice every encounter I'd had with the Waylands, though omitting any mention of the hall and its icy grip. I had that much sense at least. By the time I'd finished, he looked punch drunk.

'Have you any idea why this is happening?'

The question was tentative, but I felt a rush of relief that he was even asking it. It meant he hadn't dismissed my tale completely. 'Only the obvious one. That I've had several bad shocks recently and they've pushed me over the edge.'

'It's true that shock can do strange things.' He passed a hand through his hair. I could see he was struggling how best to respond and shock provided a neat explanation. I should have left it there, but something pushed me on.

'If it is shock, then it must be delayed. My partner died weeks ago, and these strange experiences only began when I came to Hastings.'

'You think this travelling into the past is connected to your cottage?'

'I've known something like it before,' I confessed. 'And I'd been hurt then, too, but those instances were different. Brief and indistinct. Nothing like I'm seeing and hearing now.'

He said nothing, but he didn't need to – his scepticism filled the room. I felt wretched. I'd laid myself open to judgement, trusting to gut feeling he would prove a friend when I needed one. I should have known better. I had trusted Dan, allowed him to tempt me out of my shell and look where that had got me.

'Perhaps it's true I'm losing my mind,' I flung out, angry that I couldn't convince him, angry at myself for even trying.

He gave me one of his long, steady looks. 'I doubt it,' he said evenly. 'Your partner left you very suddenly. It's most likely the reality hasn't hit you until now and it's a coincidence these strange experiences started when you arrived in Hastings.'

He had a point. Or was I allowing him to persuade me because it was easier? Because I wanted his friendship, and if I continued to insist this was more than shock, I'd forfeit his goodwill.

'Dan died a violent death,' I conceded, 'and to be honest, things hadn't been completely right between us for a while, so maybe I'm tormenting myself. Punishing myself because I didn't realise how unhappy he was.'

He said nothing but his raised eyebrows asked for more, and somehow I was able to stumble out the words. 'Since I've been here, I've discovered he was cheating on me. I hadn't a clue it was happening and I should have. It's given me this horrible feeling that my whole life with him was a fraud. It's possible, I suppose, that unconsciously I'm connecting it to the fraud the Waylands are living.'

His eyes widened and I could see this was a step too far. 'Or I could be making a quite different link,' I gabbled. 'The regressions always happen when I'm looking at a piece of artwork, so perhaps it has something to do with the fact I can't paint any longer, at least not professionally. I've never really accepted the situation and it's taken a move down here for me to act it out in some way.'

It sounded far-fetched even to my ears, and he shook his head. 'I don't buy that at all.' His brow furrowed and his face was set.

I shouldn't have come, that was clear, and I shouldn't have spilled out these crazy ideas and expected him to understand. I had thought Dan understood me but been very wrong, so why would a man I barely knew? But just as I was about to leave, he asked, 'What actually happens when you look at a painting?'

'It's not every painting, or every visual image for that matter. It seems to be those connected in some fashion to the Waylands – Sophia's embroidery, the seascape she was painting, the version of All Saints Street you have here. And it doesn't happen with a casual glance. It happens when I'm looking at the picture intently. It's as though the real world, or the world I'm living in, dissolves around me, and I walk through the image into a different life. That's the only way I can describe the experience.'

But there was a pattern to it, a purpose. The portrait of the young child had opened a path into the past, but for a reason. The girl's eyes, when I'd looked deep into them, had been searching, pleading, asking something of me. I was being told a story; I could feel it at the deepest level. But why it was being told at this moment, and why to me, I didn't know, unless as a failed artist in deep shock and owning a kind of instinctual perception, I was more susceptible than former inhabitants of the cottage. But I said none of this. What I'd said already sounded mad enough. I would make my excuses and hope we could forget this exchange.

Before I could, though, my phone rang loudly from the depths of my handbag.

'Where are you?' Julia. I'd completely forgotten. I jumped up so quickly that I sent the chair toppling. 'I'm so sorry, Jules. I'm coming. Give me five minutes.'

'Don't put yourself out. I'll take a cab.' There was a metallic sharpness to her voice and the call finished abruptly.

Gil pulled a face. 'Trouble?'

'Let's just say I'd better go.'

'Probably wise. We'll see you both tomorrow morning. Shall we meet at Das's shop around ten?' He seemed as relieved as I that we'd left my visions behind. 'Lucy is already looking for her hiking boots. For some reason, she's become convinced we'll be knee-deep in mud.'

'Fine. Ten o'clock.' I grabbed my bag from the floor and was out of the door in seconds. I hoped that by tomorrow I would have smoothed Julia's ruffled feathers.

* * *

She was waiting on the doorstep, her small overnight bag chastising me. *I'm only here a few hours*, it seemed to say, *and you can't even manage those.*

I found myself apologising lavishly. 'So sorry. My watch has gone haywire – it must have got salt in it.' Surreptitiously, I pulled down my cuff.

'Your phone appears to be working. They do have clocks on them, you know.' She wasn't going to let me off lightly.

'Look, Jules, I've messed up and I feel bad. Can we start the weekend again?'

'What's left of it.'

Then she relented and came down the steps to give me a hug. I was encased in a cloud of Chanel number five and it felt soothingly familiar. 'Are you going to let me into this seaside palace of yours or not?'

'Seaside maybe, palace a bit doubtful. But your room is very nice – it overlooks a secret garden.'

'Wow. Worth two hours on a train that wasn't sure whether it should have got up this morning.'

I let us in and made for the kettle and a much needed coffee. She followed close behind and I wondered if she was conscious of anything odd as she walked through the hall, but she made no comment. She was busy inspecting the small kitchen.

'This is jolly. I like the sunshine yellow.'

'I think it's to disguise the fact the kitchen hasn't been refurbished for years. But look outside.' The little courtyard was bathed in light, the gaily painted table and chairs beckoning. I yanked the large iron key around in the lock and threw open the door.

'Go and look,' I urged. 'I'll bring the coffee out.'

When I arrived with the tray, she had pulled a chair out of the shadow and was settling herself for a sunbathe. 'You were right. It is lovely. Thanks, Meg.' She took a mug and leaned back in the metal chair. 'This could be more comfortable though.'

'I know, but it's not worth buying another.'

'You're here for several months. It could be a good investment.'

This was my chance to confess I'd be returning to Hampstead with her tomorrow. But I didn't. We hadn't exactly made a good start to the weekend and I'd no wish to introduce another jarring note. At least not yet.

'So what's the news from Palette and Paint?' I wasn't that eager to know, but it would have seemed odd if I hadn't asked.

'As far as I can make out, everything's fine. Deepna is brilliant – but you know that. I think some of the older customers miss you, but most are fine with her. She's very good at giving just the right amount of information.'

I felt a little stung. Was she suggesting I overloaded people with advice, that perhaps the shop would run better if I stayed in Hastings for the summer? But no doubt I was being over sensitive.

'And how was Bath?' I needed to get away from talk of the shop.

She yawned. 'You asked me that before. Bath was the

same as ever.'

'And Nicky?' I had asked her that before, too, but I wasn't going to let her brush him aside.

'He's going to boarding school in September,' she said unexpectedly. 'I've got the chore of kitting him out. Mark has to go to New York on business and doesn't want to take him, so guess what? He has to come and stay at mine.'

'It could be fun getting his school stuff ready.' In truth, I couldn't imagine how anyone could send a ten-year-old away to school, but Mark had a business to run and Julia refused to commit to anything more than a token appearance.

'It's not fun, and you know it. I'm well aware what you think of boarding schools, though the one Mark has chosen seems pretty low-key and friendly. But he's a pain going off to New York like that. It would have been ideal for Nicky to go with him, but he says he's got appointments for every hour of the day and can't leave the boy alone in a hotel room.'

'That's understandable.'

She yawned again. 'I suppose. But tell me what you've been doing here. I caught sight of an easel as I passed the sitting room. Are you painting again?'

'Just a little.'

Instinctively I stretched out my right hand as far as I could and felt it give very slightly. So I hadn't imagined an improvement: the hand *was* a little more supple, though the additional movement seemed negligible.

She reached out and squeezed my arm. 'That's great. I am so pleased. Painting is what you need.'

I wasn't sure what I needed, though I was certain it was nothing Julia could prescribe. That was tetchy of me and I didn't know why. She had been a true friend during some of my darkest days. In the months after the accident, I'd been stiff and uncommunicative, submerged beneath a black fog, and no one had been able to reach me. If it hadn't been for Julia, I might still be there.

'You know,' she said thoughtfully, 'in future you could spend more time painting. We should think about expanding the business, getting more staff. I was checking the shop account the other day and we still have the pot of money from Levsky, completely untapped.'

The small pot was a commission. Levsky was a wealthy art dealer and I'd introduced him to the artist he'd been stalking for years. As a reward, he had promised a small commission on each of the two paintings he'd got Maitland Mayer to agree to. But a small commission on a painting worth thousands is a sizeable sum.

'You know how I feel about that.'

'But why? Why are you so uncomfortable about the money? You've earned it.'

'Oh, come on, Julia, I introduced Levsky to an artist I happened to meet in the shop. That's hardly earning the money.'

Mayer had been on a trip back to England and decided to visit Hampstead where he'd lived as a boy. Somehow he'd found his way to Palette and Paint and as we'd talked, I discovered that he had been a student of my father's years back.

'You only gave him a personal introduction to an artist who sells for hundreds of thousands!'

'It wasn't personal. Mayer's connection was to my father. I feel a fraud accepting the money.' There it was, that word again.

'Rubbish. Connections are there to be used. That's business and it's netted us a tidy sum, with an even tidier one due next month when Levsky gets his second picture. We shouldn't just leave the money in the bank. We should do something with it.'

'I'll think about it,' I said, though I didn't want to.

'Good. And when you've thought about it, we should buy the house next door! The agent tells me it's coming on the market very soon. Then we could extend the shop floor and carry a lot more stock. It would mean an increase in turnover and justify employing another assistant. Deepna could take on the job of manager permanently – she'd be great.'

'And what would I do?'

'You would paint, my lovely one, as you were destined to do.'

She was going way too fast. She was keen for us to expand, I'd known that for some time, but even if I hadn't felt queasy about the money, I wasn't convinced by the business case. The shop, as it stood, did well enough, but not sufficiently well to justify a large increase in retail space. Julia was a restless soul, always full of plans, never quite content with the way things were. But any new purchase required both partners of the business to agree. If I decided against, I could see some battles ahead.

'I've met some interesting people since I've been here.' I pumped energy into my voice, hoping to distract her.

'Oh, yes?'

She didn't seem too engaged, but I ploughed on. 'You know that Deepna's uncle runs a shop on the seafront – antiques cum bric-a-brac? His assistant is a lovely girl, Lucy Martinez. At least she's his assistant for the moment. She doesn't seem to have decided exactly what she wants to do.

Her brother is curator at one of the local galleries.'

Julia's ears pricked up, either because a man had been mentioned or because she thought Gil might offer a new business opportunity. 'I've been out with them a couple of times. They've promised us a walk tomorrow morning, if you're up for it.'

Her interest faded and she looked decidedly glum. 'I hope you haven't agreed.'

'Sort of. And it could be intriguing. It's the walk Rossetti loved when he stayed in Hastings.'

'Rossetti? The Rossetti?'

I nodded enthusiastically. 'I didn't know of the connection before, but apparently he was a frequent visitor to the town.'

She sighed. 'In that case, I suppose we must make the pilgrimage. As long as it's not too far or too messy. But what about tonight? Do you fancy doing something wild?'

'Wild and Hastings don't really go together.'

She stretched out her long limbs and closed her eyes, the sun's rays highlighting the auburn hair of which she was rightly proud. 'Then we'll stay in and have a take-away.'

'If that's what you'd like.'

'I don't mind, my darling. Whatever suits.'

I had the distinct feeling this was as much a duty visit for Julia as the one she had made to Bath, but I said nothing. Since Dan's death, I'd found it hard to regain our old camaraderie, but I kept hoping things would return to the way they had been. In my bleakest moments, I imagined she blamed me for his accident, though I couldn't see why she would. She had known Dan almost as long as I had and though they'd never been close, they had rubbed along, Julia poking fun at his job – *why waste your talents teaching scrubby schoolkids?* – and Dan laughing it off in his easy way.

But I knew his death had upset her, though she'd shown little emotion. At the funeral, she'd been focussed on supporting me through what had been an interminable day. I'd kept wanting to talk to her about Dan, but found it impossible. And since I'd last seen her, I had learned things that made it even harder. I couldn't speak to her of his infidelity, but could I risk divulging my encounters with the Waylands? After all, an hour ago I'd spilled out my troubles to Gil despite hardly knowing him.

She opened her eyes then, and for a brief instant seemed to look right through me. No, I thought, better not.

Chapter Fifteen

Despite my misgivings, we had a great evening. A Chinese meal and a large number of gin and tonics helped to break down whatever barrier there had been, and I went to bed a little the worst for wear but feeling I had my friend back. I wasn't sure, though, how she would take to being woken up for a ten o'clock meeting, and I was right. When I came bearing an early morning mug of tea, she groaned and threw herself to the other side of the bed.

'You have to be joking,' she muttered into the sheets.

'The walk, remember? I've promised. I'll have to go even if you're not up to it.'

I didn't know why I was dragging her out. Why I was dragging myself. After yesterday's bad misjudgement, meeting Gil would be awkward. I felt raw at the thought of seeing him again, as though I'd lost a precious layer of skin.

'How can you be so bright at this time in the morning? It's indecent.'

'If it makes you feel any better, my head is throbbing fit to bust.'

'*Everything* of mine is throbbing.' She sat up and slurped the tea. 'Do we really have to go?'

'I'll make you French toast,' I tempted.

'It's no good trying to bribe me.'

'It's worth being bribed – look out of the window. The sun is trying to break through. And think of all that fresh air.'

'I am thinking of it.' She groaned again, but swallowed the tea and looked a little less lothargic.

'The bathroom's all yours. See you downstairs in ten minutes.'

That was probably hopeful, but I'd made only a few slices of toast when Julia appeared, looking scrubbed and remarkably alive.

'I don't know why I'm up, but I'm here. Give me some food.'

She had to munch her way through two rounds and swallow a mug of coffee before she pronounced herself fit to face the great outdoors. 'I hope there's a decent path on this jaunt. I'm not exactly equipped for country walking – I left the yomping kit back in Hampstead.'

'I don't think you need worry.' I smiled. Julia and yomping was an irresistible combination.

On the way to the front door, she looked at herself in the small hall mirror. 'There must be something about this place. It's amazing but I look half decent, and after how many gins?'

'I wasn't counting.'

'And you look terrific,' she went on. 'So much better. Good old Deepna suggesting Hastings.'

I nodded a trifle vaguely, then went in search of my sun-glasses. 'Do you think I should take my overnight bag with me?' she called up the stairs.

'Maybe. I've no idea how far this place is or how long we'll be.'

'Great. You promised me a short walk. Now you're saying it could be a day-long trek.'

I rejoined her in the hall. 'I doubt it. They know you have a train to catch this afternoon.'

Now was the time to tell her I'd be travelling with her. *Don't bother taking the bag*, I should have said. *I'll need to come back and do my own packing.* But once again, I let the chance slip and we left with one small piece of luggage.

On the way to Das's shop, she linked her free arm in mine. 'Sorry I was such a grump yesterday. I had a rotten time in Bath and it's made me cow-like.' She held up her hand as I went to ask. 'You don't want to hear and I don't want to talk about it.'

'Fine. You're allowed.'

'And allowed this morning's grump, too?'

'Why not? It's Sunday. Everyone's entitled to a lie-in and you didn't get one.'

'But instead I'll get a walk, and that will blow the cobwebs away. Something to remember when I'm back on the gritty streets.' She sounded cheerful and my spirits lifted, though not for long. 'Did you think any more of my idea? About buying the house next to the shop?'

I'd hoped she wouldn't return to that. 'I'm not sure,' I extemporised. In fact, I was increasingly sure, but too happy to be back to our old friendship that I'd spoil it by being honest. I would have to tell her eventually, but not today.

'You can trust my judgement, you know. I was right about buying the shop all those years ago.'

She had been. I'd been fazed when I was told of my father's legacy, but Julia had come up with the idea of a shop and sold it to me. My mother was spiteful enough to suggest that money was the sole reason my friend had taken me under her wing. I'd dismissed the slur as another of Ruth Lacey's perennial unkindnesses; in any case, there had been no question of money when Julia first met me.

She was tough, I'd known that from the start, but she was kind, too, and had been so eager to help me get back on my feet that I didn't mind if she'd scented an opportunity. She had helped me through bad times and now I could pay back a little. And she hadn't just taken; she had lived for a whole year off her savings while she worked for free, and it was her hard work on the finances, getting the customers in, negotiating supplier contracts, that got us off to such a successful start. I owed her a lot.

* * *

Gil and Lucy were waiting outside the shop. As soon as she saw us, Lucy rushed over and flung her arms around me in a massive hug. Julia rather pointedly held out her hand. From Gil I received a chaste kiss on the cheek. It didn't seem he'd told his sister of our last conversation. Hopefully, he'd erased it from his mind and I could retreat into my shell again. I was relieved — but sad, too. He hadn't proved the friend I'd imagined; I should have been able to tell him anything and be believed.

Das came out to greet us. He was open for business, though I couldn't imagine he'd have too many customers this morning. Daytrippers were thin on the ground this early in the day. It wasn't worrying Das though; he seemed as happy as ever and willingly hiked Julia's bag behind the counter.

'Don't forget to collect it,' he warned. 'Or it will join my bric-a-brac. I could make good money on that.' He enjoyed his own joke, though Julia didn't seem to find it amusing.

She had taken in Lucy's full costume and was looking dismayed.

I looked, too. 'You found the boots then?' It was an unnecessary question.

'All she needs now is the mud,' Gil said.

'I'm equipped for all weathers. See, the sun can blaze.' She gave the long khaki shorts a pat of satisfaction, 'and the rain can rain.' A small umbrella appeared from her waistband. 'And –

'You've bought your skis in case it snows,' Julia interjected. There was an unconvincing ripple of laughter. Her tone had not been exactly friendly.

'Let's get going, shall we?' Gil broke the silence that had fallen. 'Rain isn't forecast until later in the day and there shouldn't be too much mud after the dry weather we've had. Which is just as well. Trainers are my limit.' He walked ahead with Lucy.

'And not great trainers either,' Julia whispered. 'He's a bit of a nerd, isn't he?'

I stared at her. 'I've never thought so. He's a knowledgable man and amusing, too.'

'Don't say you've developed an interest in that direction?'

'He's a decent person, that's all,' I said rather too hotly.

'But hardly in Dan's league.'

I was trying to think of something to say when Lucy turned round. 'Don't be surprised if it looks as though we're making our way out of town. We aren't, I promise.'

I'm glad she warned us. For quite some time, we had been following busy roads with housing on either side, but shortly before we left the last dwelling behind, a footpath appeared to our right. We turned down it and came out at the top of an immense green space.

'Alexandra Park,' Lucy announced.

We paused for a while to get our breath back; it had been quite a climb. I'd never even heard of the park before, but its extensive lawns and tree-lined slopes were delightful. In the distance, I could see a rose garden and what looked like a wild garden as well, and an attractive lake complete with fowl. Another piece of Hastings to enjoy. 'It's beautiful.'

'I think so, too.' Lucy beamed. 'Are you okay?' She spoke to Julia who was bent double over one of her shoes. 'Not really. I've picked up a stone.'

'Let me help.' She held out a hand for support, but Julia shook herself free. 'No need,' she said curtly.

I saw Gil look at me over their two heads, his face expressionless. He pointed to the bridge that lay ahead. 'We go over this. It leads into a nature reserve and you walk through that to get to the waterfall, though not much chance of water today, I'm afraid.'

'Great,' Julia muttered under her breath. 'A waterfall with no water.'

I was beginning to feel badly embarrassed and hoped that neither Gil nor Lucy had heard her. I couldn't imagine what had got into Julia; she seemed to have taken an instant dislike to them. Did she resent my having made friends here? But she wanted me happy, so why not encourage the friendship? And it hadn't seemed to worry her earlier when I'd talked of them. Maybe it was the warmth of their greeting that had fuelled her resentment, and the fact that Gil had turned out to be an eligible male, despite her slighting remarks. I was still smarting from her suggestion I was ready to replace Dan.

In single file we followed the path that led into the woodland, and were soon surrounded by a mass of vegetation. We were walking through a narrow valley, deeply cut and with tall, rangy saplings hanging to the sides of a steep gorge. What breeze we'd felt at the top of the park had dropped completely and the stillness was immense. Alongside the path, a stream cut a crystal ribbon through slippery banks of earth, the rushing of its waters and the odd creaking of trees, the few sounds in this strange world. There were moss-covered rocks everywhere, and huge fallen branches that looked like great prehistoric beasts abandoned by history. If I hadn't known I was in a Sussex town, I would have thought I was walking through a primeval jungle.

Ahead, a fallen tree trunk lay right across the river and I veered off towards it. Balancing carefully, I crept along the trunk, then bent down to feel the water. It was ice cold.

'That's impressive,' Gil said. 'Particularly after the boat.'

'What about the boat?' Lucy asked. 'You didn't tell me.'

'I don't tell tales. And it was only a small tumble.'

'Poor Megan. And I expect he laughed, didn't he?'

'Naturally.' Her indignation made me smile. Then I saw Julia glare across at Gil, and said quickly, 'Sorry folks, I'm holding you up.'

'We've plenty of time. Come back slowly, then we'll walk on.'

'Yes, do let's.' Julia swatted an imaginary fly from her hair.

It was another ten minutes before we came to a halt again. This time, Lucy was the guilty one. 'Let's cross over here.' We had come to a small wooden bridge.

'Why do we have to cross over anywhere? It's the same on the other side.' That was Julia, of course.

'We don't have to. Or you don't. But I think I've seen some wild orchids.' She darted across the bridge and bent to look at a clump of mauve and white blossoms. 'They *are* orchids,' she said excitedly. 'See, they've sword shaped leaves.'

She tripped back over the bridge, well satisfied. 'Aren't they beautiful? Do you like flowers, Julia?'

I wasn't sure if she was being deliberately provoking or not, but she got the response I imagined she expected. 'I do. In very large bouquets tied up with satin bows.'

The quarrel simmering beneath the surface was at odds with this peaceful, sheltered place, a gem hidden from the daily world. I didn't understand what had happened, why Julia was behaving so out of character, but I found myself wishing she would go back to London. And without me. Then I felt bad that I'd thought it.

I was glad, though, I'd said nothing about returning – I'd made an important decision while we had been walking. The morning had thrown things into focus for me and I knew I couldn't leave. At least, not for some time. Not only because of Julia's odd behaviour, but because I liked it here and the more I saw, the more I liked.

We continued to walk upstream towards a fence where the river divided into two tributaries. 'Either path will take us to the waterfall,' Gil said, 'but the one on the left is probably easier. It's a little wider, though on bad days it can be slippery.'

'Not for the fainthearted when it's raining,' Lucy put in.

'But fine today, which in a way is a shame. The waterfall in full spout is worth seeing. It's magnificent.'

We had reached the end of the path and were facing a monolithic stone wall. A great flood of water should have thundered over its edge, but days of dry weather had reduced it to a trickle.

'Is this it?' Julia who had been lagging behind caught up

with the three of us and stood looking at the small stream of water falling dejectedly to the ground.

'I'm afraid so,' he apologised. 'This is Old Roar.'

'Was someone having a joke when they named it? And Rossetti bothered to get his spats wet walking up here?'

'I don't think he would have worn spats, but he did come here.' He was dealing with Julia's evil mood with calm good humour and I liked that in him. 'Over there.' He waved a hand towards the ironwork bridge that overlooked the ghyll. 'That would have been something he'd have seen. It's a Victorian construction. Rather optimistically, it was listed in the first tourist guides of the town.'

'Optimistic is the right word.' Julia turned to go, though the rest of us lingered.

'I read this was Elizabeth Siddal's favourite place.' Lucy gave a little sigh. 'And if I close my eyes, I can see her walking beneath the trees. She was tall and slender and had this deep red hair which must have blazed in this light. I've always thought them a beautiful couple. So romantic!'

'Gloomy, more like,' Julia contradicted. 'But at least it's in keeping. Siddal was a drug addict, wasn't she? And died young.'

'Everyone took laudanum in those days and she didn't die in Hastings,' Lucy said stoutly. 'Maybe they walked here on happier days.'

'Then they must have had a taste for the Gothic. Can we go? This place is giving me the creeps.'

I thought it beautiful myself, but it was easier not to say so and we trooped back along the narrow path in silence. What should have been a delightful expedition had been one of the most uncomfortable mornings I could remember.

When we were once more out into the park, Julia made a great business of looking at her watch. 'I think I should go, but you three must stay. I can find my own way back to the shop.'

'But surely, it's too early. Your train doesn't leave for several hours,'

'I'd rather be safe than sorry, Meg.'

It was a poor excuse, but in keeping with the rest of the morning. 'If you must leave now, I'll come with you to the station.'

'There's absolutely no need. I can find it easily enough for myself. Hastings isn't exactly a metropolis, is it? And you can have fun together, romping in the park.'

Julia's moods had always been a trifle unpredictable, but now they had taken on a whole new dimension. Before I had time to think of what best to do, she had given me a quick kiss, waved a careless hand at my companions, and marched out of the park and onto the road that led back into the centre of town.

We stood in a small group and watched her go.

'Phew,' Lucy said.

Chapter Sixteen

'Come back to ours for a bite,' she followed on quickly, trying to cover the awkward moment. 'We've some great cheese and salad and a bottle of wine.'

'It sounds good, but I think I'll make my way home – let you get on with the rest of your Sunday.' I would have enjoyed seeing the house they shared in one of the newer streets of town, but right now I had to be alone.

'We've the rest of the day free,' she countered. 'Do come.' Her brother laid a light hand on her arm and that brought her entreaties to an end. I could see from Gil's face he understood. It had been a fraught expedition. The friend I'd introduced had managed to upset every member of our small party, and a few minutes ago had left me high and dry.

I was relieved when I could wave them goodbye several roads back from the seafront. My head had begun to ache and by the time I walked into the sitting room, it was pounding. I had wanted them to like Julia as much as I did, and wanted Julia to like my new acquaintances. But this morning had been an unmitigated mess, and I was left not knowing how I should act when I saw them again. Apologise on my friend's behalf, apologise on mine for inflicting Julia on them – or simply say nothing?

And what was I to do about her? After an hour in which I sat staring at the wall, I decided I'd ring her tomorrow and try to smooth the edges of what had been a difficult few days. I should never have arranged the walk, I could see that now. Julia had made the effort to spend time with me when she was very busy and still smarting from whatever had befallen in Bath, and what had I done? Instead of devoting the few hours we had to being together, I'd involved others, and others that she hadn't even known existed. It was a recipe for disaster and disaster had been duly served.

I would ring and tell her I was at fault; I'd apologise for being insensitive. I wasn't usually so tactless, and it was a shock to realise I had blundered because I'd wanted to spend time with Gil and Lucy as much as I'd wanted to spend it with Julia. But things could change. When she wasn't so frazzled at having Nicky to stay, and once I was back in Hampstead and working alongside her again, we'd recover our old friendship. We were sure to, I told myself, but I had to work to sound convincing.

I fixed myself a salad and took it out into the garden to eat. I had started to feed the birds when I'd arrived at the cottage and gradually a little band of feathers had begun their daily visits: sparrows, one or two starlings, a family of blue tits and even a robin. As I ate, I could hear them busy among the trees, flitting between branches, a few lone chirrups brightening the afternoon. The pain in my head eased and I remained in the garden well into the evening, watching the light shift and the shade creep closer. When it grew too dark and the air too chilly, the feather bed upstairs with its white counterpane and starched sheets became irresistible. It was still early, but I could sleep.

And I did, waking with a determination to waste no

more time on futile worries, but do what I enjoyed most. Over the next few days, I settled into a strict schedule: each morning I painted, retreating into an almost dream-like state, and each afternoon I sat in the garden reading or listening to the ancient transistor Das had provided. Once or twice, I ventured out to the shops to buy salad and veggies, and down to the fishermen's beach for fresh fish. The food tasted glorious and for some reason the painting was flowing. I saw nothing of Lucy or Gil and there was no word from Palette and Paint. I hadn't after all phoned Julia as I'd promised myself. It was cowardly of me, I suppose, but it felt right. These last few months, my life had disintegrated and troubles arrived in their battallions. I needed space to recover.

And I was recovering. For whole swathes of time, Dan drifted from my mind. When I'd first come to Hastings, he had occupied nearly every waking moment. Was it possible I could forget him that quickly? But I hadn't forgotten, not really; it was merely I was learning to live without him. I could say the same about Julia, and Deepna, and the shop. Even about Gil and Lucy. Sometimes it's necessary to be alone, to know who you are.

* * *

Three days after the trip to Old Roar, I was at my easel once more and putting the finishing touches to railings that marched across the streetscape. I had painted them boldly, their black a dense jet, glinting here and there with splashes of weak sunlight. Single file, they trod the raised pavement, an undulating curve that was beautiful to the eye. Those railings *were* old Hastings, I decided, elegant yet stalwart.

By lunchtime, I had fashioned them almost as I wanted,

but the sharp pains in my hand forced me to stop. I had only myself to blame. I'd been carried away by the spellbound manner in which I'd been painting, and had stood at the easel for hours each day. My injured hand had had enough, but I was amazed at how well it had stood up to the onslaught. Could it be that my fingers were less constrained, a little less inflexible, even a little more accurate?

I spread my right hand in front of me, trying to measure the reach of my fingers. It was possible that using them far more than I'd done for years had worked the magic, though when I'd tried to paint through pain before, it hadn't worked. But that was in the early days, not long after the last bandages had come off and maybe I should have kept trying and not locked away my brushes in the deepest cupboard I could find.

It was the very same scene that Sophia had painted and now hung in the Driftwood. I had chosen it before I'd ever visited the gallery and I wondered why. Had she been beside me, directing my eye? Was she beside me now, directing my fingers, giving me the strength and freedom to paint again? I was happy to think it.

Tomorrow I'd continue, but for now I would pack away my oils and go for a walk. The weather was no longer as warm, but it continued dry and a light jumper was all I would need to see me safely to Alexandra Park. I was eager to explore the gardens that had looked so attractive.

I had rescued my jumper from the bedroom floor, found my bag and had the front door on the latch, when I saw the parcel. Not so much a parcel, more a package. It must have come in the post, though I didn't know how long it had been there. It was small and thin and had become lodged beneath one edge of the doormat – no wonder I'd not caught sight of it before. I recognised Deepna's writing on the front. Another missive from Hampstead. After her last envelope, I'd told her to open all the mail and action the few orders addressed to me personally. This wouldn't be stray orders then, but a few more cards of condolence she felt I should have.

I put the package on the sitting room table, meaning to look when I got back from the park. I didn't expect there to be anything worth hurrying over and I don't know what made me sit down and open it. There was a scarf inside, a long blue scarf of fine silk, very pretty, very expensive. Deepna's note was brief: *Hotel sent this. Presume you're Mrs T, so sending it on. You may need it to fend off those sea breezes.*

But I wouldn't. It wasn't my scarf. And it didn't belong to the illusory Mrs Travis. I knew who it did belong to, though, and before I had laid it down on the table, large tears were rolling down my cheeks.

* * *

I don't know how long I sat weeping, until finally I came to a stop. I couldn't have kept crying, there weren't enough tears in me. There weren't enough tears in the world to assuage the grief I felt. Julia. Julia was Mrs Travis, the owner of a scarf left behind from a fun-filled weekend. Julia was Dan's mistress in a liaison that had been going on for at least six months. A woman who was my friend, my rock, the inspiration for the life I now led. Her betrayal was a thousand times worse than Dan's. How could she have done this to me?

'Don't jump. Your door was open.' It was Gil Martinez.

I sat bolt upright, my hand scrabbling for the scarf to hide it away, back in its wretched package. I was in a sad state and he was the last person I'd expected to see, the last person I wanted to see.

'Sorry, your door was open,' he said again, lingering on the threshold. I had left it on the latch when I'd taken the parcel into the sitting room, how many hours ago?

He walked further into the room and saw my face, and in an instant was beside me. 'What is it, Megan?'

How to account for my sorry appearance unless I told him the truth? But I no longer felt able to confide in him, and this would be such an admission of naivety, it would be difficult to tell anyone. How could I have been so stupid not to notice what was happening between my lover and my best friend?

He came across to me and knelt down beside my chair. 'Don't say, if you'd rather not, but it might help.'

Somehow I told him. I'm not sure even now what enabled me to, but I stumbled and hiccuped my way through the unhappy tale and when I'd finished, he reached out for my hands and held them fast. His warmth was comforting. No words, no murmurs of sympathy, just a strong hold that told me he was there and felt my misery.

'It must be why she's seemed so strange lately. Keeping her distance and then behaving as she did last weekend.' I blew my nose hard. 'One minute the friend I used to know, the next someone I didn't recognise. And the two of them weren't even very good friends…' My voice tailed off.

'Don't try to make sense of it. They were dishonest and clever at being dishonest.'

'And I was stupid. Unbelievably stupid. I thought I knew them both and I didn't.'

I had always known Julia for a restless creature and perhaps I should have anticipated trouble, realised that one day she might begin to see Dan in a new light, as someone else to conquer and make hers. I wasn't sure where that thought had come from, but it rang true nevertheless.

'It's not stupid to trust. It's a decent, honourable feeling.'

'So what do I do now?' My shoulders slumped as I thought of the morass I had to confront.

'Dan is dead,' he said bluntly. 'All you can do is decide how you'll think of him in the future.'

'And Julia? She's my business partner as well as my best friend. Former best friend.' It was a sad amendment.

'Take your time to work out what's best for you. For you, mind. Not for her. And not even for the business.'

He stroked an errant strand of hair back from my tear-stained face and got to his feet. 'And I thought I was bringing you good news this morning.'

'What is it? I could do with good news.' My voice was still wavering, but I'd begun to sound more like myself.

'I hope you'll be pleased.' He sat down opposite me in the matching chair. There was a pause before he said, 'Did you know Wayland's name before I mentioned the painting we hold at the Driftwood?'

His question startled me. He'd dismissed my ramblings, or so I had thought, but here he was reopening the subject.

'Only from seeing flashes from the past – the ones I told you of.'

'And you'd never read of him before?'

'No, never. Why do you ask?'

'I'm trying to build a picture, if you'll excuse the pun. The fact that an artist called Wayland lived in Hastings around 1850 is in the public domain, but *you* didn't know it. You only knew of him by hearing his name in this cottage.'

I wasn't sure what he was getting at. 'That's true, but the man I've seen may not be the Wayland who painted your picture. I feel he is, but I could be wrong.'

'Wayland isn't a common name, and certainly wouldn't have been in a small place like Hastings. If you were to discover a Wayland was living in your cottage at that time, it would be pretty conclusive evidence that the man you see is real – wouldn't it?'

'I suppose, but how would I find out?'

'It's what I've been pondering.'

I was amazed. He had seemed so decided that my weird experiences were solely down to shock. 'I came up with someone I could contact,' he continued. 'Will Fenton. He's an archivist by profession, but from time to time he researches the local area. I thought he might uncover something.'

If he had, if he could prove the Waylands were as real as I felt them to be, it would be precious. More precious still, though, was knowing Gil hadn't ignored my story but acted on it.

'Even if your friend has got nowhere, thank you for trying.' My thanks ran more deeply than Gil knew; he was the friend I had thought him after all.

'I came to tell you I'd heard from Will and my good news is that he's managed to trace your Waylands.' I leaned forward, caught by the possibility there might be objective proof for a story that was almost impossible to believe.

'The people I've seen were real ?'

'It seems they might be. And you were right to think they'd lived in this very cottage. Will started with the electoral register, but found no mention of them. That's not surprising. Spencer Wayland was unlikely to be a householder and eligible to register. But then my friend burrowed into the rental rolls for Hastings and discovered a couple called

Wayland rented this cottage some time in 1849, into 1850. They don't appear in the 1851 census, so presumably by that date they had made sufficient money to rent a better place. You said they were beginning to taste success.'

'She was at least.'

'Ah, yes. And that brings us to the delicate matter of whether or not to challenge prevailing assumptions.'

'That it was Spencer who painted the pictures? It's probably better for your job you say nothing. Otherwise you'd have to cite the mad woman you know, who sees and hears people from the past.'

'And yet the evidence is clear. A couple called Wayland lived and painted here, so the work in the Driftwood was almost certainly done by one of them, and if what you've seen is true, it was Sophia. And that fits, since every known Wayland is a landscape. As a woman, Sophia wouldn't have painted figures, she wouldn't have had the opportunity to study the human body. So do I ruffle feathers or not?'

'Not! You can't be sure what I experienced was true. I may have seen real people and they may have been the painters we think, but it doesn't follow that what I heard them say and saw them do *is* real. Tell me honestly, Gil, can you believe it?'

'It's fantastic, I grant you, and I'm a cautious man.'

He wasn't just cautious. He was thoughtful and intelligent and had shown a natural degree of scepticism, so how could he come even close to accepting such a notion? 'But is it truly possible I can see scenes that took place all those years ago?'

'That's something I didn't ask my archivist. I think he might have done a double take if I had. Thinking logically, you knew nothing of these people, so if you hadn't seen

137

them, how would you have known they even existed?' He smiled across at me. 'I was wrong to close my mind.'

I felt amazingly happy. Somehow it mattered hugely that Gil was with me. 'And what of their story?'

'If I believe you've seen and heard them, why wouldn't I believe their story?'

'It worries me that what I've seen is true. I think the Way-lands could be headed for trouble. In a way, I'd be almost glad if my mind were making it up.'

'It seems that it isn't. We may have to accept – extraordinary though it is – that you've found a way to walk back into the past.'

'I'm a time traveller? Is that what you're saying?'

'Something like that. Who knows? There are theories.'

'Such as?'

'Well, one is that time is just another dimension and that all points in it are equally real. In other words, there's no objective flow of time. The theory has it that future events are already there, so if that's so, why not past ones? What you see, what you hear, depends on where you are in the time continuum. For most of us, that's simple. For you, not so much.'

It was a wild idea, but comforting nevertheless. I managed the glimmer of a smile for the first time since he'd arrived. 'I like that notion, that I'm part of the flow of time.'

'Far better than being crazy,' he agreed.

Chapter Seventeen

Gil left shortly afterwards, but not before he had invited me to Rye. He and Lucy often had Sunday lunch with their mother and, if I felt up to it, I'd be very welcome. A new scene might do me good, he said. Hastings had once been the new scene that would do me good, and I wondered how many more I'd need before I found any kind of peace.

I spent two days brooding before I decided to go. The world I'd shared with Dan had been built on sand, revealed as a fraud. Now that fraud had grown even greater and its enormity was difficult to take in. Julia's betrayal cut me into a thousand pieces and try as I might, I could find no forgiveness. My mind kept replaying the past few months in the light of what I now knew, circling endlessly and always coming back, it seemed, to the night of the accident.

What had happened that evening, before the policeman was standing at my door, his face grave from impending bad news? There had been no art therapy course, that was clear; Dan had invented it and told me at the last moment, I suppose, to ensure I'd no time to check, if I'd had a mind to. He had been meeting Julia at the Thornton Manor Hotel, as he'd done so many times before. What excuses had he used then? I racked my brain, but couldn't remember. Whatever they'd been, they must have sounded plausible. I was trusting, but not wholly gullible.

The two of them had been meeting that night, but Dan had never arrived. Julia must have been seething. She wasn't a woman you stood up. She had probably waited an hour, maybe two, then driven home. Was she home, I wondered, when I'd rung to tell her the dreadful news? She hadn't been at a party, as she'd claimed; her excuse she had been drinking and couldn't come with me to identify the body had been, like so much else, a lie. I'd put the sharp intake of breath, the initial silence at the end of the phone, down to shock, which indeed it had been. But there had been so much more to that shock than I could have dreamed.

She hadn't come with me to the morgue because she couldn't trust herself to seeing Dan lifeless. I wondered if she had genuinely cared for him. Perhaps for a little while. By the time the funeral came round, she had got a grip on herself and journeyed through the day without emotion, except for the kindness she'd lavished on me. Was that her way of deflecting her own pain? Perhaps I was being unfair. Perhaps she had felt pain for me, too. And guilt.

It was impossible to know; impossible any longer to know her, if I ever had. I felt sure it had been she who'd instigated the relationship with Dan. He had always been wary of Julia – he told me once he found her frankly terrifying. She was too slick, too sharp, too go-getting. Well, she had got him in the end. I imagined she'd made a pass and he had succumbed. He couldn't have been particularly happy with his life, I knew that now, and maybe they'd had a few drinks together when I wasn't around, and one thing had led to another. But it hadn't stopped there. It must have been too exciting for them. An adventure, a thrill, the thrill of keeping it from Megan. Julia would have liked that aspect. He was mine, so she would have him.

I was only just realising what a strong part of her nature possession was. It was the same with the business, although I'd never seen it that way before. The money to buy and set up the shop had been mine, but I'd made her an equal partner. Yet that hadn't been enough and she had wanted to run the firm on her own terms. She still did for that matter – the insistence on extending, for instance.

And then there were friends. For years, she'd been a sufficient friend for me, but I had only to think of the way she'd behaved towards Gil and Lucy to guess what might have happened if I'd made friends elsewhere.

The more I considered it, the clearer it became that Julia hadn't wished me to have anything that wasn't hers. I remembered an exchange we'd had shortly after I'd learned of my inheritance. *It's a matter of luck*, she'd said. *Your father made money and passed it on to you – it could have been anyone's father. It could have been mine. I could have been the one sitting on a large bank balance.* Was that resentment talking? Jealousy? A feeling she deserved what I had, deserved more than she'd been given in life?

I would never know. Gil had said I must figure out for myself what my relationship with her would be, and I'd very quickly figured it out. I didn't want to speak to her, I didn't want to see her. I couldn't work with her, that was certain. One day, the past might be forgotten between us, but I couldn't imagine when. It was her duplicity that stuck in my throat, the lying and the scheming. If she and Dan had genuinely fallen in love and told me, it would have hurt, but I would have coped. But not this. Deceit eats away at you, and if I were to remain whole, I knew I had to say goodbye to her. To the friendship I'd cherished for so long.

* * *

By Sunday the weather had improved greatly and the sun was already climbing the sky when I left for my day in Rye. I'd never owned a car, far too bothersome in London, but I'd imagined that Gil did.

'I haven't driven for years,' he said, wrong-footing me. 'And on the salary the Driftwood pays, I doubt I'll be driving any time soon. There's a direct train to Rye and Mum's house is only a ten minute walk.'

He was waiting for me at Hastings station. I'd not been back there since the day I'd walked through the rain storm to the cottage, and it was an odd feeling. The last time I had crossed its forecourt, I'd been staying for one night, two or three at most, but here I was three weeks later and more reluctant to leave by the day. Julia's betrayal had only increased my unwillingness to go back.

Lucy leaped into view, waving a ticket at me. 'I've got yours, Megan. Let's go. Platform two. The train is due any second.'

It was a short journey, twenty minutes at most, and for much of it we travelled inland through a wide, open landscape, marshland it seemed, but shortly before we reached Rye the track headed back towards the coast. More wide, open space. This time, though, the view was of sea, mile after mile of water, waves lapping quietly at the shore and bright with sunlight.

I had my first proper view of Rye after we emerged from the station. And I loved it. Streets of old houses, some of them half-timbered, some of them very old indeed, straggled their way uphill to a church that must have been visible for miles.

'Interesting it's a church in prime position and not a castle.' We had begun the climb and I was already slightly out of breath. 'I would have thought there'd be a fortress to defend the town.'

Lucy drew alongside me. 'It is a kind of fortress. It's called the Citadel.'

'The church is called the Citadel?' I wondered what kind of religion prospered in Rye.

'The Church is called St Mary's,' Gil offered from behind. 'Citadel is the name for the old part of Rye, the part that's built on the original rock. If you climb to the top of the church tower, you get a marvellous view of the town. And the countryside – for miles around.'

'And there is a castle, in any case,' Lucy put in. 'It's just you can't see it from here. It's called the Ypres Tower. It's part of the Citadel and so is Mum's house. She lives in a cute square by the church.'

'It sounds lovely.'

'It is. It's a Mum kind of place,' she said happily.

The pull uphill was steep and the church above us loomed large, far larger than I'd expect for a small town, and I said so.

Gil put me right. 'It wasn't thought large when it was built. Rye was an important place then – one of the cinque ports that provided safe harbour against attacks from the French. That's why it was allowed to build its own defences like the Ypres Tower. The town is a good two miles from the sea now, but then it was surrounded by water.'

'There's a harbour, you say? I'd like to see it.'

'We'll have a walk after lunch,' he promised. 'The historic part of the town is relatively small.'

Lion Street led directly to the main entrance of the church, and for the first time I saw the face of St Mary's clock. It was enormous and a stunning blue.

Lucy pointed at the two golden cherubs housed in a pediment above, each with a hand on a small bell. 'Those are the Quarter Boys, Mum told me. They strike the quarter, but not the hours.'

'They've also written a message.' I read aloud the words carved between each cherub. *For our time is a very shadow that passeth away,*' and pulled a face. 'A bit doleful for a sunny day.'

'Always good to be prepared,' Gil said, as we turned into Church Square.

And what a delight it was, a large expanse of green, enclosed by a low brick wall, built goodness knows when. On one side of the square, a row of half-timbered houses, once residences of mediaeval merchants, I imagined, and on the other, a pink-washed rectory and tile-hung cottages, each fronted by their own small patch of garden rioting with colour.

'This is it.'

We were standing in front of one of the smaller cottages, an enormous climbing rose showering gold over its dainty porch. The front door flew open and an older version of Lucy was hurrying down the path towards us with a smile that could have lit an entire town. There were hugs and kisses all round, the warmth of her welcome balm to a bruised soul.

She shepherded us through the tiny sitting room and the even tinier space that must have served as the dining area. 'The weather is so wonderful today, we'll eat in the garden. The chairs are all out. Lucy, take Megan and Gil, help me with this tray. I've made some lemonade.'

Lucy gave a little sigh, but escorted me out of the back door and into the most magnificent small space I had ever seen.

'Sorry about the lemonade. Mum is teetotal.'

'It will be perfect on a day like this.'

'It *is* pretty good lemonade,' she said judiciously.

'And so is her garden.'

I looked around appreciatively at the mass of foliage and flowers. Roses climbed white-plastered walls, intermingling with honeysuckle, and somewhere I could smell jasmine. A single narrow path led first to a small murmuring fountain of blue stone, and then on to a pergola which until recently had bloomed with wisteria.

'Megan thinks your garden's great.'

Mrs Martinez had arrived with a large jug of cloudy lemonade, followed by her son bearing a tray of glasses.

'Thank you, Megan. I spend far too much money on my garden, but I love it.'

'What are all the flowers? I don't know half of them.'

'Let me see. Delphiniums and hollyhocks at the back of the border, then there's foxgloves, lupins and phlox in the middle – they'll make quite a show in a month or so. And I've put in purple cornflowers, too, and white daisies, to add a little more colour.'

'Not that you'll need it.' Gil gave a slight shake of his head.

'Not that I'll need it,' she repeated. 'Here, Megan, do have a glass. But I love colour. And you must, too, as an artist. Painting is a wonderful skill. I admire it so much. You must come over and see me on your own – I can feed you and you can paint Rye. It's very paintable.'

I smiled at her enthusiasm. 'I'm no artist, I'm afraid. Just

145

a seller of artists' supplies.'

'That's not what *I've* heard. And please call me Rose.' She couldn't have had a more fitting name.

'When is lunch, Rose?' her daughter asked.

'Mum to you. Or even better, Mama.' She laughed. 'Are you hungry, petal?'

'I am ravenous. And I smell roast chicken.'

'You do. I hope that's okay. I wasn't sure what to cook, but chicken is fairly innocuous.' She turned to me. 'So how are you finding Hastings?'

I saw a crease appear in Gil's forehead. Was he worried I might start talking about the strange world I'd been drawn into?

'I've grown to like the town very much.'

'Megan is staying in Das's old cottage in All Saints Street.' It was clear she still knew nothing of the time travelling, and I was grateful.

'That must be charming. The whole of Hastings Old Town is charming.'

'The cottages are a tad spooky.'

'Nonsense,' her mother scolded. 'They've simply been lived in.'

I wondered whether Lucy had felt that coldness at the end of the dark passage. If she had, she'd never mentioned it. Was the aura of the cottage simply a part of its being lived in, as her mother said? By the Waylands among others, though not it appeared for long. But the icy grip I'd experienced, and the constant uneasiness I felt when passing through the hall, suggested it was more than living that had happened there.

'Come with me.' Rose grabbed her daughter's hand. 'You can help me serve. I hope it's all right if I don't do serving dishes?' The question was for me.

'It couldn't be better. And please fill my plate. I'm ravenous, too.'

When they had gone, I said. 'Your mother fits this place so well, Gil. How did she come to find it?'

'She had to live somewhere – move house, I mean, when my father upped sticks and left. We were living in London at the time and the places she viewed there were far too expensive. And she's never really liked big cities. So it made sense to look for somewhere in the countryside. She already knew Sussex a little and though Rye was a bit out on a limb, the town was reasonably priced, and that was important.'

'It's handy she has you and Lucy in Hastings.'

He gave a small smile. 'Near enough to see us regularly, but far enough to live separate lives.'

'I think Lucy told me she'd followed you and your mother down here?' I had never been completely clear as to when or how his sister had come to surface at Das's emporium.

'More or less. It's a shame she did, but it's what she wanted.'

'A shame?'

'While she's in Hastings, her career is on hold. Das is a great fellow, but working in his shop isn't going to get her far. She has an MA in Conservation and she should be using it, but the right jobs are in London.'

I wondered if Gil knew about the advertisement Das had ringed, wondered if Lucy had done anything about it, but I thought it best to say nothing.

'She's probably like your mother and doesn't like cities.'

'It's not that.' He paused a while and when he spoke, he sounded hesitant. 'Lucy is bright and bubbly on the surface, but she can get very down. She was badly affected when Dad

147

left. She was his princess, I guess, and she found it difficult to cope. I was at uni when he went and the whole divorce thing didn't impact on me that much, but she was still quite young, still at school. She went to university the following year, but then dropped out and it took a lot of talking and a lot of patience on Mum's part to get her to go back. She seemed to need to cling to one or other of us, preferably both.'

'So when you moved to Hastings and your mother was already in Rye, she came too?'

'Pretty much. I'm hoping one day there'll be a job that will tempt her back. And if it's offered, that she'll be brave enough to accept.'

'What are you two gossiping about?'

It was Lucy herself, bearing two large plates of food that smelt very good. Rose followed behind with two more. 'Here we are, my dears. They're fresh grown vegetables, Megan. Not mine, I don't have the space, but my neighbour in one of the biggies on the other side of the square grows acres of them. The gardens there are enormous and they face south, so they get every bit of sun going.'

I delved into the broccoli and carrots as commanded, then the chicken and roast potatoes. 'It's delicious,' I managed to say between mouthfuls. And it was, made more delicious I'm sure by good company and beautiful surroundings. A trifle with fresh strawberries followed and then a large cup of coffee.

'I can't eat another thing!' I protested, when Lucy appeared from the depths of the kitchen with a plate of mints.

'Can't eat chocolate! Such shame. Where's the woman in you?'

'I'll find her once that heavenly meal has gone down a little.'

'You must walk it off, then you'll be ready for jam and scones,' her mother decreed.

Gil groaned. 'Why do you do this? We'll be lucky to get through the train door.'

'Go on with you. Out of your chair and walk.'

Lucy, who had just sat down, went to get up again and then checked. I saw her mother waggle her eyebrows at her. 'Darling, you can help me in the kitchen. Gil can be Megan's guide. He knows his way around the town and there's plenty to see. Henry James lived around the corner in Lamb House, you know. And we've had artists here as well as writers – Turner, and didn't Millais come, Gil?'

'I believe he did,' he said drily.

Chapter Eighteen

When mother and daughter had carried the dishes back into the house, I dared to look at him and we both burst out laughing. It broke the tension.

'I'm sorry. My family's clumsy matchmaking is the last thing you need at the moment.'

'Don't worry. It doesn't bother me.' And it didn't. I'd been through so much worse, and the day was too perfect to fret over trifles.

'My mother doesn't even do it very well, but I'm thirty and for her that's a watershed. She's beginning to give up hope.'

He looked younger than that, I suppose because he was tall and slim and his hair had a boyish flop to it. 'You've never made time for romance then?' My tone was deliberately lighthearted.

'It's been difficult these last few years. Life has been pretty unsettled.'

'Even in London? You were there a fair time.'

'Four years and there were several girlfriends, but it never worked out.' His face clouded. There had been one particular woman, I guessed, and I wondered if I dared ask. In the end, I didn't have to.

We had left Lucy and her mother banging dishes in the kitchen and were walking along the paved path towards Lamb House when he said out of the blue, 'She was married, the girl in London. Or rather, she'd been married, but she was going through a divorce. At least, that's what I thought. She had a little daughter, Ellie. Just a toddler.'

'That couldn't have been easy.'

'Actually, it was fine with Ellie. I loved her to bits and missed her badly when we split. But split we did.'

'Because your girlfriend didn't get a divorce?' I hazarded.

'In the end, she decided against, though it took her long enough. She may even have gone back to her husband. She was thinking of it – she said it would be for Ellie's sake.'

'But you didn't think so?'

'I had a good relationship with the child and I believed we could make it work. Maybe she honestly thought she was acting in Ellie's interests, but sometimes people can deceive themselves.'

'Neither of us seem to have been too lucky.'

'Us and thousands of others. But here's Lamb House. It's main claim to fame is that Henry James owned it. He bought it around the end of the nineteenth century and wrote his last books here. Then after his death, E F Benson was a tenant.'

'The Mapp and Lucia novels! They're fun. Rye was called Tilling in them, if I remember.'

'Yes, an old local name, and the house became Mallards in the book. It's the most elegant building in Rye, I think.' We stood for a while, admiring the Georgian symmetry. 'You should come back and take a look inside. The house is open to the public a few afternoons a week and the garden is beautiful... There's Mermaid Street on our right – it's worth a walk down but expect the cobbles to be painful.'

He wheeled me towards a narrow street that ran steeply down towards the river. Very old houses lined either side, one of them a sprawling, timbered building that had given the street its name. I stopped to look. The date over the entrance proclaimed it had been rebuilt nearly six hundred years ago and looking at its ancient timbers and sloping roof, I could believe it.

'The inn was a well-known meeting place for smugglers,' Gil said. 'The harbour is two miles down the river now, but that wasn't always the case.'

'Rye had smugglers? The town looks much too proper for that.'

'It might today, but in the eighteenth century it was infamous. The fishermen here were very poor and life was a struggle. Many of them took up smuggling as a side line, until preventive methods became more effective. There were numerous gangs in the area – the Hawkhurst is probably the most notorious. They hung out at the Mermaid to plot their dirty deeds. It was the place they went to ground when they were being chased. There's a secret passageway in the bar that goes up to one of the bedrooms.'

'An escape route.'

'One of many. There are passages beneath a lot of the Citadel, and almost all of them lead to the sea.'

We were near the bottom of the hill now and I caught my first glimpse of the river as it snaked its way seawards. There was a busy road to cross before we could inspect the collection of boats astir on the rising tide, but even from here I could see the glow their coloured sails made against the glinting water and the flat, muddy banks.

'It seems a popular mooring place.'

'Sunday sailors,' he said derisively.

'And you're not?'

'*Touché.*' His eyes shone. 'I think it's time we took another turn in the rowing boat. I want to see that spectacular dive you do.' I smacked him hard on the arm.

'Ouch! Be careful or I'll tell mother and you won't get any jam and scones.'

'You're so lucky.'

'Because I'll get the jam and scones?'

'Because you've got Rose.'

I'd been struck at how close both children were to their mother. I envied their easy relationship with her, Lucy in particular, cuddling and touching, laughing and joking at each other's foibles. It seemed ideal. Rose wasn't her daughter's best friend, I saw that. She was a mother still, but she was the rock on which Lucy and perhaps Gil, too, had built their lives. Her love seemed unconditional. She didn't blame anyone for her abandonment, didn't expect her children to order their lives around her. She had made the best of what life had handed out and it was a pretty good best. The comparison with my own mother was painful.

Would it be as painful for Sophia? She had spoken wistfully of her parents, but there had been a realism, too, that the young couple had burnt their boats and must make their way in the world alone. Perhaps if Sophia had a child, her mother might yield and give her daughter the love she needed. *If* she had a child. The last glimpse I'd had of her, hadn't looked hopeful.

A smart yacht with a red hull and blindingly white sails was tied up close to the walkway, and Gil stopped to admire it. 'I'm glad you like my mother.'

'I do, very much. I like your whole family. It's so very different from what I've known.' I sounded as wistful as Sophia.

'When did you last see your mother?'

'A few years ago.'

He pursed his lips. 'That's quite a time.'

'She had a row with Dan one day, and after that I never saw her.'

'Not even at his funeral?'

'No, she didn't come. Like I say, I haven't seen her since that quarrel.'

'What was it about?'

'Dan took her to task and she didn't like it. She didn't like him, she never had – not that he was at all bothered – but her visits to the shop, sometimes every day, made me nervous and that did bother him. He had the temerity to suggest she didn't visit so often, or at least that she phone ahead to check if it was convenient. That didn't go down well. She exploded and went for the jugular – her furies are quite spectactular – but Dan surprised me by being every bit as horrible to her as she'd been to him. The row was awful but it did put paid to her visits, and my life became much easier once she stopped interfering.'

He didn't speak for a while and when he did, it left me feeling ruffled. 'I suppose you could see it as natural – your mother calling on you so often. You were just starting out with the shop and perhaps she was concerned for you. She might have thought she was being helpful.'

To an impartial listener, his words were reasonable, but I wasn't impartial and never could be. 'You're saying I should rethink my mother? You don't know her. She didn't call to be helpful, she's not in the least the helpful type, unless you count constant criticism as help. She has to be in control. She came to meddle and make me doubt myself. She loathed

I'd inherited my father's estate and hated especially that I'd been able to buy the shop.'

He looked puzzled. This wasn't a mother he could recognise. 'But why?'

His question was understandable, though to me the answer was as clear as day. 'The legacy gave me independence. My father left me sufficient to buy the business – at least to put down a deposit and grab a mortgage – and then to buy in the necessary stock. For the first time in my life, I could make a decent living and more importantly, I could move out of the family home.'

'And that's what she didn't like?'

'She hated it. And I'm not overstating her reaction. She hated the fact I would have a life separate from hers. Hated I had a future that wasn't built on resentment of the past or grief over what might have been. I was starting out to run a successful business. And I did. Buying the shop was one of the best things I've ever done, but she never encouraged me, never praised me. Until that row with Dan, she was constantly there, ready to carp and find fault.'

'He did you a favour then.'

'I suppose. She'd wanted me to walk away from the moment I met him. I had chosen him for myself, you see, and she'd had no part in it. And when he moved in with me, things got even worse. She didn't much like Julia either. She was grateful to her for saving me from myself, but once I was back as a functioning person, she wanted her to disappear and not return.'

'You could say her judgement about those two wasn't that far amiss.'

'Except at the time neither of them had done anything to warrant her hostility. She wanted my full attention and was jealous of anything or anybody that got in the way.'

'And this was because she'd lost your father?'

'You tell me. You're the psychoanalyst.' I sounded unpleasantly tart. He was refusing to see my mother for what she was, and I didn't like it.

He took hold of my arm and gave it a small squeeze. 'I've upset you and I'm sorry. You know your mother and I don't. But I've seen the effects of divorce close up and I suppose I've some fellow feeling. I know how destructive it can be.'

'It can be liberating, too. In a roundabout way my parents' divorce worked for me – eventually. It gave me freedom.'

The riverside path had ended and we were walking back into the town. He took my arm again as we crossed the main street to walk up the steep, narrow road that ran parallel to Lion Street. When we had panted our way to the top, the church was on our right.

'Back again', I said brightly, hoping we had finished the earlier conversation. But apparently we hadn't.

'I'm guessing this, but I don't think your mother knows Dan is dead. Am I right?'

I said nothing, though I could feel him willing me to answer. But he didn't ask again and a few minutes' walk brought us to his mother's cottage. The door was ajar and the smell of fresh baked scones filled the air.

'I should have worn a smock,' I joked. 'I'll have to buy elasticated trousers for my next visit.'

He smiled faintly, but then seemed to relent. 'Don't let her bully you into eating.'

'Did you enjoy the walk, Megan?' At least Rose had no trouble smiling.

'I did. Rye is a lovely town.'

'Another one of Lucy's small but beautifully formed creations,' he said. 'Where is she, by the way?'

'She had to leave.'

'She didn't mention she was leaving early.'

'I know she didn't, dear. Come out into the garden again. It's still very warm.' She led the way through the house, saying over her shoulder, 'Half way through the washing up she remembered she'd agreed to meet up with friends in Hastings.'

Gil looked at me, a bland expression on his face. 'That's a shame. Now Megan and I will have to travel back alone together.'

Rose made a great business of tidying the chair cushions, touching the teapot to see if it was warm enough, handing out the scones, anything to distract. But her cheeks were pink with embarrassment. She had been found out.

I pretended not to notice anything amiss and dived into a scone. It was as tasty as I'd expected, and we had made our way through half the plateful when Rose jumped up to make another pot.

'Thanks, but no more tea,' Gil said. 'It's time we were off or we'll be stranded in Rye, waiting for a train that never comes.'

'Of course you must go. Time's getting on. But it's been lovely to have you here, Megan. Please come again – and you don't need to bring him, you know. Come with your paints and enjoy a day in the town.'

'I'd like to. Very much.' And I meant it.

* * *

As Gil had prophesied, the train was a long time coming and it was nearly dark by the time we arrived back in Hastings.

'I'll walk you to the cottage.'

'There's really no need. I'm not likely to meet the mad axeman between here and All Saints Street.'

'I hope not, but I'll still see you home.'

He was determined, and if I were honest, I liked the idea of being walked home. It was a long time since that had happened. The air had cooled considerably and we set off from the station at a brisk pace, reaching the seafront in record time. There was still a mix of people around, couples mainly, strolling in the dusk and enjoying the last of what had been a glorious day. I saw the Cutter Inn a short way ahead. The boating pond opposite had closed for the day, but the inn's lights were already gleaming and several brave souls were drinking their beer on the outside terrace. Instinctively, we came to a halt as we drew abreast and looked through the window.

'There's Lucy,' Gil said. 'So Mum wasn't telling porkies, well not entirely. She did have friends to meet.'

I bent my head to get a better view and saw Lucy's laughing face at one of the tables near the bar. She appeared to be having a great evening.

'Do you fancy a drink?'

'No,' I said slowly, and then more slowly still, 'No, thank you.' I could hear my voice fading, even as I tried to speak.

Through the glass, the Cutter's bar seemed to be losing its form, losing its colour. I tried hard to focus, but the window in front of me had narrowed, its panes growing smaller and its frame assuming a different shape. I peered into the dimly lit interior, half closing my eyes in an attempt to find Lucy again. There was a red glow somewhere in the room, the lick of flames, it seemed. I couldn't understand why. It was an evening in late May and it had been a beautiful day. There was no way it was cold enough for a fire, and a roaring fire at that. I felt a draught of air. A figure edged past me and went into the inn, the wide skirt of the woman's dress brushing against my leg as she passed. Then I understood. I had walked through that invisible veil again.

I peered into the interior once more and there was Spencer Wayland. He was drinking and there were already several empty glasses on the table. As I watched, he threw back his head in a loud guffaw. I heard it quite clearly. The man beside him had made him laugh; the man beside him was Rossetti, not quite as hearty as his companion but still smiling. Sophia was walking towards them, and as she approached Rossetti rose to his feet, surprise written on his face. But then he was bowing to her and offering her a chair, and in an instant she had slipped into it.

Chapter Nineteen

'**M**rs Wayland! What a pleasant surprise.'

She was gladdened by Rossetti's welcome. He had risen from his chair on catching sight of her, but her husband had not and *his* face declared her presence was anything but pleasant. He was angry, she knew, and she felt her stomach do a small somersault.

She looked from one to the other. 'I hope you will forgive my intrusion.' She hated to sound a supplicant, but if she were to succeed in her mission this evening, she had no choice but to be deferential.

'There is nothing to forgive, Mrs Wayland. Your company is most welcome and we have done with talking business.' Rossetti pushed her chair home. 'Before you arrived, I was telling your good husband of another lady, one I hope will be in Hastings soon. I wish very much to introduce her to you – I am certain you will like each other.'

Despite her nervousness, she was intrigued. 'And who is that?'

'She is a Miss Siddal. I met her through my friend, Deverell. Do you know Walter Deverell, Wayland? No? He is the best of good fellows and came across Miss Siddal in a milliner's shop of all places. *A stupendously beautiful crea-*

ture, he told me, and he was right. As soon as he saw her, he wanted her for a model, for his painting of *Twelfth Night.* But he had such trouble rendering Lizzie's hair that he asked me for help. I'm not surprised, her hair is magnificent – the most brilliant red tresses. Naturally, I was magnanimous and painted them for him!'

'And you say Miss Siddal is coming to Hastings?' Lizzie sounded as exotic as the man extolling her beauty.

'Nothing is arranged at the moment, but I am hoping it will be. And very soon. But I'm talking far too much. May I get you a lemonade?'

'Thank you. I would enjoy a glass.'

Rossetti had gone only a few paces when Spencer turned on her, as she had feared.

'What are you doing here, Sophia? It is not seemly for a decent woman to be seen in a public house.'

She lowered her gaze. He was right. It was better not to think what her father would say if he could see her in such a place. And her mother, too. That was even worse. But she must not think of it now, but remember her cause was noble and work to placate the man she had married. Her plan depended on it.

'I have seen so little of you these past few weeks, Spencer, and I feared you would return to London this evening with Mr Rossetti. I came to persuade you to stay in Hastings a little longer.' It was a weak excuse, but it would have to do.

Spencer's face lost some of its frown, but his fingers beat an impatient tattoo on the table. 'Such nonsense. I shall be here a while, you must know that. I am come back to check on Lord Ecclestone's painting – and there are still arrangements to make for its despatch.'

She lowered her head and said in her softest voice, 'I

should have waited for you to return to the cottage, I know, and I am sorry to have angered you. I'm afraid that when you are away, I become too lonely.'

He unbent a little further and patted her hand. 'I understand, my dear, and I am sorry, too – for having left you so long. But I am here now for several days and we will work together.' When she made no response, he tightened his grip and said genially, 'I must congratulate you. In my absence, the Ecclestone painting has progressed extremely well.'

'I'm glad you think so.'

She tried to keep the strain from her voice, but failed. She loved to paint, but not like this. Not in a way that crushed the life from her.

'It's important I deliver the work on time,' he intoned. 'Too often artists are viewed as unreliable, but that cannot be the case with me. Particularly as it was Rossetti himself who introduced me to Ecclestone.'

'I am the one who must deliver the painting on time.' It was a rebuke, her spirits not entirely vanquished, but he seemed not to notice.

'Yes, of course, my dear. But we are a team, are we not? It is I who find the clients, and you who bring their dreams to fruition.'

'For the moment,' she murmured.

He looked disconcerted. 'We have begun to build a name for ourselves, and I think you must agree that things are going well. Very well. Why would you want to destroy such success?'

'I've no wish to destroy anything, but I am painting more than I have ever wanted, and I am tired.'

'My poor darling, of course you are. I have been lacking

in thought – the last thing I wish is for you to be fatigued. When you are finished this latest work, you must rest a while. I know the weather tires you, but you are far enough advanced to complete the painting within doors and in the studio you will be protected.'

A Pre-Raphaelite style required her to study nature face-to-face and reproduce its every detail in intense colour. It was how Spencer had taught her to paint – he was right, though, that weather tired her. Hastings was a fine town, but in summer the sun scorched her hands, and in winter the wind was strong enough to shrivel her cheeks.

She worried now she might have betrayed her feelings too clearly and counselled herself to be more careful. Her husband must not suspect her scheme. Her face softened and she lowered her eyelashes, as though flattered by her husband's care for her. He seemed pleased with what he saw and reached out, wrapping a loose curl around his finger and bringing it to his lips.

'You have excelled yourself with this painting, my dear, and I know Lord Ecclestone will be delighted. With his per-mission, we will send it to the Free Exhibition in the New Year. The Exhibition has done us proud in the past and you can be sure his lordship will encourage much of London society to attend a viewing. Then once the painting is hung in his home, he will invite his particular friends to visit. The Stade will become almost as well known in London as it is here. That should ensure us commissions for years to come.'

Her mind felt battered and an immense weariness suf-fused her body. For the moment, her plan lost its impor-tance and she could no longer pretend. 'If there are more commissions, why do you not fulfil them? Then I could return to my embroidery.'

Startled, he dropped the curl and almost swept his glass from the table. He was shocked, she could see, but why? Surely that had been the agreement between them, from the day the painting of Old Roar, chosen by Rossetti as a worthy exhibit, had proved an unexpected success.

'Embroidery? What can you be thinking? You are a highly proficient artist and your style has proved much in demand. Ever since Old Roar, landscapes of Hastings and the Sussex countryside have had a ready market.'

The painting had sold on the second day of the Exhibition and there had been any number of disappointed customers. Spencer had not been able to hide his delight and, before she could stop him, had promised he would fulfil any commission they cared to offer. But once those immediate commissions were completed, he had promised, hadn't he, that she would be allowed to fade into the background? Yet now, it seemed, he was expecting her to continue without end. It was journeyman work, tiring her body and destroying her creativity. She had only to look into the mirror to see how badly the forced pace was affecting her health.

Even worse, was the constant worry. She was aiding a fraud, there was no dismissing it, and it was only a matter of time before she and Spencer were found out. What would her father say? Her mother? They would be horrified she had become a party to such deceit. If only she could speak to them, but they were lost to her for ever.

'Every canvas we sell is a fraud,' she blurted out.

This was not what she had meant to happen, but fatigue had pushed her to recklessness. She tried to cover her distress by bending her head and studying her dress intently. It had been painstakingly sewn in the small hours of the night, and she noticed its liberty print carried a new smear of the vermillion red she had used for a sailing boat.

'Fraud is a most ugly word and quite untrue.' His tone was steely and she knew he was furious she had dared to challenge his judgement. 'We have sold our paintings as the work of S Wayland, which indeed they are.'

'But women do not exhibit publicly and everyone will assume the paintings are by you. So why can they not be?' She put every ounce of persuasion into her voice. 'You are the artist, not me.'

It was manifestly untrue, and she felt bad knowing it. Her husband had been generous with his time. He had taught her everything he had learned at art school and with such enthusiasm that it broke her heart now to think of it. He had been so encouraging, so amazed at how quickly she had understood and applied the technical aspects of painting, that he had pushed her on and on until she had become his equal in skill. More than his equal. But that same skill was trapping her and she had to find a way out.

There was a deep silence and Spencer moved uneasily in his chair, swaying slightly as he did. 'You have said yourself you are overtired. That is the problem, and no wonder. You must rest.'

'It is not only rest I need.' It is a child, my own child, a small inner voice said. But aloud her words were temperate, her tone grave and determined. She had cast the die and there was no going back. 'I would like you to fulfil any future commissions.'

For a moment, he said nothing, and when he spoke it was in a voice so tight it hardly escaped his mouth. 'You know that is not possible.'

'But it is. It is what we agreed. When we receive the next commission, you should send one of your own canvases.'

She was aware, as she made the suggestion, that by doing so, they were likely to fail. Spencer had managed to sell a few of his works locally, but only a few, and now even that source had dried up.

'This is not how we planned our life.' She had not wanted to sound so desperate, and she saw her husband look around for his friend. Rossetti's presence would put a stop to a conversation he wanted to end.

'Do you think, I do not realise it? But those plans were made before we knew how successful you would be.'

There was a resentful edge to his voice he could not conceal. He had been thrilled when Rossetti had selected her painting for the Exhibition, but she knew he had thought it a fluke that would not be repeated. He had been wrong.

'You can be as successful, I'm sure.' She wasn't sure, but she must give him the confidence to believe. Increasingly, he spent less and less time at his easel and these last few months, none at all. And no time in Hastings either. She dared not imagine where he had been or what he had been doing.

'I think we both know that to be untrue.' There was a bitterness she couldn't ignore and one she had not heard before. 'Whether we like it or not, we must face the truth. You have become the breadwinner.'

And now there was no mistaking his rancour. She could not blame him. The more skilled she had become, the more she had realised her husband would always be the inferior artist. And if she had realised it, he had, too.

'Unless...' She paused, wondering if she dared go on. There was no doubt Spencer was regretting their marriage – and maybe that signalled his rebellion was over. 'Unless, perhaps, you were to go to your father and ask him to reconsider his offer of employment.'

She waited for the explosion and it duly came. 'Go to my father! Go cap in hand, and ask for a job I despise! What kind of man do you think me? I have failed at art, you say, therefore I must be good at stockbroking? Let me tell you, Sophia, I will not sell myself so despicably.'

But you are expecting me to sell myself, she whispered silently. She must stay calm, though, speak rationally and try to make him understand. If she could resolve this impasse, she would not be forced into a double deceit. It was wicked to dupe the public who bought her work, but she had come tonight intending to make Spencer her victim, too.

'If I am to be the breadwinner, let me earn our living by sewing. I would much prefer it.'

It was a strange thought, but true. She had never imagined she would miss Madame Vionnet's establishment, but now the large, square room in the basement of the Mayfair town house, its tables littered with trims and patterns and shears of every size and shape, was remembered with pleasure. It had become a haven to which she longed to return – the light coming from the wide window, so perfect for sewing, the air thick with fluff and thread. Then the excitement of new materials: bolts of sprigged cotton, bright silks, fine crêpes, delivered to their door.

'What you can earn as a seamstress will be paltry.'

'Maybe, but it will keep us in food and rent.'

'And is that all you want? Enough to keep a roof over our heads? Where is your ambition? If we continue to sell paintings, we will have sufficient money saved within the year to return to London and rent a fine house. Then society will come flocking to us in droves.'

A year. And no end after that. She put out a hand and grabbed him by the arm, a small dam breaking within her. 'I cannot go on, Spencer. I speak to you from my heart. My life has become a drudgery and every ounce of creativity is spent.'

'What nonsense! If that were so, we would not have people wishing to purchase your work.'

'It is the way I feel.'

'You are saying you refuse to paint?' His voice was brittle.

'I will complete this last commisssion, but then let me sew.'

She sounded braver than she felt. Spencer had a bullying streak that before her marriage she had not imagined. She should have done. He was the only son, the heir his parents had longed for, and whatever he'd wanted he had been given, indulged as much by his elder sisters as by his parents. Florence and Henrietta had been married off to wealthy men, one had acquired a title, and Spencer was supposed to have followed suit. But he hadn't. He had abandoned a lavish existence, the mansion in Mayfair, the Berkshire estate, to be with her. He had given up much and she must never forget it.

She would make a final appeal, throw herself on his mercy and hope to change his mind, or she would do something she might live to regret. 'It is not that I refuse to earn our living, dearest. I will do so willingly. I will make our future a happy one, I promise. You may continue painting and I will support you in your endeavours in every way I can.'

'But not in the way I have chosen. It is clear to me our future lies in art. Your art. Yet you question my decision.'

She schooled her face to express nothing, but her heart

was slowly cracking. How could he not understand this life was bad for her? How could he put money before her happiness? And what of the child of which they had talked? He had kept from her for weeks now, and she was convinced he wished to ensure she would not fall pregnant and endanger his grand plan. But what of her grand plan, the baby she so much wanted?

The thought gave her the courage to continue. 'I have no wish to quarrel but –'

'I have no wish to quarrel either. And we will not.' It was said with finality. 'You must accept that I know best, Sophia. I am your husband and you will do as I wish.'

'I am sorry to have been so long with your lemonade, Mrs Wayland.' Rossetti was striding towards their table, a small tumbler in his hand. 'The landlord here is an old friend, you see, and he would talk so. I must be told every small detail of Hastings news from the last few months.'

She bit her lip. Mr Rossetti's absence should have helped, but it hadn't. She had been unable to persuade her husband, and now she had nothing to lose and must go ahead.

'Thank you. The drink is most welcome.' She took a delicate sip of the lemonade. 'Why not another glass of wine, Spencer?'

Her husband looked pleased. Wine was a far more attractive proposition than arguing with a recalcitrant wife, and no doubt he assumed her small rebellion was over. *Women's troubles*, she could hear him thinking. He rose to go to the bar, his gait a little unsteady.

'Perhaps that should be the last one,' Rossetti remarked, a knowing smile on his face.

In response, she cloaked herself in haughtiness. 'I think Mr Wayland should be his own judge. I have never known my husband to disgrace himself with drink.'

'Of course not,' he said hastily. 'A man is naturally entitled to his enjoyment.'

But when Spencer returned with a new carafe of wine, Rossetti rose to leave. 'You must excuse me Wayland, Mrs Wayland, but I have an early departure in the morning.'

After he had gone, she drank her lemonade slowly while Spencer downed another two glasses, barely a word passing his lips. When he reached for a third, she judged it time to go.

'There is one small aspect of Lord Ecclestone's painting I am finding troublesome, my dear. I have been wrestling with it for a while and I need advice. I haven't liked to mention it before – I know how busy you are – but if you could spare a little time…'

His smile was askew, but it was a smile and she took heart. 'You have only to ask. A team, that's what we are.' The voice slurred a little. 'Did I not say that?'

She agreed solemnly and helped him to his feet, then watched with some anxiety as he weaved a path to the inn doorway and shouted a loud goodbye to whoever was listening. The fresh air proved a sobering element, but even so by the time they'd reached the cottage he had forgotten he'd been asked for any such advice. He stumbled into the hall, shrugged off his overcoat in an exaggerated gesture and twirled his hat to land on the bentwood coat stand. He was starting towards the kitchen when she stopped him.

'I am sorry I questioned your judgement, Spencer. You were right – I *am* extremely tired. I hope you will forgive me.'

He was magnanimous. 'My little wife, why would I not forgive?' He bent to kiss her, his mouth sliding sideways across her lips. 'It is as I've said, you need rest.'

'I do, but I need you more.' He blinked at this declaration. 'Shall we go upstairs?' She tried to put particular meaning into her voice and hated herself for doing it. More trickery, but this was too important to shy away. 'You will be back to London in no time at all and I miss you so very much.'

In the candlelight she could see the gleam of his eyes and, for once, they looked hungry. 'Yes, let us go upstairs.' His voice had become husky. 'I fear I have neglected you shamefully and I must put it right.'

Later, she lay beside him listening to the irregular rhythm of his snores. Lay beside him, wide awake and motionless, hoping yet fearing that he had truly put it right.

Chapter Twenty

I felt Gil's strong grip on my arm. 'You saw them, didn't you?'

'Yes.' My voice was little more than a whisper. 'They're still haunting me. Or I'm haunting them.'

Puzzlement, incomprehension, a fleeting disbelief were all there in his face. I'd thought him convinced of my walk back into the past – he'd had a friend research the Waylands after all – but now I wasn't sure. Deep down, maybe, he still clung to the notion that my 'aberrations' were down to shock. But he'd been with me this time when it happened. He had seen its effect, and it was one that couldn't be dismissed. He was being forced to believe the incredible.

'I don't understand.' His grip had loosened, but his voice was still urgent. 'I thought it was visual images that triggered these encounters.'

'It *was* a visual image. I was looking through the window and it formed itself into a frame. The scene I saw was akin to a painting.'

He gave a small nod, but his face still expressed bemusement. 'So what happened?'

'They were in the inn. Rossetti was there.' My voice slowed as I tried to make sense of what I'd witnessed. 'I'm not sure why. He appeared to be in Hastings on some kind of mission.'

'No clue as to what?'

'He mentioned Lizzie Siddal. That he hoped she would come to the town soon – he may have been making arrangements. He seems to have met her very recently.'

'Then it must be around 1850. The winter after Wayland sold the first painting at the Free Exhibition.'

'Do you mind if we walk? I need to get my legs moving.' I couldn't stop them trembling, but I didn't want him to know. The scene had been so vivid, and unusually painful. It was as though I'd been experiencing the feelings Sophia concealed beneath her words. And they hadn't been good.

'Yes, we should move. It's getting chilly.' The door of the Cutter swung open and in the sudden beam of light, he saw my face. 'I'm so sorry, Megan. I wasn't thinking. You must feel shaken up.'

'A little,' I admitted.

'Come on. Let's get going.' He tucked my arm in his.

'Whatever year it was,' I said, as we strode along the seafront, 'the weather was very cold. There was a fire blazing and the customers were in heavy clothes.'

'Definitely 1850. I remember reading it was a harsh winter. The Great Exhibition was being planned for the following May and preparations were delayed because of the snow. That would accord with what you saw.'

'From their discussion it seems that selling a picture at the Free Exhibition led to other commissions – for Sophia, at least.'

'I'm not surprised. The Pre-Raphaelites rendered nature dramatically, and from what I've seen of reproductions, the Wayland painting of Old Roar was spot on. Sophia managed to nail the style wonderfully.'

'She may have done, but she wasn't happy about it.' We had reached the bottom of All Saints Street. The brisk walk had done me good and I wanted to share what I'd learned.

'How do you mean?'

'I think she was planning something. It looked to me as if she was deliberately getting her husband very drunk. Well, perhaps not very drunk, but enough to throw caution to the winds and give her the baby she wants. I'm not privy to her thoughts, but in a weird way I could feel them this time. That was new.'

'So where did you leave the happy couple?'

'Going upstairs to the bedroom.'

He gave a small laugh. 'I hope you didn't follow.'

'No, I was spared the details, but it doesn't look good. Her husband is adamant she carries on painting. It's netting them a good deal of money and he likes money. From what I learnt the first time I met them, he is used to wealth.'

'And she doesn't like the money?'

'It's not that. It's more she wants a different kind of life. Painting is a pleasure for her, I think, or it should be, but the constant labour of turning out commissions is proving destructive. And Spencer gives her no practical help – he seems to have been away in London for weeks. It's bad he's not pulling his weight, particularly now when she's decided it's time for a baby.'

'I guess he can't make her paint. When I looked up the records for the Free Exhibition, there was no mention of a Wayland painting after March 1851. There was a landscape exhibited then, a work commissioned by a Lord Ecclestone, but after that, nothing.'

'That's the picture she's been working on. She agreed to

finish it, but refused to paint any more. I know you say her husband can't make her paint, but he's a Victorian patriarch and he could make her life so miserable she will do as he wants. Don't forget, they've committed fraud together, so he has a hold over her.'

'She has the same hold over him.'

'Perhaps, but if they were found out, her fall would be the heavier. She's a female artist who's not been content with turning out genteel water colours for the family. She has dared to exhibit publicly and sold her work to the highest in the land. That's not just unwomanly, but makes her guilty of defrauding unsuspecting clients. Important clients. At least, I suspect that's how society would see it. Spencer would be in trouble, too, but he could melt away and without his support, she would be lost. Don't forget, she may have a baby to protect.'

'Sounds like trouble is brewing.'

'Big trouble would be my guess. I hope she'll be okay.' We were outside my front door and stopped by the railings. 'Could you speak to your archivist again? I know the Wayland trail went dead in 1851, that they weren't living in this house after that year, but there must be a trace of them somewhere. Could he find them, do you think?'

'I can ask him and he can try. It will cost me a fair few pints, but then it's worth it to stop you worrying over dead people.'

'They're not dead. You said so yourself – they're living in a parallel universe.'

'It wasn't quite what I said but I get your drift.'

He stood looking down at me for what felt a long time. It seemed he was deciding whether or not to speak. 'What about the people who worry you in this universe? The

175

person I should say.'

'Julia? You see, I can speak her name without bursting into tears. Great progress. I haven't been in touch. I was going to phone her, but in the end I couldn't face it. I *have* made a decision though – I intend to sell the business. It will be messy – she's an equal partner – but I know she'll agree if she does well out of it. I'll ask my solicitors to employ an agent, and once the shop is sold, they can deal with sharing the assets.'

The street light was throwing shadows across his face and making him look solemn, even disapproving. 'That's quite a decision after you've put so much into making the shop a success.'

'It's the only thing I can do. I can't continue to work with her and I can't afford to buy her out. Even if I managed to get a bank loan, which is unlikely, she would make it impossible. She would fight for every penny and I'd be left with a fraction of a business.'

'From what I've seen of her, she'll do that anyway.'

The shrug of my shoulders expressed exactly how I felt. 'The professionals can sort it out. It should be a clean split, but it probably won't be. And if she goes away with more than she's entitled to, I don't care. I need to get out.' To a quiet life in a quiet town, I added to myself. And a man I thought more of each day.

'I can't blame you feeling that way. Your life here hasn't been exactly easy.'

'And I was supposed to be getting away from it all! Deepna assured me that Hastings would do me a power of good.'

'I can't think it has.'

'Then you'd be wrong.' I went on tiptoe and planted a

firm kiss on his mouth.

'I'll file that away. For future reference.'

* * *

He had made light of my kiss and I was glad of it. It had been wholly impulsive and so out of character I couldn't believe I'd done it. What had prompted me? The scene I'd witnessed in the inn and my fears for Sophia? I'd felt anxious and disturbed and Gil had understood, even while he struggled to accept what I'd seen. Over these last few weeks, he'd given me a sense of security I'd never had before, and that was a powerful feeling. But there were other emotions, too, and they weren't as positive. I felt too jangled to sleep immediately and made for the kitchen. The end of the hall as I passed through felt very cold, colder even than usual. It was the contrast with the warm evening outside, I told myself.

I took the drink upstairs and plumped down on the bed to think. The kiss had stirred bad emotions and they wouldn't leave me alone. There was guilt for one thing. Guilt at feeling happy with another man so soon after Dan's death. Unjustified, but it was there nevertheless. Maybe if Dan hadn't died so brutally, it would be different. There would have been time and space in which to detach myself – his affair with Julia would have eased the way. But losing him so suddenly, I'd had no time to disentangle my feelings, no time to stop loving him and come close to loving someone else. It was a mess, I decided, and the best thing I could do was pretend the kiss hadn't happened and lose myself in painting.

* * *

I had been working for an hour the next morning, when

the lion's head knocker summoned me to the front door. It was Das. I hadn't finished my invitation for him to come in before he bounded through the hall and into the sitting room. Seeing the easel, he made an immediate dash for it. In the last week or so, the work had progressed by leaps and bounds, I'd been careful not to overtire my hand, but in other ways painting had been a perfect therapy. Whenever I lifted a brush, all thought of Julia and the hideous events of this year fled. I had been putting the finishing touches to the sky when Das knocked.

He stood looking at it for a long time. 'This is most beautiful,' he said at last. 'A most beautiful scene of old Hastings.' It was the man who loved Georgian antiques who spoke, but then the businessman came to the fore. 'I could sell this work easily.'

'It's not for sale.' His face fell a little. 'It's a present, Das. I've painted it for you.'

'Me?' He was genuinely flabbergasted. 'Why me?'

'To thank you for your kindness. You've allowed me to stay for a peppercorn rent when I've no doubt you could have let this cottage for a great deal more.'

'That is only a little kindness and this is too much.' He looked at the painting again. 'Beautiful,' he repeated.

I felt strangely light and frothy, as though invisible shackles had melted in the warmth of his praise. It was the first picture I'd painted that had come close to what I'd once been capable of.

'We will hang it here in the cottage. On that wall there.' He pointed across the room to where the picture of the young girl hung in shadow. 'That can go,' he declared. 'It's not a painting, you know. It's just some sewing.'

Just some sewing, hour after hour of painstaking thread

work. 'It's an embroidery and I like it. Could we not leave her in place and hang the picture on this wall.' I gestured to a space adjoining the bay window.

'If you wish. It is your home. But the sewing is nothing. The picture was here when I bought the cottage. No one wanted it so I kept it. Holidaymakers don't appreciate fine art and it filled a space.'

There was an irony there. And also sadness. Why had this beautiful work been left behind when the Waylands moved? Why would Sophia have abandoned it? She had spent hours creating the image, had hung it with such pride on her wedding day. It had meant something to her, something big and important. Yet she had walked out of the door, leaving it to succeeding owners and tenants to do as they wished. Thank goodness they had given it little notice, or by now it would have found its way to a council dump.

'Can I make you some tea?' I asked Das. I was unsure why he'd come, but it seemed this was a social visit.

'No, thank you. I won't disturb the artist at work. It was your tenancy I came about.'

My heart did a small droop. It was almost June and Das would want to clear the cottage for his holidaymakers. I would have to find new accommodation, but at this time of the year it was likely to be expensive and, despite the cottage's uncomfortable quirks, I doubted I'd find anything that suited me as well. One thing was certain, I couldn't go back to London – not yet.

I thought he looked uncomfortable and tried to help him out. 'You'll want me to pack up soon?'

'No, no. Not at all. I am suggesting you stay. And the rent – no need to worry. You have paid me for the next few weeks with this beautiful present.'

'But your holiday tenants?'

'I'm sending them to another property. One I own in the newer part of town. It is much bigger and they are sure to prefer it. They are a large family.'

'Are you certain?' It seemed drastic. They might have preferred a character cottage to a bland bungalow on a new estate, and I didn't want Das to upset them.

'Absolutely. We want you to stay. Lucy wants you to stay.'

So that was what was behind his surprising visit. He adored Lucy and wanted to keep her happy. 'That's very kind of you, Das. I'm sure I'll be staying a while,' I assured him.

'Good news, Miss Megan. The summer is fun here, perhaps a little mad.' He shook his head at the thought. 'But you will enjoy it.'

I wondered aloud what it was I'd be enjoying. 'There's a festival very soon. You can be part of the procession. It's the Jack in the Green procession.'

'And what exactly is that?' I didn't much like the sound of it, whatever it was. But Das was enthusiastic.

'Jack has a giant cloak of leaves and a crown of flowers. He has many followers – a gang of giant figures – and he leads them through the town. It's all good fun.'

'And what does the procession do, other than walk through the town?'

'There's much, much more. Singing and dancing and drumming and food and beer. The Bogies try to keep Jack safe while they make havoc.' It was sounding less than fun, but Das was not deterred. 'There's a big stage and the Bogies lead Jack there and then he is killed.'

'Really?'

'No, not really. It's pretend. It releases the spirit of summer.' He must have read that somewhere, but he said it with panache.

When he'd gone, I wiped my brushes and packed away the oils. I would take the rest of the day off. I had no worries now about moving, and could take time to plan how I'd go about selling the shop. It hurt me to do it, hurt a lot, but as I'd told Gil I had no other option. If I hadn't made Julia an equal partner, I could have paid her a severance fee. But I had made her a partner. I'd acted from the best of motives and landed myself in an unholy mess: she had as much right as I to say what happened to the shop. If she decided to be awkward, I dreaded the brawl that might ensue. But I would sell, come what may. I was surprised at how combative I felt.

In the last few minutes, the sun had crept out from a blanket of grey and I thought it warm enough to sneak an hour in the garden before lunch. Except that now I was staying, it made sense to buy a more comfortable chair, just as Julia had suggested. Maybe two, if I felt bold. I had seen a garden shop in one of the roads leading up to Alexandra Park. I would walk there now and if I found something I liked, get them to deliver.

I spent a delightful hour trying out one garden chair after another until the proprietor became distinctly edgy. I think he suspected me of being a vagrant looking for somewhere to camp. When his pacing became too intrusive, I fixed on a couple of recliners covered in a beautiful deep blue linen. They would be perfect for the small courtyard. I realised when I went to pay that I'd managed to come away from London with the credit card used to buy supplies for Palette and Paint, rather than my personal card. My spending in Hastings had been modest and so far the cash I'd come away with had been sufficient. But I would have to use the business card for now and even things up when I finally made it back to London.

The owner tried my card in his reader, but nothing happened. No comforting whirr of machinery signalled acceptance. He tried again, and once more nothing. He looked at me hard.

'It was fine when I last used it.' I felt ridiculously guilty. 'I may have scratched it in some way and that's why it's playing up.'

'Mebbe. I'll have to telephone.' He sounded surly.

'Fine. If there's a problem, I'll get cash from the bank.'

He went out to the back of the shop and when he returned, handed me the card, his expression one of gloom mixed with resignation. He'd always known me for a tricky customer.

'You'll have to get cash,' he said. 'The card is declined.'

'But why?'

'How should I know?' His expression was sour. 'Cash though.'

'I'll be back,' I said curtly. 'Please reserve the chairs for me.'

I was still annoyed at his attitude when I reached the cottage and was half inclined to forget the purchase altogether. But I didn't like that I'd had a problem with the card. If I'd had a problem, then maybe Deepna had, too. And that was serious. It was the account she used to order supplies for the shop. I should have kept a better check on finances, I knew, but the distractions since I'd been in Hastings meant the shop had largely faded from mind.

I got through to her straightaway and explained what had happened. So far she'd had no trouble, but then she'd not placed any orders for a week or so and she promised to check what was going on and let me know. As far as I knew,

Julia paid our credit card bill every month. From early days I'd decided to leave the banking to her – she was the finance director, after all – and I was always worried that if I got involved, I might make mistakes. Send a cheque to the wrong person or transfer money into the wrong account. Julia was the one who had access, but she was the one I didn't want to ask.

'When you phone the card company, Deepna, get them to send you a print-out of the account,' I said. 'I'd like to know just how this mistake happened.'

Chapter Twenty-One

I've always had the ability to know when to stop painting, the moment when continuing to fidget with a picture would be detrimental, and the day after Das's visit that moment arrived. I put my brushes to rest and went in search of a framer's. I'd never seen one on my walks around the town and it took a fair degree of ingenuity to run the shop to earth. After several hours of being directed here, misdirected there, I was rewarded by finding a small business plying its trade along with others in a charming mews. It was on the far side of Hastings, almost at the boundary with St Leonards, and I was feeling hot and sticky by the time I marched across the cobbled courtyard. It was worth the trip, however. The owner seemed to know exactly what he was doing and promised me the painting within a few days.

I strolled back to the cottage feeling satisfied, though a little deflated. The work was complete and in the absence of a new venture, I was at a loose end and without company. Not that solitude was a new thing. I'd spent many days alone since coming to Hastings, days painting, reading, walking, not caring whether or not I saw another soul. I'd needed the space to be alone, but now it was making me restless and casting around for distraction.

Rye presented an answer. Rose Martinez had proffered an open invitation to me and my sketchbook, and I decided I'd visit in the next few days. When I telephoned that evening, Rose was delighted. She had worked late the whole of the previous week, she said, and in exchange had the next day off.

'I'll come another time,' I was quick to say. I'd no wish to monopolise her one free day, but she seemed not to mind.

'You must come tomorrow. It's perfect timing.'

'Then I'll bring my own sandwiches.'

'Certainly not! No one visits me with a sandwich box under their arm!'

I'd arranged with her that I'd do my sketching first and call at the cottage around one o'clock. That meant I had two hours to walk the town, two hours of pure enjoyment. Without company, I could stop wherever and whenever I wanted. I spent a long time drawing the river and its boats, then the quirky streets that wound their way to the top of the Citadel – and the Ypres tower, its four rough stone turrets looking out across marshland to the English Channel, a brilliant defence against marauders.

Last of all, I walked back to the church and after sketching the clock and the quarter boys, climbed to the top of the spire and took in the view. The sky had cleared and I could see for miles: in the foreground, rows of uneven red roof tiles, chafed and greened by the weather, then the sinuous river winding its muddy way through flat grasslands to the ribbon of sea in the distance. I sat down and filled several pages of my sketchbook. It was only when the clock struck a single loud chime that I realised I'd made myself late for lunch. I scrambled down the wooden staircase and out of the church door. It was fortunate Rose's cottage was only yards away.

'I'm sorry I'm late.' I was at her front door and panting.

'A few minutes, my dear. Nothing at all.' She wore a faded print dress and easy sandals and looked completely comfortable. 'How are you? Have you made many sketches?'

'I have. I'll show you.'

'Wonderful! After we've eaten, perhaps. I'm sure you must need sustenance after a morning spent working.'

I wasn't sure hours of sheer pleasure could count as work, but Rose was smiling and waving me towards the small alcove that served as her dining room.

'I thought it best we eat inside today. The sun is too fitful and whenever the sky clouds over, the temperature falls at least ten degrees. Now sit yourself down. Water, juice?'

'Water is fine, thanks.'

The water duly came and with it a large dish of lasagne, its cheese topping bubbling an invitation. 'I thought we were having a snack.'

'We are not. We are having a decent meal.' An equally large bowl of salad arrived at the table.

'You shouldn't have, Rose. This is your free day and you've spent all morning cooking.'

'Nowhere near all morning. Lasagne is a breeze. I've spent hours in the garden doing what I love and now you're here for lunch. An ideal day.'

Rose had the happiest of natures. There had been darkness in her life, but she had refused to let it win.

'I've had Lucy on the phone this morning,' she said brightly. 'She had to try several times. I was in the garden and didn't hear it. No mobile you see. But eat up.'

Together we made inroads into two generous servings of

hot lasagne and it was a while before she continued. 'I knew it must be important for her to ring twice. She tells me she's applied for a job.'

'She has?' I hadn't seen Lucy since the last time I came to Rye and imagined she was still deep in stock-taking.

'Did you know about it?'

'Only a little. Das, Mr Patil, showed me an advertisement for a job he thought she should go for.'

'He is a dear. And he's right. I'm so pleased she's done it. I'll be even more pleased if she's given an interview and goes to it.'

'You think she might not?' I remembered what Gil had said of his sister's need to stay close to her family.

'There's always the chance. She's gained a lot of confidence this last year, but the job is in Surrey and that would mean a move.'

'And you're not sure she'll want that?'

'I'm fairly sure she won't, but it's possible we can persuade her – Gil and I. I think the very fact she's gone for the job at all signals she's willing to be persuaded.'

'It would mean you'd see less of her.'

'It's worth it if she gets her life back on track. It's fretted me knowing she's marking time. And if it all comes to nothing, at least she's had the courage to try. Gil is as keen as I to see her succeed and he'd be the one to miss her most. I know they can be quarrelsome – brother and sister stuff – but he loves her dearly.'

'Sharing a house is a good arrangement,' I mumbled, my mouth full.

'It has been, but arrangements change. Life changes.' I caught her studying my face, the smile for once absent. 'It's how you deal with change that matters.' Was she thinking of Dan? I daresay her children had told her what was behind my stay in Hastings.

'I thought at one time Gil would settle in London, but then he decided on the job in Sussex.' Her voice was casual, but I guessed she'd introduced the topic for a reason. And I was right. 'The Driftwood was an amazing promotion for him, of course, and it came at the right time, but his leaving London was a sad business. Did he tell you?'

'A little.'

She put her fork to one side. 'It was very upsetting, the way it ended. He'd known Lisa for several years. He was very much in love with her and when she decided to break with him, it came as an enormous blow. I liked her. Lucy liked her. We were looking forward to her being part of the family, but there, it wasn't to be. And perhaps the choice she made was right. Her little girl needed stability, and even the best divorce is disruptive. I know Gil felt they could make it work, but I'm not sure. We can never really understand what children feel – my guess is that fathers are missed far more than we know.'

I wondered if she was thinking of her own daughter and I wasn't sure how to respond, but she brushed past it and said, 'I've strawberries and cream for dessert. Can you manage a bowl?'

'I think I might, though I shouldn't. The pasta was wonderful.' I helped gather plates and cutlery and followed her into the kitchen.

'Lucy was jumping with excitement – she's getting ready for the festival. She spent two minutes telling me about the job and ten ticking off the names of everyone who'll be cavorting beside her. Sometimes I think she's little more than a child herself.'

I was trying to remember what Das had told me. 'That's the Jack in the Green procession?'

'Jack in the Green is part of it, but it's a four day festival. Lucy is working on her costume – all very secret, but I think she intends to be a Bogie. How about you?'

I laughed. 'I'm not into fancy dress.'

'But you'll go?'

'I expect so, but I'll go as me.'

When the strawberries had taken due punishment, I showed her the sketches I'd made. Her finger went unerringly to the scene I had drawn from the top of the church.

'They're all excellent. Every one of them would make a brilliant picture, but this is my favourite.'

'Mine too. When I get back, I intend to make a start.'

'That's good news. I'm so pleased you decided to stay. I wasn't sure you would. Lucy said she felt you might not.'

'I had a few doubts,' I confessed. 'But in the end, it seemed the best plan.'

'It's made Lucy happy. And Gil, too.' She didn't say any more. She didn't have to.

* * *

When I arrived back at Hastings station, it was still quite early. I was eager to reclaim my picture, so I turned in the opposite direction to the cottage and arrived at the framer's as the owner was closing for the day. He checked through the stack of pictures awaiting collection and laid mine on the counter for approval. Even to my hypercritical eye, it looked good. The frame was a moulded wood, silver flecked slightly with black, and a perfect setting for the colours of All Saints Street.

'How are you going to get it back?' He was looking at my

189

bulging satchel.

'I'll manage.' I was filled with the need to have the picture home, even if it meant a painful trudge with my satchel on one arm and the painting under the other.

'Tell you what. I'm shutting up shop right now. I can give you a lift along the seafront. Will that help?'

It would, and when he'd dropped me at the bottom of All Saints Street, the walk to the cottage door took only a few minutes. I dropped my satchel where I stood and tore off the brown paper wrapping. I would hang the picture immediately. The old picture rail had survived – more benign neglect, I imagined – and the framer had found me the right shape hook.

It was a matter of minutes and I had it up. Now that it was hanging, the picture didn't look like the one I had worked on for weeks. It looked as though it had been there forever, as though it had been hung by Sophia herself. She had painted the self-same scene, so why not? Together with the exquisite embroidery, it created a small shrine to the dead woman. I walked over to look at her picture again, wondering how she had come to stitch the beautiful face of this girl child. Was it someone she had known or was it Sophia herself? I hoped against hope she would get the baby she wanted and that all would be well.

Whatever her future, it was decided. It had happened. Or had it? I struggled to believe time was only another dimension, with all points on it equally real. If that were so, if future events were already there, then the course of a human life was decided from the outset. That was too deterministic by far. Yet Sophia's story had a horrible inevitability – from being a blissful bride she had become a doubtful wife and then a woman who deceived for her own ends.

Was that true of everyone's story? My own was not dissimilar. Dan had migrated from lover to liar and cheat, Julia from friend to traitor. Inevitability had cost me the man I loved and the friend I thought had loved me. And I had an uncanny feeling that it wasn't yet over, that the final act was to come, for myself and for Sophia.

I gazed again at the portrait of the young girl. The image was stitched with so much tenderness I found tears forming in my eyes, convinced that here was Sophia's vision of the child she believed would one day be hers. In some strange way, it was mixed with Rose's evident love for her daughter, and with the maelstrom of feelings my own mother stirred. I had been a girl child once and it hurt to imagine how she had felt about me. How she felt about me now. I couldn't lose Gil's words that all she had wanted was to be useful, to be part of my life.

On the surface, I had been generous. Whenever I was forced to speak of my father, I'd make light of his absence, and if my injury were ever noticed, I'd emphasise its accidental nature and praise my mother for doing all she could to make amends. I would say that in no way did I blame her. But my heart told a different tale. I did blame her, at a deep, atavistic level. I blamed her for keeping my father from me, for destroying the life I should have had, for not being a true mother.

A loud ringing made me jump. I snatched up the satchel and spilled its contents over the floor while I tried to find my phone. It was Deepna, but an unusually hesitant Deepna.

'I've got the print-out, Megan. The one for the credit card.'
'And?'
'Our limit was breached because of air tickets.'
I was quiet while I tried to work out what tickets they

might be. I hadn't been abroad for well over a year.

'Two tickets, singles,' Deepna continued in a strangled voice, 'to Buenos Aires, first class.'

I felt winded, punched in the stomach. Yet another miserable blow. But I mustn't let it matter to me, must try at least to sound as though it didn't.

'No wonder our credit limit was breached.' It was a feeble attempt. Deepna said nothing. I was sure she knew, or at least guessed, the truth. 'We must pay the balance as soon as possible.'

My tone was brisk, businesslike. Julia should be the one dealing with this, but neither of us mentioned her. It seemed as though a silent agreement had sprung up between us and I'd no idea if Deepna had even seen her. I wasn't going to ask.

'We must owe a fair amount of interest,' I went on, 'but pay it all. The card will be clear then for when you need to order again. In the meantime, use the cheque book in the safe – it's for emergencies and you're on the bank's list of signatories.'

'Fine.' There was relief in her voice. She wasn't going to have to deal with the tangled relationships she sensed were at the bottom of the problem. 'I'll do it tomorrow.'

I threw the phone down and slumped onto the old Victorian couch. Buenos Aires. How strange that Argentina kept cropping up. Was that where everyone went to escape? It was certainly where Julia and Dan had been going. On one-way tickets. I wondered when they had planned to leave. Perhaps they'd been meeting that disastrous Friday to finalise their getaway. No wonder Julia had behaved so oddly these past few weeks. She hadn't just lost a lover, she'd lost the new life she had planned. Dan's death had turned her world upside down every bit as much as it had mine. Almost I could feel sorry for her. Almost.

What I didn't feel was any real shock. Or anger, or desire for revenge. It was what I'd been expecting: a closing curtain to the life I'd once had, the final act of a rather bad play, where from the outset you guess the plot and one scene inevitably follows another just as you knew it would.

Chapter Twenty-Two

The festival started that Friday and I decided in the early evening to walk down and see for myself what it was all about. I thought the town would be reasonably quiet, most people returning from work or cooking supper. I couldn't have been more wrong.

I'd not even reached the bottom of my street before I heard the clamour: the shouts of stall holders announcing their wares, the strains of distant music and the loud buzz of a crowd enjoying itself. Overnight the seafront had been transformed: every bench, every lamp post, every street sign, sported its cargo of greenery. Fast food stalls had taken root along the promenade and the air was spliced with an aroma of hot dogs and onions. More sweetly, a Dutch counter was doing a roaring trade in pancakes, and the first beer stall I encountered had a queue almost to the Cutter. A troupe of Morris dancers passed me, their foreheads beaded with sweat, their handkerchiefs limp. Incongruously, a giant begreened figure loped alongside them.

From the open door of the Cutter, came the wail of saxophones and a crowd of young people spilled onto the pavement, each nursing several bottles of beer and shouting wildly. One of them bumped heavily into me, another pressed a ticket into my hand for live theatre. It didn't appeal and neither did the mayhem. I'd seen enough and was about to go when I heard Lucy's voice. I searched the crowd without much hope of finding her, but suddenly she was there in front of me, her head thrown back in laughter and her cheeks a hot pink.

'Great, you've come, Megan.' She was clasping the obligatory two bottles.

'I was about to go. It's a bit rowdy for me.'

'Don't be a grouch. The fun's just beginning.' She swayed towards me.

I pulled a face. 'How many of them have you had?'

'Sssh, don't tell Gil.'

'Don't tell Gil what?'

He had walked down from the Driftwood and cut along the seafront in time to see his sister being hoisted shoulder high on a tide of partying young men.

'I'm celebrating,' she announced from her perch, her voice almost inaudible in the din.

'Celebrating the job?' I asked.

'Sort of. I went for the interview today.'

'That's great, Lucy. I hope it went well.'

'I excelled myself.' She slid to the ground and swayed towards me again.

Gil put out his hand to hold her steady. 'Give the celebrating a break for a while,' he advised. 'Or leave it till you get the job.'

The crowd surged once more and this time it engulfed all three of us. Somewhere in the middle of it, a scuffle broke out. Gil frowned and took my arm.

'Come on, let's get out of here.'

'Lucy…,' but she had already disappeared.

'She'll be fine. I know most of the guys she's with.'

He slipped his hand in mine and together we walked eastwards towards the fishermen's beach. Away from the centre, it was a good deal quieter and when we stopped at a small wine bar a short way from the Stade, there were few other customers.

At the counter he paid for a bottle of wine and helped himself to a couple of glasses. 'The weather's fine. Shall we drink outside?'

It sounded good. The evening was warm and far too inviting to spend in a stuffy bar, and I followed him to a comfortable niche on the wall that ran below the promenade, a little above the shingled beach. The sounds of revelry were muted now, overtaken by the slap and hiss of waves. For a time, we sat in silence while the evening quiet gathered itself around us. In the distance, the misty shape of boats filled the horizon, while overhead gulls made desultory swoops across the beach looking for anything the fishermen might have cast adrift.

'Is the whole festival like tonight?' I'd downed half my wine and was feeling mellow.

'Pretty much, though Monday can be even more boisterous. That's the finale. Sometimes it gets too much. I guess you have to get into the spirit of things to enjoy it.'

'And do you?'

'Hardly ever.' He gave a wry smile. 'I'm a misery, but I'm in good company. The great and the good in Victoria's time weren't keen either. The festival lowered the tone – Hastings had gentrified itself by that time. I probably belong back then, with your Waylands.'

'What did the Victorians do – shut themselves away on festival days and bolt their doors?'

196

'Better than that. They changed the law and put a stop to the celebrations altogether on the grounds of public disorder. There's always an increase in crime at these events, but really it was too much sex they objected to. And far too much drink.'

'It wouldn't seem they managed to suppress it entirely. The event has carried on.'

'It disappeared for a long time. It wasn't until thirty years ago someone had the bright idea to revive it.'

'Das said something about the festival being to welcome in summer.'

'That was its origin, I think. Part of the May Day celebrations – they happened everywhere, but Hastings was unusual. The different guilds competed to see who could make the most elaborate garlands. They'd pile more and more greenery into them until eventually the garlands became so elaborate they were covering the whole man. Hence Jack in the Green.'

'And Lucy is part of the procession – your mother mentioned it.'

'She always is. She loves it.' After a while, he said thoughtfully, 'I heard you'd gone to Rye. Did you come back with many sketches?'

'I did. I had a wonderful day there. There's one drawing in particular I'm going to work on.'

'I'm glad. You need to paint.'

He turned to face me and the sun dipping below the horizon caught his dark brown hair in its last rays. His grey eyes, flecked with green, were beautiful, and I wondered how I'd ever thought his face unremarkable.

'Here, have another glass.'

I should probably have refused, but I was too happy,

sitting close, aware of his bare arm against mine. I wondered if he felt as comfortable.

'Lucy has been working on her costume,' he said. 'The kitchen is a complete wreck, but as far as I can see she'll be wearing a bucket of green face paint and three buckets of cabbage leaves. I suppose it's always possible she may have something else up her sleeve.'

'I'd like to see the finished result.'

'I'll take you on Monday, if you're feeling brave. I have to go up to London tomorrow and I'm staying overnight, but I'll be back for the big event. The procession starts from here and ends up at the castle mid-afternoon. There's a big festival area on the West Hill.'

'Is that where Jack is slain?'

'It is. He's the main man, but he has an entourage that stretches for miles – Morris men, the Bogies of course, and the May Queen, and God knows who else on the day.'

'The Bogies sound frightful. What exactly do they do?'

'They're Jack's attendants. They guide him through the streets, and at the same time play music and sing and dance. And at some stage the May Queen gets crowned.'

'That's quite a programme.'

He gave a small laugh. 'Never say Hastings doesn't celebrate summer!'

'Crowning the May Queen is a bit odd, though. It doesn't seem to fit the general anarchy.'

'That's because she's another piece of Victoriana. Jack in the Green wasn't the only lusty fellow the Victorians cleaned up. The May Queen was originally a Lord and Lady of the May, a pair of sexy jokers. But then the maypole was once very different, too – a phallic symbol thrust into the earth – and look what happened to that.'

198

'They didn't like people having fun, did they?'

'Not working people at least. Do you still fancy going?'

'If it's okay with you, but you'll be in London for two days and you might rather stay home.'

I hoped the ploy wasn't too obvious. I needed him to talk about his trip, know why he went up to town so often. The thought that it might be to see Lisa and Ellie, that he could still be in touch with them and Rose not know, was unwelcome. It had begun to matter to me.

'Monday should be fun and I'd like to take you. The trip up to town isn't exactly heavy lifting, though it could prove tricky. It's hard to believe, but I'm still hunting the Jepson. Since the last fundraising event, the owner has had a much better offer from a big gallery in Germany, but he's still keen to support the small guys and keep the picture in the country. Negotiations have been protracted, shall we say.'

'Is the Jepson why you went to London a few weeks ago?'

He nodded. 'Deals like this take time. A lot of time.' Then he looked at me sharply. 'Why the interest? Do you suspect me of a dalliance?' He pulled down the corners of his mouth in mockery. 'Now there's a Victorian word for you.'

Since that was precisely what I did suspect, I felt myself flush from my feet upwards. 'It's your business,' I managed to say.

'I was hoping it wasn't.'

'What do you mean?' I thought I could guess, but I didn't want to make a fool of myself again.

'You kissed me a few nights' ago.'

His directness took me aback. 'I -'

'Didn't intend to,' he finished for me.

'I did intend to, but then I thought I shouldn't.' I would be as honest as he'd been. My life already contained too many lies.

'You're still in love with Dan, is that it?' He said it without expression.

'No.' I was stunned to hear how definite I sounded. 'Dan belongs to another life, at least it feels that way. When you didn't kiss me back, I thought maybe I'd made things awkward between us.'

He shook his head. 'I wanted to. You've no idea how much. But I didn't feel a passionate clinch was quite what you needed at the time. You were upset by what you'd seen at the Cutter. It felt wrong to rush you.'

I inched a little nearer, though it was hard to see how I could get much closer. We had edged so far together in the last few moments that we were almost in each other's laps.

'And what about the earlier kiss?' I reminded him. 'The night we came back from the boat trip. I wasn't upset then.'

'I shouldn't have done it. You might not have been upset, but you were a woman on your guard and with good reason, as it turned out. I kissed you that night without thinking. It was stupid – I might have frightened you off for good.'

'But you didn't.'

'No,' he said consideringly. 'I didn't, did I? So how about giving it another go? This time, we might do it properly.'

He didn't wait for an answer before his arms were round me, pulling me tight into him, his face hard against my cheek. Then his mouth found mine and for a long, long moment I allowed myself the touch of warm, firm lips. I was stunned by my response, and for an instant the breath was knocked out of me.

My hand reached up and with my finger I drew the outline of his face, tracing a path from forehead to cheek and coming to rest on his lips. 'Hmm, wine.' He sucked at my finger. 'Tasty in every sense.'

Then he'd pulled me tight against him again, and this time we kissed like lovers. A fisherman walking by stopped and we looked up to see him grinning at us.

'Perhaps this isn't the best place.' I was hot and flustered.

'Then we must think of somewhere else.' He was smiling as he helped me to my feet. 'I'll walk you home, but then I better make tracks. I've an early call – I'm on the milk train tomorrow.'

We made our way back to All Saints Street, walking hand in hand and keeping an easy silence. At the bottom of the steps, I turned to say goodbye. 'I'll see you on Monday then?'

'You will. Around midday? We have unfinished business, Megan Lacey.' And he kissed me again.

Chapter Twenty-Three

Two days later, he was on my doorstep at midday sharp. He gave me a quick hug. 'How are you? Did you tackle the festival again while I was away?'

'I didn't. I've been a coward and stayed put, waiting for my white knight to arrive.'

'Well, here he is, minus the horse, I'm afraid.'

He followed me into the sitting room and, while I gathered my belongings together, walked across the room and stood looking at the two pictures that now hung on adjacent walls.

'I have no idea why,' he said, 'but these work together. They shouldn't. One is an embroidery, the other an oil. One a portrait, the other a townscape. It's extraordinary, but I'd say they belonged to each other.'

I could have told him why they belonged, but saying that Sophia was in both sounded too fanciful. I believed it though.

'How was London?'

'Large, noisy, manic.'

'And the Jepson?'

He shook his head. 'Sadly, I won't be bringing it home to the Driftwood, but not because my negotiating skills are lousy, though they probably are. The owner decided in the end he couldn't bear to part with the painting, so no sale to anyone.'

'That's disappointing.'

'And a waste of many man hours. You win some, you lose some, though cliché does nothing to soften the blow.'

I slung my handbag across my shoulder and reached for a denim jacket. Through the window I saw clouds tinged with storm, but it was far too warm to wear anything heavier. I would have to hope the rain went elsewhere.

'I'm longing to see Lucy and her cabbage leaves. How is she by the way? I've seen nothing of her since you left.'

'You won't have. The Bogies are like a secret society while the festival is on, and she's very much part of the group. I caught up with her when I got back last night and she seemed in good spirits. She had a sore head for a few days after Friday's binge, but she's fine now, if you can call being plastered in green, fine. Let's go and find her.'

Out on the street, a couple ran past us, a little late for the parade. The woman had on a flowing gown with flowers and leaves in her hair, her partner in pantaloons and tricorn. Both of them carried totems topped by a crown of leaves.

'Don't you wish you'd dressed up?' he teased.

I tucked my arm in his. 'I'm happy as I am.'

And I was – very happy. I still found the speed at which I had walked out of one life and into another disconcerting. Had it happened so quickly because I'd been living an illusion? But who was to say this was reality? I had been wrong about Dan, and so very wrong about Julia – might I also be wrong about Gil? Every day, though, I felt more detached from my former life, my sole link with it now the business and what was to become of it. I had been dragging my feet, even though I'd made the decision to sell. It seemed so irrevocable. But I had to act, contact the solicitors and give them my instructions. I would do it tomorrow.

We wound a slow path down to the seafront, following in the wake of other latecomers. 'What route does the parade follow?' I couldn't see how it would take all afternoon to reach its destination.

'It snakes its way round and round the Old Town for several hours. At some point, it comes back to All Saints Street, and then down High Street again. That's just before it climbs up Croft Road to West Hill and the festival area. Whatever street it's in, there'll be hundreds of onlookers.'

There were. From the moment we reached the seafront, we had to push and jostle our way through crowds five deep. Catching up with the procession was not going to be easy, but after twenty minutes of hot and sticky manoeuvring, I noticed the noise of the crowd had grown louder, along with the beating of drums, the jingling of bells and the clapping of sticks. Several troupes of Morris dancers entertained the crowds as we walked, the men in white with crossed ribbons over their chest, the women with pink and mauve tabards. In their hair were ribbons and flower garlands. They looked amazing, a far cry from their popular image.

Das was outside his shop as we drew opposite and I waved across at him. Seeing him triggered an important question. 'Did Lucy hear about the job?'

Gil gave a slight shrug of the shoulders. 'They rang to offer it while I was in London – Saturday morning. She came on the phone to me straight afterwards. She was in a terrible state, then she called Mum and then she was back to me. They must have been keen to ring her at the weekend.'

'It doesn't sound as though she was keen to accept.'

'I don't know and that's the truth. After the frantic phone calls, she switched off – literally – and went into green Bogie mode.'

'There she is!'

We had caught up with the rear of the procession at last and I saw Lucy dancing wildly in and out of a group of black-clothed figures. They wore black painted masks and carried long wooden truncheons. One of them was playing an accordion which seemed wholly surreal. But then the whole festival was surreal – I had never seen anything like it.

She caught sight of us then. 'Megan, it's you! And my lovely brother. Don't you look a couple!'

I wish she hadn't said that, though it was what I'd been thinking when I had caught sight of us in the shop windows as we'd passed.

'Come on over here,' she yelled, 'and meet my zombies.'

We were duly introduced to the group of living dead who gave us a spontaneous performance with their cudgels, clashing sticks loudly to the out of tune accordion. Luckily for us, a strolling jazz band soon usurped their place.

'We must catch up,' Lucy said to me as quietly as she could over the din. 'I've not seen you for an age.'

'You've been too busy being a Bogie – oh, and chasing jobs.'

'You heard? What do you think?'

'I think it's your call.'

'*You* were brave. I've been thinking about that. You had a real knock-back with your accident, but you got over it.' I didn't like to tell her I'd carried the fragments of that knock-back ever since. 'So, I think I should. I'm going to ring them in the morning. Tell them I'm their woman.'

Gil, who had been exchanging banter with one of the zombies, heard her last words and his face filled with genuine pleasure. He strode across and gave her such a strong hug that he swung her clear off her feet.

'Now look at you,' she scolded. 'You're all green.' The green paint had indeed coloured the pale tee shirt he was wearing. 'What will Megan think of you?'

'I'm hoping to find that out, just as soon as Jack has been slain.'

My face turned scarlet, but luckily Lucy was whipped away that instant by a fellow Bogie. She was evidently falling down on her duties to attend to Jack.

'Hungry?' he said close to my ear, saving me further embarrassment. I was hungry, unexpectedly so, and we made our way to a nearby stall selling frites and mayonnaise along with small salad boxes. 'We have to have the salad, to excuse the chips,' he said.

At that moment, I didn't mind how much lettuce I ate. The storm clouds had drifted away and the sun was bright. Everywhere people had smiles on their faces. A large group of women dancers were advancing along the street towards us, their black bodices and long skirts of yellow and orange making them seem a swarm of exotic bees. Only the flowered headdresses and false plaits said otherwise.

'I'm sorry about the Jepson,' I said, when we'd made inroads into both salad and chips. 'Will you be able to use the funds for a different picture?'

'I'll have to. We had a grant from the Arts Council, but a lot of the money was from public donations, some of it quite small amounts, but adding up to a substantial haul. We can't return it and people will want to see something for their money, if possible something with a link to the town.

But I have to admit that at the moment I'm stumped.'

He took my empty cone and salad box and threw them into the nearest litter bin, then linked arms with me for the uphill climb. 'This is where it gets interesting.'

We were half way up West Hill when the noise became overwhelming. If I had thought it loud before, it was now cacophonous. Musicians were everywhere, in white suits and black top hats, playing trumpets, violins, more accordions, but it was the drums that made my spine tingle. A pagan pattern of beats split the air and by the time we'd reached the centre of the procession, I couldn't hear myself think, let alone speak. There must have been at least a thousand people following Jack, many of them wearing green make-up and leafy costumes. Some of the men were naked to the waist, a crown of leaves on their heads, their chests daubed with green paint. The whole was a riot of sound and colour. I saw Lucy in the distance, dancing in and out among her fellow Bogies, as they guided Jack towards his fate. He was a gigantic figure, stumbling and twirling like a drunken Christmas tree.

'Is he on stilts?'

'No, but it's difficult for him to walk. He's beneath a kind of cage that's covered with leaves and somehow he has to remain upright. The Bogies' job is to make sure he does.'

We were nearing the castle ruins perched on the top of the hill and the singing and dancing had spread across the entire area, helped in no small part by a stall that was selling an ale brewed especially for the festival.

'It's called The Thirst of May,' Gil told me. 'I won't offer you a glass – in this sun, it means a monumental headache. But you can take home a piece of Jack's greenery for luck, after he's met his end.'

'When will that be?'

'Any time now. Listen.'

The drums had become even louder, if that were possible. Then quite suddenly, they halted. Everyone fell silent. Dancers stopped mid-step, musicians mid-note. Jack was led up to a dais, Lucy and her fellow Bogies helping him to navigate the few steps. Then as he stood there, the drums began again, this time a never ending roll. The death roll. A man stepped out from behind the Bogies waving a large sword and with one slashing movement cut through the top of Jack's leaves. The huge crowd let out a communal gasp. Then drums still beating, Jack fell to his knees. He had been ceremonially slayed.

Someone called out, 'The spirit of summer is released.' A loud cheer and Jack stood up and began with his attendants to throw layers of his green costume to the waiting crowd.

'Sure you want a piece?'

'Why not?'

My luck today was as good as it could get, but I couldn't rely on it continuing. Anything Jack could do to make it more certain was fine by me.

The symbolic death over, people turned to walk down the hill, still cheerful but considerably quieter. Gil and I followed in their footsteps and were soon back in the centre of the Old Town, where the stalls we had passed earlier were doing a roaring trade. Witnessing the drama must have whetted a hundred appetites.

On the corner of All Saints Street, a flower seller had set up shop. I hadn't seen her on our way to the parade, but now I stopped to look. Beneath the stall's striped awning, banks of summer flowers, a harmony of bright colour and brighter scent. But towards the front, there were simpler bouquets, cellophane twists containing a single rose.

Before I knew what he was doing, Gil was handing money to the woman and presenting me with a long stemmed flower. A rose. A rose of rich, deep burgundy. I laughed and he put on a hurt expression. 'No mockery, please. I'm your white knight, remember.'

'I'm not great at playing the damsel, I'm afraid.'

'Try – you might like it.'

I did as I was told and buried my nose in the softness of the flower. Its perfume drowned me. When I drew back a little, I could see the way each of its petals interleaved so cleverly it formed its own labyrinth, the petals closing in on themselves more and more tightly, leading me to the rose's very centre and to the secret it concealed. But then the flower was at a distance, half hidden in a mist, and I was no longer holding it. There were shouts of revelry still, but the sound of carriage wheels, too. A woman, heavily pregnant, was standing at the bottom of All Saints Street. She was holding the rose, my rose, and looking hopelessly into the face of the man who fidgeted uneasily beside her.

Chapter Twenty-Four

'I thought you might like it,' Spencer said. 'That particular shade of red. Do you recall? I bought you a rose like this on the day I proposed.'

'I do recall it. We were walking in the gardens at Kew and it was very hot. You proposed beneath the shade of an oak tree.' It should have been the happiest of memories, but she could inject no pleasure into her voice.

'You must put the flower in water when you get home. The cream lustre vase should work admirably. The rose will be a small remembrance until I return.'

'Return? But are you not coming home with me now? Surely you are staying?'

'I will be back in Hastings in no time at all.' His voice blustered a little.

'You have already been away far longer than you promised, Spencer, and now you are leaving again? I do not understand.'

He passed his hand over his face, as though to disown the truth of her statement. 'Have I not assured you I will be gone a short while only?' He sounded irritable.

'How short is short?' She felt unutterably weary, shifting her weight from one foot to the other in an attempt to relieve the nagging pain in her back.

'I cannot say exactly. A few days maybe.' He paused for an instant, and then assumed a new liveliness. 'But you may be certain it will be soon. And when I return, I shall bring with me new friends.'

'Really?' For a moment, her interest was caught. 'Is the mysterious Lizzie to put in an appearance at last?'

'I doubt it, my dear, though I know that Rossetti is trying hard to persuade her. But others will come – William, he is Gabriel's younger brother, and Millais, too. After the furore around his latest work, he might enjoy a small respite. Has the chatter reached Hastings yet?'

She looked blankly at him, but he appeared not to notice and continued to hold forth. 'In London, *Christ in the House of his Parents* is on everyone's tongue. It has been seen by many as quite shocking – too Romish or too blasphemous. Still, it's an ill wind. Since Dickens denounced the painting, Millais has become very much the man of the moment. Everyone wishes to know him.'

'If he is now so great a man, he will not wish to be bothered with such a humble place as Hastings.' She shifted uncomfortably from foot to foot again and for the first time her husband appeared to notice her discomfort.

'You must come and sit for a while.' He guided her down a few steps to the sea wall and brushed a handkerchief over the stone parapet. When she had sunk down in some relief, he said, 'In fact, Millais is most anxious to see the town. And anxious to meet you. But that is for the future. In the meantime, there is much we need to discuss. I called at the cottage, but you were not there and I have wasted a good hour searching for you. Now I find you walking the streets – no wonder you look so sickly.'

It seemed he could not resist the urge to put her in the wrong, or was that guilt talking? 'I have been walking the streets, as you put it, to find you. You did not come at the hour you promised.'

'There were reasons,' he muttered.

She could guess at those reasons. She had seen the woman loitering outside the Cutter Inn as she'd passed minutes ago, a tall willowy creature, with untied hair and a shocking freedom in her dress.

'Time is pressing, but we have found each other now.' His tone had changed to bracing. 'And we must plan. We have much work ahead of us.'

She half closed her eyes and wondered if he any longer inhabited the same world as she, but said nothing. Instead she took time before she opened her eyes fully again, then looked steadily at him and held his gaze until he was forced to look away. An unbecoming red flush travelled down his face to a neck that had grown thicker of late.

'I am working for us while I am in London,' he protested, though she had remained silent. 'You must never think I am not. And I bring exciting news. The Duke of Woodbridge!'

'And who is he?' The name meant nothing to her.

'He is only the richest aristocrat in the whole of East Anglia *and* one who likes our work. He is willing to honour us with a commission.'

Why did Spencer speak so? As though it were he who sat for hours at an easel, whose fingers ached and shoulders pained. As though it were he whose head was burdened with worry their deceit would be uncovered. Whose heart drowned in the sadness of a dream gone sour. She had tried so often to make him understand her wishes and failed. This time she must leave him in no doubt: she would not fulfil this new commission

'It is a most flattering offer, but I fear you must disappoint the duke. In a few months, our baby will be with us and she must receive all my attention. There will be no time for painting; I have already put my brushes to dry.'

He took a step back, his eyes betraying anger and his mouth tight-pressed. Then he began to stride this way and that, his pace jerky, his limbs uncertain, until he had described a square and arrived back where he started.

'I would not wish to accuse you of a lie, but so it is. I have called at the house and there is clear evidence you have been at work.'

'It is a small thing – a picture for my own self.' Foolishly, she had left the paints on display, though the canvas had been well and truly hidden. She had no wish for Spencer to see it.

'I am heartened to know you feel well enough to sit at your easel, whatever you may be painting. It bodes well for the duke's commission. And that must be completed, Sophia. The trips I make to London are necessary, but they are expensive. We must sell our work to pay for them, and for much more, of course. The Duke of Woodbridge will pay handsomely. Very handsomely. When the work is finished, we will have a large enough sum in the bank to set up a London home at last.'

She compressed her lips to stop a retort. The sum in the bank seemed never quite sufficient for this mythical house; there was always another commission, another painting.

He squared his shoulders and looked straight ahead, as though he were about to take an oath. 'I promise that once we are established in London, my travelling will cease – there will no longer be a need.' Then shoulders relaxed, he bent towards her. 'That will make you happy, my darling, will it not?'

'I have no desire to live in London. I am happy here, but I need you by my side. It is not good for me to be so much alone.'

'Have I not promised that in time I will be by your side? Until then, if you are lonely, why do you not ask your mother to come to you?'

She was astonished. How could he suggest such an impossibility when it hurt her even to think of it?

'My mother renounced me the day I eloped with you, or do you not remember?' Her voice was shaking. Her mama, she knew, would never disobey her husband's wishes even though she might wish to, even though her daughter needed her now more than ever.

'Then you must comfort yourself that a new future is coming. London! Think of it!' He took her by the shoulders and gave her a gentle shake. 'It has been our dream from the moment we married.'

She had no recollection of this being so. Their dream had been far more modest: to make a good enough living to keep a roof over their heads and to be happy together.

'Perhaps our dreams must change,' she suggested in a quiet voice. 'We have a baby to think of now. The sea air will be more healthy for the little one than noisesome streets.'

He pounced on this. 'There I cannot agree. We will buy in one of the better quarters of London, one that is calm and clean. The child will thrive in the bustle of a big city, you will see. And for his sake we must do all we can to advance our fortune - *his* fortune, too, as he grows to maturity.'

'He is a girl.'

'What do you mean?'

'We are having a daughter.'

'How can you know that?'

For a moment, her face was serene. 'I know.'

Bewildered, he shook his head. It was clear she had become inexplicable to him. Become? Perhaps she always had been. More and more she had begun to realise this truth. She longed to be home again, really home, with people who understood her. With her father reading by the fireside, pipe in mouth, and her mother bustling in the kitchen. Her mother. Her heart ached to hear her sing as she worked, to feel the older hands smooth her brow and plait her hair. But she could expect no mercy from them – what mercy had she herself shown?

Her face must have expressed something of what she was feeling, for unexpectedly Spencer sat down beside her and took her ungloved hand in his. It was their first moment of intimacy since meeting; his love for her was not, it seemed, quite dead. She felt the warmth of his touch and yearned for the strong clasp she had known, yearned for things to be as they once had.

'The point is, my dear, I have already consulted with the duke. Last week, I spent several days at his country estate. In summer, you know, he entertains a large house party. His guests are the very best of society and I found it most agreeable – the food, the pursuits, the company. Most agreeable.'

For a moment, it seemed, he was lost in pleasurable memory. 'The man is an excellent client for us. In time, he may even become our patron. When you are come to London, I will find some way of introducing you. It will be difficult, but not impossible. Who knows, if the duke takes a liking to you, we may win ourselves an invitation to Woodbridge next year.'

A slight noise at that moment had her turn her head. Out of the corner of her eye she glimpsed the figure who had been waiting outside the inn; the woman had walked ahead and was loitering on the pavement opposite. Her presence made a mockery of partnership, a mockery of love, but it gave Sophia courage.

'Who knows indeed?' Her tone was caustic. Spencer, though, was too entranced with the scene he'd conjured to notice his wife's scorn.

He jumped up from his seat on the sea wall and began to pace back and forth in a burst of nervous energy. 'But this will happen only if we deliver what the duke wants. He saw Lord Ecclestone's picture, the one of the Stade, and was most taken with it. The duke is an amateur sailor and a view of the fishermen's beach with working boats is something for which he will pay well. The work is to be hung in his private snug and will be seen by his closest contemporaries. They are certain to spread the word in the right quarters.'

'Why does he not buy Lord Ecclestone's painting, if he likes it so much? It would be a good deal simpler.'

Her husband looked at her as though she had lost what small intellect he believed her to possess. 'Lord Ecclestone does not wish to sell. How could you think that? And the duke wishes his own particular ideas incorporated into the painting. He has spoken to me at length and, since I returned from Suffolk, I have been working on preliminary sketches. They are left at the cottage. I thought it safer to bring them myself, than entrust them to the mail.'

He thought her stupid so she would be. 'But why bring them at all? They have nothing to do with me.'

What smile he had managed vanished in an instant. His head lifted imperiously. 'When I am next in Hastings,

Sophia, I shall hope to see the painting begun.'

A deep rage took hold of her. How dare he break his promise that the Ecclestone commission was the last, and then command her – and it was nothing but a command – to begin again.

'The painting of the Stade was the last I was to do. I have little energy, a few hours each day perhaps, and these are taken up with my own work.'

'Then you must put it aside. The duke is by far more important than a personal whim. Once the painting is finished to his satisfaction, we will be secure for years to come. That is a prize indeed.'

She did not believe him. There would always be more money to chase, more commissions to complete. She would not paint for the Duke of Woodbridge whatever the outcome.

He stood waiting for a response and when she gave none, he spoke again in a voice that was a little too loud. 'I must go now. I have to be in London for dinner tonight. This encounter has delayed me badly; it is fortunate my friends eat late.'

'And does she eat late, too?' She nodded her head towards where the woman stood, her face bright and mocking, her lips a rosy red and the long russet hair flying free.

'She is unimportant.'

'Is she so?'

'She is a friend of Gabriel's whom I have promised to escort to London.' His tone was peevish, resentful of the need to explain.

'A young married man escorting a single woman on his own? I am sure it is of no moment in the circle in which Mr Rossetti moves, but it would once have been unthinkable to you.'

'You have become narrow-minded. That is the danger of living so retired. These days, I move in company where such conduct is perfectly acceptable.'

'But not to me.'

'Your scruples are foolish. I have changed and so should you. We must live as artists.'

'On the contrary, I must live as a mother.'

'What has that to do with anything? A mere biological imperative. Our life must be greater than that. I have no desire to be harsh, but you know well I had no wish for a child. If you had not been so careless...'

That made her smile. 'Me? Careless? Let us hope that she is not careless, too.'

The woman had grown tired of waiting and was strolling towards them. Sophia, burning with anger, turned her back on her husband and walked away.

Chapter Twenty-Five

I'd grasped the rose so hard that a thorn had pierced the cellophane wrapping and drawn blood.

'Here.' Lucy had arrived and was waving a tissue at me. 'You're bleeding – and badly.'

I looked down in bewilderment. The flow of blood from my finger seemed far too heavy for a mild injury, but I took the offered tissue and dabbed away as much as I could, then wound the paper tightly around my finger. Even through her layers of green paint, I could see Lucy was looking worried. It should have been a mere pinprick, but the blood was still trickling down my hand. Gil stood to one side of us, looking as dazed as I felt. He knew where I'd been, though not what had happened.

'You should wash that,' he said very quietly. 'You may have picked up part of a thorn.'

'I'll take Megan for a cup of tea and she can use the washroom.' Another voice had joined us; I hadn't known Rose Martinez was attending the festival.

'Mum is why I came to find you.' Lucy had regained a little of her bounce. 'To tell you she was here and looking for you.'

'Mum *is* here and ready to help.' She turned to me. 'If

you fancy a sit down, there's a very pleasant tea room in the square that runs off the top of High Street. A good brew should put the colour back into your cheeks.'

I'd begun to shiver but managed to nod, and Rose took control. She wrapped a scarf around my shoulders, then waved her children away 'Go home, both of you, and make yourselves respectable.'

'I am respectable,' Gil protested 'I'm not the one plastered in green.'

'Just make sure your sister is fit to be seen in public again. Go on, shoo.'

I allowed Rose to take me by the arm and walk me up High Street and into a small square I didn't know. Even through my confusion, I had the strong feeling she'd engineered this tea party. I was unsure why, but too shaken to mount any resistance.

Straight ahead, I could see the bright blue façade of the teashop, standing proud in a cluster of white plastered buildings. Rose held the door open for me.

'I always have tea here when I come to Hastings. It's a trifle dainty, but flower posies and gingham tablecloths make one feel all is well with the world.'

I was still carrying the rose between my fingertips, but as soon as we'd found a table I laid the flower down on the window seat beside us.

'How is your finger now?'

I looked down at the bloodsoaked tissue. 'Messy, but it seems to have stopped bleeding at last. I'll wash it clean in a moment.'

'That was quite an onslaught. Roses are beautiful, that one in particular, but their thorns can be treacherous.'

I thought of Sophia and the treachery she was facing.

Another small part of her drama had been played out this afternoon, and her situation appeared to have gone from bad to worse. The worst yet. For her, the rose meant danger. It had been bought to placate, to reassure her of her husband's love. To buy her off? If he thought a flower would work such magic, he must be very stupid.

It seemed he had arrived back in Hastings only that day, but was leaving again and this time with another woman. His excuse was puny and Sophia's suspicions had to be right. Spencer was cheating on her and daring to pretend otherwise. He was treating his wife as a dolt, who would accept whatever was handed to her as long as her husband spoke gently. But I knew she wouldn't. She was bright, she was hugely talented, and now she was rebellious.

Since those first heady days of marriage, I had seen her become ever more questioning, even mutinous. But did he realise it? She had refused to paint this new commission, yet it was clear he'd not believed her. He would expect her to do as he'd commanded – and what if she didn't? Would he abandon her and the baby when it came? The baby had been an act of defiance, too; I'd guessed as much the last time I'd seen her. She had plotted her pregnancy as nearly as she could, and the plot had worked. I worried it would prove her undoing. As far as I could see, her story could only end unhappily.

'A penny for them.' I had been sitting oblivious to the fact that a tray of tea and two chocolate eclairs had arrived at the table.

'I'm sorry, Rose. I've been daydreaming.'

'Judging by your face, the dreams weren't too pleasant.'

I tried to order my expression into something more amenable. 'No, really, I'm fine.'

I could see she didn't believe me, but she made no comment and poured tea for us both. I had been too busy fretting over Sophia that for a moment I'd forgotten the way I'd been hurried to this table. Rose had dismissed her children so summarily that she had to have an ulterior motive. She tackled it after the first cup.

'Are you feeling a little better now? I thought tea would do the trick – it's always good after a shock. But I wanted to talk to you, too. You must be wondering why.'

'The question did cross my mind.' I managed a weak smile.

'I don't want to put you on the spot, but I'm in a worry and I think you might help.'

'I can try.' I was willing though wary.

'It's about Gil.' My antennae switched to alert. Was this a new bombshell? 'He has never discussed his private life with me and I wouldn't want him to, but it doesn't stop me from picking up hints here and there. And the hints – more than hints, I think – is that he likes you very much.'

'Good,' I said quickly. 'I like him, too.'

'There's liking and liking.' I wasn't sure what she was suggesting and it was a while before she made her meaning clear. 'I wonder if you realise how much Gil cares for you? How serious he is?'

Did I? The question had me floundering. He'd held me in his arms, he'd kissed me passionately, and it was clear he wanted to go to bed with me, but he had never told me exactly how he felt and I hadn't wanted him to. That would have forced me to speak my own feelings aloud.

'It's a tad early to be serious – for either of us,' I said. 'We met little more than a month ago.' A weak defence but the only one I had.

'That's exactly my point. It's a very short time in which to know someone. And it's unusual for him, in fact completely out of character, to form a strong attachment so quickly. The thing is, Megan,' and she leaned across the table, her eyes searching my face, 'I don't want him hurt again. I spoke to you a little about Lisa, but I never mentioned how devastated Gil was by the break-up. It's taken him years to get over it. He's had other girlfriends, but nothing serious. You're the first person who has really meant anything to him.'

'And you think I'll hurt him?' I was disconcerted she felt I had that kind of power, disconcerted, too, that she assumed I would treat his feelings carelessly.

She heard the edge to my voice and reached for my hand, giving it a friendly squeeze. 'Not deliberately, my dear. Never that. But you could hurt without realising. I'm aware of what happened to you before you came to Hastings. You lost the man you loved and maybe a new relationship is too soon for you, though not for Gil. It's a question of timing.'

She was a concerned mother, who didn't want to see her son heartbroken, and I understood. In her eyes, I must still be mourning Dan and have no room in my heart for a successor. She knew nothing of the revelations that had pushed my grief into the past. Nothing either of an older story that was affecting me profoundly and shaping my thoughts and feelings.

I tried to reassure her. 'I like him very much, Rose, but we've known each other only a few weeks and we met at a difficult time. Gil understands that.'

The difficult time had grown a lot less difficult since I'd learned of Dan's infidelity and Julia's betrayal, but I wasn't going to speak of it. Gil was still a half open book for me and I needed time to know my own heart a great deal better.

Rose would have to be content.

'Another cup?'

'No, thank you. That was a life saver. And the eclairs have given me a sugar high. I needed it after the excitement of Jack. Did you see him slain?' I hoped it was a neat change of subject.

'I did see, though the climb up West Hill nearly did for me. I glimpsed you and Gil walking at the tail end of the procession, but I hid myself in the middle of the crowd. I didn't want Lucy to see me and be inhibited.'

She was laughing and I joined in. 'I don't think there was much danger of that.'

'It was fabulous though, wasn't it? I haven't been for several years, but when I do come, I'm always amazed at the spectacle. Completely bizarre but wonderfully invigorating. Next year you must invite your family. I'm sure they would enjoy it.'

'I've no real family. Only my mother.'

'Invite your mother then. She's in London, isn't she?'

'I doubt she would come all this way for a day.' I was back-pedalling as hard as I could.

'Not for a day, certainly, but she could come to stay. She would love the sea, everyone loves the sea, and Hastings would make a pleasant change from the city.'

'I'll mention it,' I said, though the promise was an empty one.

The idea of inviting my mother to Hastings struck me as impossible, but then I wondered why. These last few weeks since Gil had defended her to me, she'd been constantly in my mind. Ruth Lacey was a problem, she had always been a problem, and my response had most often been to walk away. Those moments when she'd shown an uncharacteristic gentleness, when she'd wanted to do the right thing, had rarely compensated for the impossible demands and terrifying rages. It was hardly surprising that whenever I'd tried to do her justice in the past, the feeling hadn't lasted, and we were still in the same stalemate we had been for years. Should I attempt to break the impasse or simply accept this was the way it was?

Without my realising it, mothers had become the background music to my life. In part, it was meeting the woman who sat opposite and seeing the fashion in which she mothered; in part, seeing how difficult Sophia's life had become and how much in need of *her* mother she must be.

Rose was on her second cup of tea when Lucy reappeared, duly scrubbed, her brother in tow. 'Are you two still gossiping?' She pulled out another chair. 'Can I have a cuppa?'

'There's not much left,' her mother said. 'If Gil wants one, too, we'll have to order another pot.'

'He doesn't drink tea.' His sister wagged a finger at him. 'I don't now at least.'

Lucy nudged her mother's arm. 'I've got some news, Mum, and I'm coming home with you so we can talk.'

'What now? You'll be very late getting back.'

'I shall stay over – a big treat for you.'

Rose smiled. 'Of course, it's a big treat, but won't Das need you tomorrow?'

'He's shutting up shop for a couple of days, so I'm all yours. We have something to celebrate.'

Her mother looked expectant. 'Is it the job?'

'Not now. I'm going to tell you everything when we get to Rye. These two have their own thing to do.' She wore a wide grin and her eyes were dancing.

Gil scowled at her. She'd been teasing, but she was right

– Rose's questioning had made me brave and I knew I must speak to him about me, about us.

Rose looked around the group and then said with decision, 'If we're going, Lucy, we'd better go now.'

Chapter Twenty-Six

Somewhere a clock struck five as we dropped down on to the promenade. The sky had cleared and the late sun was hot on the nape of my neck. Now the revelry had moved elsewhere, there was a stillness to the world. The sea was a glassy calm and the few boats near to shore seemed spellbound. We drifted along without talking, happy to share the quiet of this warm, hushed evening, and had reached the bottom of All Saints Street before either of us spoke.

'I'm sorry for the matchmaking again. Lucy is even more clumsy than my mother.'

I hugged his arm. 'I don't need an apology. I'm happy to be with you.'

'But they shouldn't do it. It's embarrassing. More than embarrassing. They both know your partner died in dreadful circumstances – you must think they're utterly insensitive.'

'A month ago, I might have done. I might even have dissolved into tears. But things have changed, I've changed. I can see more clearly now.'

'That Dan wasn't the man you thought him?'

'He wasn't and Julia wasn't the friend. I was myopic and saw no further than my nose.'

'You're too harsh on yourself. And you've got through it – that's what's important.'

'It's battling through that's changed me, I think. After the intial shock, I've managed somehow to put every miserable discovery to one side. I'm still mortified to think how idiotically trusting I've been, but it's as though it happened in a different life and has nothing to say to me any more. It's a weird feeling. Almost as though I've been reborn.'

'Sounds inspiring rather than weird.'

'Well, liberating, that's for sure!'

'Who would have thought Hastings could have that effect?' He was joking, but I answered him seriously.

'It has – and from the first day I arrived. I stepped into a new world and began living someone else's life as well as my own. Only small snatches, it's true, but enough to understand Sophia's story and give me some insight into my own. I think it's made me more aware of who I am and where I'm going. And the advice I'd give her is the advice I've given myself.'

'Which is what?'

'To cut free. To forget the mistakes I've made and be brave enough to start over. Not so easy for a Victorian woman, but more than possible for me.'

'I like the sound of starting over.' He stopped and pulled me towards him, kissing me full on the lips. Then nuzzled my cheek. 'I like it very much.'

'*I* can manage it, I only hope Sophia can. I suppose your archivist friend hasn't come up with anything?'

'I haven't seen him for a while, but I'll give him a ring tomorrow.' He took my hand and together we walked uphill to the cottage. 'I guess the rose I bought took you back to Sophia?' I nodded. 'You worried me, Megan. You seemed almost traumatised. Far more shaken than the last time. What was it that was so bad?'

I took my time before I answered. It had been worse. What I'd seen had upset me badly: Sophia's deep unhappiness, her vulnerability, the way in which she was being bullied. I had been overwhelmed by an urge to help her, a determination to fight her corner, while knowing all the time I was helpless to do so. I'd entered her world but I could play no part.

But was that true any longer? My role had begun to shift; the change was subtle but disquieting, my experience this afternoon crystallising what had been lurking just below my level of consciousness. It was a mark of how much I trusted Gil that I was about to confess thoughts and fears that sounded frankly insane. I tried to sound casual, though what I was about to say was anything but.

'You're right that today was particularly bad. Each time I've seen Sophia, it's hit closer to home.' I paused in an effort to get my words right, and he murmured a small encouragement. 'It's as though I'm becoming more and more immersed in her. The first few times I found myself in her world, I stood at a distance – when I saw the Waylands the day they were married, when I saw her painting on the sea-front. I was an observer, a bystander, if you like.'

He frowned. Was I about to test his open mindedness to destruction. 'And then?'

'Then at the gallery when you found me, I'd been looking at a townscape Sophia had painted, but *I* was painting the self-same view and found myself drawn into the scene itself, as though I were part of it. And outside the Cutter Inn, I felt the brush of her skirt as she sidled past. The actual feel of her skirt.' I looked at him to see how he was taking this. He was clearly puzzled, but otherwise waiting for me to continue.

'Today was different again. The rose you gave me was the rose Sophia was holding. I know it couldn't have been the exact same rose, but it was the same colour, the same size, the same shape. One minute I was holding the flower, then she was. It felt as though the years, the centuries had collapsed, and I was as much a part of that world as Sophia. I was sharing her feelings, sharing the moment with her.'

'And then you were bleeding profusely?'

I felt a rush of relief. It seemed he had understood. 'And so was she – bleeding, I mean – inside at least. I felt my fists balled in anger and saw that hers were, too. Do you see what I mean? It's as though it's no longer enough for me to be drawn back into the past and learn what happened, I have to become part of what happened. It's scary.'

'Is it possible your mind is pushing you to become more involved?'

'You think the impulse is coming from me?'

'If not, who else?

'I don't know. But it's not from me. It's not what I want.'

'It's not what your conscious mind wants,' he amended.

I shook my head. I couldn't be more certain. 'It's a force pushing me into her life, as though I have to be there. As though she wants me to know her – her plight, her pain, to bear witness for her.'

'That *is* fanciful.' His open mindedness was coming to an end and I had to concede he had good reason. It was altogether madness to think what I was thinking.

We walked on, but a little before we reached the cottage he came to a halt. 'What *did* you see?

When I told him, he took a while to think. 'I wonder what she was painting? Evidently a picture she didn't want her husband to see.'

'It was a work she was committed to, that's for sure. She must have been around six months pregnant, and sitting at an easel couldn't have been easy. I wonder if her mother knows about the baby? Her parents have washed their hands of her, but perhaps they'll soften when they realise they have a grandchild.'

'Unlikely. Victorian family morals were unforgiving, at least in the class that Sophia comes from.'

'Her father might refuse to see her, but her mother? Surely, she'll relent. I hope for Sophia's sake she comes to her. The girl needs her more than ever, particularly now she has dared to gainsay Spencer.'

'I doubt her defiance will last. She'll almost certainly bow to the inevitable. Most women did.'

'I disagree. Not about most women, but about Sophia. I don't think she'll bow. She has made a decision and that's to go against her husband's wishes. She is determined to keep what energy she has for her own work.'

'So what's your guess? What is this mysterious work?'

'I'm guessing she is painting her baby.'

'But she hasn't had it yet.'

'"It" will be a daughter. Her dream child. She's already embroidered a portrait of her as a young girl.'

'I'm not even going to question how that could be.'

But he did have a question for me and it came out of the blue. 'How about you? Did you never want a baby?'

I cast around in my bag for the door key. I needed time before I answered. 'I toyed with the idea,' I admitted. 'Until Dan made it clear he was appalled. I never mentioned it again, and at the time it didn't seem to matter. Maybe because our life together was never real and a baby would have made it so.' I tried to sound indifferent, but for the first time it struck me that my silence on the subject had been part of a desperate need to keep our relationship going.

He looked down at me and I found myself unwillingly drawn to those thoughtful grey eyes. 'Does it matter to you now?'

It wasn't a question I wanted to face, but I knew I had to be honest. 'It's beginning to.'

I felt myself blushing like a gauche girl and fumbled hastily with the key. Inside the house, he took me in his arms. 'I'm glad it matters,' he said simply.

We were at the foot of the staircase and it seemed the most natural thing in the world to walk up hand in hand and, once in the bedroom, slowly undress each other.

* * *

If I'd thought about this moment, and in the secret recesses of my heart I knew I had been flirting with it for weeks, it was to imagine a lovemaking that was gentle and tenderly considerate. Why I don't know. I suppose it was to do with Gil and his perennial calm, the way he listened and gave his full attention, the way he had navigated our friendship so delicately, never intruding but always there.

But I'd been wrong. It was as though up until this moment, we'd placed an embargo on our deepest feelings – I'd done so because I couldn't bear to think myself so shallow that I could love another man within weeks of Dan's death and Gil – well, for much the same reason, I guess. His few kisses, and I remembered every one, had hinted at something more, suggested a passion that might be at odds with the unflustered surface he presented to the world.

But in truth, they had been nothing more than a taster

and I should have known that. Weeks spent being tender and considerate had bred a fierce hunger in him and, as it turned out, had bred it in me, too. Initially, he tried to reign himself in but it wasn't what I wanted, and I showed him so. Any pretence had gone and we loved each other completely.

By the time we fell apart, I was half asleep. He tucked himself against me spoonwise, and folded me tight. My eyes were slowly closing, when out of nowhere the image of a baby fixed itself in my mind. Today was the first time I had ever spoken of the possibility. After Dan's hostile response, I'd allowed myself to set aside any suggestion of a child. I guess I'd wanted to fit his idea of me, his notion of the life we would lead. But I no longer had to conform to another's template and one day, I decided, I would have that baby.

Is that how Sophia had felt, so certain of her need that she was willing to risk everything? It was clear she was in a dangerous situation and I hoped against hope her mother would come, that somehow they would find their way back to each other. Would my mother come if I were pregnant? What kind of grandmother would Ruth make? I fell asleep pondering questions I was unlikely ever to answer.

* * *

I must have slept for a couple of hours and would probably have gone on sleeping if my mobile hadn't rung in my ear. The early evening sun was spilling across the large feather bed – I hadn't had time to pull the curtains – and I lay bathed in its rays and cradled in Gil's arms. He hadn't stirred and I tried to stifle the noise by tucking the phone half way under the pillow.

'Megan? Megan Lacey?' The voice was vaguely familiar. 'Mark Greenfield here.'

'Hallo, Mark,' I stuttered, wondering what on earth Nicky's father wanted with me.

'I'm after Julia. She's not on her landline and she's not answering her mobile. I rang the shop and spoke to Deepna, but she hasn't a clue where the woman is.'

'How did you get my number?' I was fuzzy with sleep and it was the first thing I thought to ask.

'I had it on my phone for some reason,' he said impatiently. 'Do you know where Julia is?'

'I don't. I haven't seen her for several weeks.'

'Neither has anyone else.' He sounded harassed and extremely irritable.

'Is it important?' My eyelids had begun to droop again.

'Of course, it's important.' It was obviously the wrong question and he exploded down the phone. 'I've Nicky here and nowhere for him to go. She's supposed to be having him while I'm in New York, but I can't get into her flat and I can't raise her anywhere.'

'I'm sorry.' I wasn't sure what I was supposed to do.

'Surely you must have a clue. You work with her. You're partners.'

'Soon to be ex-partners, Mark.' I wasn't responding well to his tone. 'And I have no idea where you'll find Julia. I'm sorry for the dilemma you're in, but frankly I don't care a fig where she is.'

'I see,' he said stiffly. 'I'm sorry to have troubled you,' and rang off.

For the first time, Gil shifted beside me. I'd begun speaking too loudly. It wasn't Mark's fault, but the mention of Julia had stirred memories I had every reason to forget. I'd told him the truth: I couldn't imagine where she had got to. A sudden holiday perhaps she'd forgotten to tell Deepna about? But surely she wouldn't take a vacation, knowing she was committed to having her son to stay while Mark was in New York. It was a mystery – and then it wasn't.

The ticket to Buenos Aires. She would still have it. I hadn't bothered trying to get a refund from the airline because it meant retrieving the paperwork, and to do that I would have to confront her. She would still have the ticket and I knew with complete certainty she had gone to Argentina. It sounded outlandish, but it was the only explanation. Why waste a first class journey to South America, she must have thought. But to go alone, after she'd planned the trip with her lover, a man not a few months dead, suggested a heart impervious to feeling. But then, I knew that of her. I had always known it. I'd excused her occasional abruptness towards me and to others, her lack of interest in her son, the indifference with which she spoke of her mother and of mine, as being just Julia. Her flight to Argentina was perfectly in keeping, and it was my error for not having recognised before how damaging her coldness could be. Well, good luck to her. I was sorry about Nicky, but Mark would have to cancel his trip and stay home with the boy. I wasn't going to tie myself into knots over it. I snuggled up to Gil and once more slept.

Chapter Twenty-Seven

We woke after dark and Gil scavenged around the kitchen cupboards for something to eat, returning with cheese and crackers and milk and what was left of a chocolate cake. Not exactly food for an untroubled sleep, but we were too tired to care and once hunger pangs were appeased, tumbled gratefully back into bed.

I slept late and by the time I'd opened half an eye, Gil had left for work. He must have tiptoed around because I'd heard not a sound. Or perhaps it was that I was utterly fatigued. It had been a tumultuous day with a suitably tumultuous finale. I didn't get up immediately, but stretched myself across the bed and gave the ceiling a lazy contemplation.

It felt good. Good in a way I don't think I'd known before. Julia and her escape to Argentina was a niggle at the back of my mind, but it was a small niggle. It would mean complications over the sale, of course. The solicitors might find her difficult to trace, but once she ran out of money, I was sure she would make contact. It was over. She was over. This truly was a new beginning. I would scour the cottage from top to bottom, I decided. And once my nest was clean and uncluttered, I'd begin the process of turning an indifferent sketch of the landscape around Rye into something of which I could be proud.

First to the kitchen to collect a bucket and mop. I was half way along the hall when I felt the intense cold. I was used now to the chill at this dark end of the passage, but today it was icier than ever. The evening I'd returned from seeing Sophia at the Cutter, the evening she'd determined on her dangerous plan, it had struck me as oddly cold. I'd put it down to the weather, or to imagination. After the dreadful night I had spent during the storm, I knew I was overly susceptible to any hint it might happen again.

But this morning, it wasn't imagination. The cold was so intense that even though I was wrapped in several layers of clothing, I could feel my skin smart. Gil had said nothing last night when he'd gone to the kitchen, but that didn't surprise me. I'd realised some time ago that other people didn't feel it. It was only me, just as it was only me who saw Sophia. And yesterday I had seen her again, facing a cata-strophic quarrel with her husband, and a perilous future alone with a baby still to be born. This spot, this part of the cottage, or rather my reaction to it, was an echo of what was happening elsewhere. The blacker Sophia's future became, the colder it grew, confirming what I had always known instinctively, that something bad had happened here. And if it had happened in the past, it would be happening again – to me, and very soon.

My mood plummeted, but I wouldn't let this new anxiety destroy the world to which I'd woken. It took a consider-able amount of caffeine though, before I could pull myself together and make a start. I filled the bucket, snatched up the materials Das had provided and, holding the mop ahead of me like some knight with his jousting lance, I plunged back across the hall and up the stairs. I must have made a comic picture, and would have enjoyed it myself if I'd felt at all like laughing.

I tackled my bedroom first, lips set and shoulders hunched, but as I worked the tension gradually eased. By the time I had finished upstairs, I was singing aloud while I swiped cobwebs, washed skirting boards and flicked dusters. Then I felt a trifle foolish – this must be what feeling loved did for you, I thought wryly. It brought home to me how little I had felt loved during that last year with Dan. We had fallen into a pattern, one I hadn't questioned. I hadn't dared to look too closely, I could see that now; I had been determined to make myself content with the situation. No wonder neither of us had been truly happy.

After a couple of hours, the cottage was sparkling, or most of it at least. I ignored the hall entirely, whisking through it to get back to the kitchen as quickly as I could. The cold I'd experienced this morning had been breath-stopping, but even so it hadn't matched the frozen pull on my soul the place had exerted on the night of the storm. I guessed that whatever had happened here, whatever was activating this frightening phenomenon, became supercharged when an electrical storm was in the offing, and I prayed I'd be spared another.

I made a salad lunch and took it into the garden to eat. The day hadn't yet decided what to do with itself; one minute it was hot and sunny, the next a dark cloud would block every shred of warmth. But I decided to take a chance and once I'd washed up, I collected my sketch book and began work at the blue painted table.

After a few hours, I'd half-filled my book with detailed drawings. The composition of the canvas was coming into focus – I was thinking in colour now and feeling increasingly excited. I flexed my right hand. It had stood up well to the hours of drawing and I'd been right all those weeks ago to see an improvement. I hadn't dared to think about it since, but now spreading my fingers, wriggling them back and forth, bending my palm from vertical to horizontal, I knew with certainty that for whatever reason, my injury had become less of an obstacle.

Buoyed up, I went indoors to make tea – the clock showed it was already past four – but through the kitchen window the sky was darkening once more, and this time the first spats of rain hit the glass. I tore back into the garden. The wind had risen and loose pages from my sketch pad were soon airborne and flying like small white birds around the walled enclosure. I chased after them, grabbing a page here, a page there, when a laugh from the back door brought me to a halt.

'There's one more – over there, behind the old rose bush.'

'You should be at work,' I scolded him. 'Not standing in the doorway laughing at me.'

'Sorry, I would come out to help, but I don't like getting wet.'

'Shut up and make the tea. The kettle's boiling.'

In a few seconds, I'd arrived back in the kitchen, wholly dishevelled. 'Why are you here anyway?'

In response, he grabbed hold of me and kissed me so hard the pages I'd rescued were crushed all over again. 'Do you really need to ask?' He slackened his hold only very slightly.

'You're early,' I accused, but I couldn't stop myself smiling. 'And look what you've done to my drawings.'

He took them from me and held them up one by one. 'They're good. Very good. I think you should put St Mary's tower on the left and make it quite dominant, then the ledge below its window will frame the landscape.'

'That's exactly what I intend to do, kind sir. Here, can you stir the teapot?'

'Tea leaves. A novelty.'

'I'm becoming quite the housewife. I've cleaned the entire cottage this morning.'

'I'm impressed but...'

'But what?'

'Shouldn't I be able to smell my supper cooking? That must be a mistake.'

I gave him a playful punch. 'Your mistake. Haven't you seen the schedule? It says you're tonight's cook. Lucy says you're a maestro.'

'When the mood takes me, I can knock out a decent chilli, but not today. Far more interesting things to do.' And once more he pulled me close. 'After we've drunk this, let's walk – the rain should have stopped by then. We could call in at the Cutter for a drink on our way back, and grab a pizza next door.'

'Surely not a take-away!' I held up my hands in mock horror. 'Lucy says the only shop-made pizza you eat is in Italy.'

He grinned. 'What is this with Lucy says? Am I in for an evening of my sister's ramblings?'

'Not if you're good. Is she back from Rye yet?'

'I've no idea. I imagine she'll stay on with Mum until tomorrow if Das isn't open. The two of them have a lot to talk about.'

'The job, you mean?' I hoisted myself on to the kitchen stool and sipped my tea. 'Do you think she has made the right decision?'

'I do, don't you?'

'It's right for her career, but she's very attached to you and your mother, and the job will mean a move.'

'She can visit at weekends. To start with, I'm pretty sure she will. But after a month or two she'll have made friends and her trips home will dwindle. And that will leave me with half a house to fill.' His look was meaningful, but I didn't respond. I couldn't. If I were to move into Gil's house, it spelt permanence and I wasn't sure I was ready for that.

'Think about it,' was all he said, taking the cups to the sink and washing them vigorously. He bent down and peered through the kitchen window. 'We can go – shower's over. The fabulous blonde locks won't get wet.'

The way his eyes rested on me made my heart hammer. Rose had said her son knew only one way to love, deep and lasting, and despite the damage I carried I longed to love him back in the same way. I hoped I could.

The rain had stopped but the wind was ferocious, and as we gained the promenade, it became a battle to stay upright. The sea was wild, its gunmetal waves pounding shorewards, riding high over wooden breakwaters and hitting the shingle with a sharp slap. We kept to the seafront all the way to St Leonards, the wind blowing from the west hard against us as we walked, but it was fresh and bracing and I could feel my cheeks glow. Marine Court was where we decided to turn. I'd loved its modernist architecture from the moment I'd seen it, and we stood for a while, gazing at its sleek lines.

'It's brilliant,' I said.

'Did you know it was designed to resemble the Queen Mary? In the Thirties that would have been Cunard's new liner.'

The building's sharp white prow, etched deep against the dark skyline, seemed to glide forward as I watched. 'On a day like this, it feels as though it might actually be sailing.'

'Perhaps we should hitch a lift?' But when we turned, it was to fly towards Hastings without effort, the wind at our backs pushing us onwards. At the boundary between the two towns, Gil stopped. 'Time for a rest?'

'I could walk for ever.' It was true. I was finding wind and waves exhilarating.

'You'll walk even better after a gin. Let's try the Rope and Anchor.'

In fact, we managed two gins before spilling back onto the promenade and going in search of the much derided pizza. Back at the cottage, the evening drifted by, dozy and intimate. We didn't bother to make excuses to go to bed early; we were there as soon as the dishes were washed and the doors locked. When I closed my eyes that night, I was in his arms and folded in a firm embrace. I could get used to this was my last thought.

Chapter Twenty-Eight

I shooed him off to work around eight o'clock the next morning. He'd left half a dozen things undone the day before and was eager to get to the gallery. I was as eager to make a start on the new project. I'd spend the morning priming the canvas, making sure that when I began to paint, the colours would sing. Oils become increasingly transparent as time goes by and an opaque white surface reflects back the maximum light. It was fortunate I'd bought with me a good quality primer I'd barely used, and was soon covering every inch of the canvas, top to bottom, with careful brush strokes. I worked slowly and methodically. If the canvas were poorly primed, the oils could sink in and leave dull patches on the surface of the painting; a smooth coating would allow my brush to flow and provide the necessary grip or 'tooth' for the colour.

I had left the gesso to dry before I began on a second coat when there was knock at the door. Gil again? I'd locked it this morning, not wishing to be disturbed, and had to hurry into the hall to answer. What could have happened for him to return within a few hours? But it was Deepna who stood on the threshold. The sight of her shocked me. Her thin, wiry figure was a familiar one, but this morning I barely recognised her. She seemed to have shrunk in stature and the smooth skin of her face had folded into deep worry lines. When I took her hand and drew her into the hall, I could feel her body tense beneath my fingers.

'How lovely to see you, Deepna.' I tried to ease the moment with trivialities 'And on such a beautiful morning. You must come into the garden and enjoy the sun.'

She said nothing but allowed me to lead her to the back of the house.

'Have you come to see your uncle?' I said over my shoulder. I had a sudden thought that Das might be ill and had called his niece down from London without my knowing. When she still said nothing, I fell back on an old staple. 'I'll make some tea.'

But before I could turn towards the kitchen, she had reached out and grabbed me with a grip so fierce it numbed every muscle in my arm. 'No, no. I have to say this now, Megan, or I won't be able to tell you.'

'Say what? What on earth's happened?' I was beginning to feel queasy.

'The credit card.' She blurted out the words, then stopped speaking, her breath coming short and irregular.

'Yes, the credit card,' I prompted. 'You were going to pay it off.'

'I tried to. But before I could, the bank stopped a payment to one of our suppliers – they were furious – so I didn't go ahead. I thought it must be a mistake and I needed to find out what was going on before I sent a cheque to the card company. But the next day, another two payments were stopped.' Her face had become frozen, her lips barely moving. 'Then the bank manager rang the shop and asked to see me straightaway. That's when he told me.'

'Told you what?' Queasiness had turned to outright nausea. Something screamed at me that my life was about to fall apart – again. Only this time for good.

'He told me the account had been closed.' Her voice had become no more than a whisper. 'He thought we knew.'

'The account closed?' I was trying desperately to make sense of what she was telling me. 'How could he think that? How could he think we knew?'

'He assumed we had decided to clear our account and bank elsewhere. He was cross that nobody had thought to talk it over with him.'

'*He* was cross. Didn't it occur to him it was highly unusual to withdraw funds in their thousands? Did fraud never cross his mind?'

'He didn't raise questions because of who withdrew the money.'

I'd had to bend close to hear these last words, but Deepna had no need to say more. I knew, knew everything. My limbs were cotton wool and my stomach knotted in pain. I slumped heavily against the wall, trying to keep myself upright.

'Julia?'

Deepna hung her head and a whispered, 'Yes,' came from her mouth. For minutes on end, we stood in the hall looking vacantly at each other, both of us paralysed by the sheer awfulness of the situation. At length she said, 'I've tried to get hold of her, but she's not answering her phone. I haven't seen her for a week, maybe ten days.'

'And you won't.' My voice was robotic. 'She's in Buenos Aires. That's why Mark can't reach her either. She has taken the money and flown to Argentina.'

Tears began to trickle down Deepna's cheeks, but I

couldn't cry. I had to find a way out. 'What about the money from Levsky?' Deepna shook her head.

'That's gone, too?'

'There's no money left, Megan.'

'But there was a second payment due. The commission Levsky was paying for the last Mayer painting.' I couldn't seem to get my head around what she was telling me.

'It was paid a few weeks ago, but it's gone.'

'Gone,' I repeated.

Then through the bewilderment, the anguish, a rush of pure fury, rip roaring fury. How dare she? How dare Julia ruin a woman who had done nothing but offer her friendship? If she had been there in that dark, narrow hall, I would have struck her. A blow so hard, it would have knocked her senseless. But she wasn't there, and my body trembled with a useless, uncontrollable passion.

'I am so sorry.' It was Deepna's turn to soothe. Very gently, she took my hand and led me out into the garden where I slumped down onto one of the metal chairs. What a good job I had never gone back for the recliners. And how stupid that was. My world had collapsed and all I could think of was recliners.

After a while, she tried to talk to me again. 'A lot of our suppliers have closed our account with them and some are agitating to be paid for past orders. I didn't know what to do so I shut up shop and came to you. I haven't called at my uncle's yet. I didn't want to worry him.'

She was being sensible and I tried to match her. 'You did right. The fewer people who know, the better. We must get through this as best we can.' I had no idea how we would, but I had to give her some reassurance, ragged though it was. It was clear she felt a personal responsibility and that wasn't right.

I staggered to my feet. 'I'll make that tea and heap it with spoonfuls of sugar. That's the cure for shock, isn't it?'

But once back in the kitchen, I could have sunk to the floor and cried my eyes out. All the work I had put in, all the contacts made, the hours spent with clients, the enthusiasm and hope for a new business. All gone. And my father – is this what his life's work had amounted to? A shop with dwindling supplies I couldn't pay for and a business whose mortgage I could no longer meet.

I switched on the tap, but not a dribble of water. It was an old ascot system and had been temperamental of late, sometimes refusing to fire. Up until now, though, I'd always managed to run the cold stream at least. Today would be different. Today was my nadir. I poked around at the back of the boiler and found a thin pipe that seemed disconnected. But if so, why was the boiler not leaking water? I poked around some more, then gave up. Deepna wouldn't get her tea and I would have to find a plumber – or Das would.

While I had been scratching round at the back of the ascot, I'd dislodged some of the emulsion and a small chunk of plaster fell into the sink. Now Das would need to repair the wall as well as the boiler. Perhaps I could replace the wedge of plaster so the damage was unnoticeable. It's strange the way the mind works in moments of extremis, concentrating on the humdrum when ruin is all around.

But as soon as I pressed my head against the wall, I could see there was no way I'd manage to conceal the damage. The fallen plaster had revealed a wallpaper beneath the emulsion paint, a design of soft, yellow roses interweaved with light green foliage. Edwardian, I thought. I scratched at it, though why I don't know. My mind had switched off and was floating free of anything and everything. There was another wallpaper beneath the yellow roses, this time a Gothic pattern of dark lozenges linked by a chain of snake-like ribbons. This one had come from a much earlier date. I gazed intently at the curlicued diamonds amid their blood red swirls, and then I was there in the kitchen with Sophia,

Chapter Twenty-Nine

'**W**hat do you call this?' Sophia's hand was shaking, but she tried to keep her voice steady.

Her husband looked at her outstretched palm and gave the smallest of shrugs. 'It looks very much like a necklace. Is there some uncertainty?'

She could have hit him and hit him very hard. 'If there is uncertainty, it lies elsewhere. But you know that well.' She looked with distaste at the string of gems, its rubies glittering blood across her hand. My blood, she thought, the blood I've expended to buy this. 'What is this trinket doing in your pocket?'

'Let me ask *you* a question. What are *you* doing in my pocket? If you choose to violate my privacy, you cannot pretend shock at what you find.'

'I don't have to pretend. I *am* shocked. I know this necklace was not bought for me.'

'You are right, it was not. But you are wrong in imagining the worst.'

'Do I have to imagine? It seems clear enough.'

'Only to a parochial mind. You do not know the true situation and have jumped to a most offensive conclusion.'

He came towards her then and reached out for the necklace, but her hand closed over the stones, their sharp edges biting her flesh. They stood face to face for what seemed an endless moment, and then she saw his hand drop and his expression soften. When his hand reached out again, it was to brush back a lock of hair that had fallen across her forehead. She saw he had found his most winning smile and pinned it to his face.

'Your pregnancy is making you erratic, my dear.' His voice was warm, and smooth as liquid honey. 'Give me back the necklace and I will explain everything.'

'I'll not bargain with you. You will explain.'

Her voice was flat and she kept her hand wrapped tightly around the bauble. She was gaining strength from somewhere, it seemed. Her legs had stopped their disconcerting tremble, and the blood was flowing freely in her veins. Her uncompromising tone had its effect on him. He took a step back, raking his fingers through locks he had allowed to grow long and luxuriant.

'Very well, I will. The case is simple enough. A friend asked that when I was next in Hastings I collect this piece of frivolity from the jewellers' shop on the promenade. He left it there for repair and I am to return it to him once I am back in London.'

She gave a small, joyless laugh. 'This piece of frivolity as you call it, is a valuable necklace. Do you think I am so stupid I cannot see that? What man would leave precious jewels for repair in a small provincial town when he could walk down any West End street and find a master jeweller to do the job?'

'It was inconvenient for my friend to do so.'

'Inconvenient for you, I think. You are lying to me, Spencer. This friend has no existence beyond your imagination. You are the owner of this extravagent piece of jewellery. It is you who purchased it – and purchased it for your mistress. Am I not right?'

Clear-eyed, she looked across at him and beneath her gaze he seemed to shrivel into himself, his hair lose its lustre and the lines on his face furrow more deeply.

'What if I did?' He had turned belligerent. 'I have a right to happiness. You are the one who has ruined our marriage. You deceived me, tricked me into fathering a child for whom I had no wish. Did you think I would not realise? And now you wish to blame me for my reaction. What did you expect when you set out to deceive?'

'That you would welcome the child when she came. That together we would be a family.'

He shook his head furiously as though to dislodge the idea from his mind. 'You knew well that was not what I wanted.'

'It is what you should have wanted. But rather than be here to welcome your child into the world, you prefer to spend time with a woman you have scooped from goodness knows where. A prostitute, no doubt.'

'She is no prostitute,' he spat out, his fists clenched, 'but an artist's model.'

'Model, prostitute, what is the difference? You accuse me of ruining our marriage, but you are the one who has broken your vows, and broken them cruelly.'

He hung his head at that, and she could see that despite his bombast he felt remorse. When he spoke, his voice was filled with sadness.

'There is no point in these recriminations, Sophia. It was wrong for us to marry. I was young and foolish and wished to be done with my parents' control. I thought unwisely the difference in our backgrounds would be of no matter – but it is.'

'My family is honest and diligent and there was a time when you valued them. If my background was acceptable then, why now do you call it into question?'

He shifted impatiently on his feet. 'I cannot seem to make you understand. All my life I have known nothing but freedom and that is how I must live. I cannot bear to be hemmed and hampered by the pieties of your class. I must be allowed to come and go as I please, to make friends where I want, to love where I wish.'

'And where does this magnificent freedom of yours leave me? What freedom do *I* have? What happens to a woman who has married for love, but now finds herself condemned for it?'

'We are in a bad situation, I acknowledge. A divorce is impossible, but I am willing, happy even, to continue our marriage even though it be in name only. I have no wish to see you destitute and you may remain in this cottage and raise our child here. I doubt there is anywhere else you can go. You have only your parents, and they are unlikely to receive you.'

She knew that well enough. And knew there would be no divorce. She had neither the money nor the contacts to pursue a successful action. And even if she had and won her case, what would be the result? She would end a wrecked woman, a mother without a child, for surely with the law on his side, Spencer would take revenge and ensure their daughter was lost to her, given over to his parents' ruinous care.

Her silence prompted him to enlarge on the scheme he was formulating. 'Why cannot we settle our lives to please us both? We can work together – we are still a team. I will continue to find commissions and you to paint them. Our partnership will grow and there will be enough money for you to employ a wet nurse and, when the little one is older, a nanny. You can live in comfort, be free of household cares, be happy with your child.'

There was a pause before he added, 'But I must be free to enjoy my life as I wish. What do you say?'

She was rigid with anger, but chose not to answer his question. Instead, she asked her own. 'How did you get the money for this piece of vulgarity?' She unfolded her palm and allowed the wicked glow of rubies to fill the kitchen.

'That is not your concern.'

'It is very much my concern since I suspect it was money earned from my paintings that purchased it.'

'It is money I earned. I am the one who procured the commissions.'

'And I am the one who fulfilled them. Whatever money has been earned, half of it must be mine.'

'I could dispute your claim and I would have the law on my side. As your husband, your property is my property, your money my money. But I shall be generous. I am prepared to grant you your wish.'

'I do not consider that generous. I have the moral right.'

He turned away and looked out of the window, his lips forming themselves into a sneer. 'Your insistence does you no credit. A fixation with money is one aspect of your class I heartily despise.'

'Those are fine words, but empty ones. I will have my half of the money and I will have it now.' It cut her to shreds to realise the bright hopes of her heart had come to this. But if she were to be an abandoned wife, she would need every penny.

A sulky expression had settled on his now fleshy cheeks. 'You will have it, I promise.'

'When?' In defence of her unborn child, she was ferocious.

'It may take a while, but once the duke's commission is delivered, you will have it.'

'But there is already money in the bank. Money for the London house we were to buy. Do you not remember? Or is that another lie you told?'

He pulled himself up to his full height and tried to look dignified. 'It was not a lie. I had every intention we should move to London, but in the interim I have considered the plan well and decided against. We are no longer suited, my dear, that is the sad truth. We can no longer share a dwelling with any degree of comfort.'

She sank down onto the wooden chair. She had been standing too long and her back throbbed painfully. 'There was a day when to live in the same dwelling was the sum of our dreams. Or have you forgotten?'

'I have not.' He lowered himself into the seat opposite. 'I am truly sorry our plans have not unfolded in the way we expected, but our lives have diverged. I need to be in London. I cannot bear to live this slow parochial grind, while it would seem Hastings suits you well. That being so, is it not sensible to proceed as I have suggested?'

'And the money?' Her thoughts were fixed on how much she would need for the child's future, for a safe, warm home and an education that might one day allow her daughter to carve a better life for herself.

'As I say, you will receive the necessary monies as soon as the Duke of Woodbridge receives his painting.'

'So the money in the bank has gone? You have spent every penny?'

His silence said everything. She scraped her chair back against the red tiled floor and very slowly rose to her feet. Then walked back and forth between window and table. When she turned for a final time, it was to say baldly, 'There is no Woodbridge painting.'

He jumped, as though a fire had been lit beneath him, sending the wooden chair flying. His complexion had turned an unhealthy grey. 'What do you mean, no painting? You must have finished it by now, or you are nearly finished.'

She shook her head, looking through him as though he no longer existed. The Spencer she had known had ceased to live for her. 'There is no painting. It was never started.'

'That cannot be,' he jabbered. 'Are you quite mad?'

'Why are you surprised? I was clear I would not undertake the commission. I told you plainly, the day you bought me the rose. The day you brought your dollymop to Hastings.'

'But you didn't mean it. That was petulance talking.' He had staggered to the kitchen door and was holding onto its frame, seemingly for support.

'On the contrary, I meant every word.' For a moment, she felt the most glorious surge of triumph. 'You must tell the duke there will be no picture.'

'I will not. I cannot tell him so. And you have been working, I can see.' He raised an accusing finger, pointing to the smudge of indigo in her hair.

'I don't deny I have been painting – but not for the Duke of Woodbridge.'

'Then he can have what you've painted,' he gabbled wildly. 'It may not be what he ordered, but I must give him something or lose all credibility. At the very least, it will whet his appetite. He will appreciate your artistry and will be willing to wait for what he has commissioned.'

'You will not have the painting.' The harshness of her voice cut the stifling air in two. 'The painting is for no one but me. But this, this you can have.' She threw the necklace across the room and, as it fell to the floor, its red petals broke and scattered.

'That was foolish.' He had recovered some of his poise. 'Foolishly destructive. And it will not stop me from taking what I need.'

Before she knew what he was about, he had marched out of the kitchen to the foot of the stairs that led to the attic. She hurried forward to stop him, but her movements were slow and lumbering and he was half way up the staircase by the time she had put her foot on the first step.

She remained there, immobile, her heart beating wildly, her breath coming in short gasps. He would not take the painting, surely. He could not. Not when it meant so much to her. He had already taken her heart and broken it. He had taken her future and ruined it. He could not take something she held every bit as precious: the portrait conjured from her dreams.

When he re-emerged at the head of the staircase, she was waiting. He had rolled the canvas, the oil barely dry in places, and carried it underneath his arm. When she saw it, she let out an anguished cry and, as he came towards her, lunged forward to make a grab. Her large belly unbalanced her and she toppled into him. His new patent boot slipped on the stair and before she realised he had lost his footing, he had tumbled past her, hitting his head on the wooden architrave of the stairway and losing consciousness. He fell with a loud thud on to the flagstones of the hall. The canvas flew from his grasp and landed at her feet. She scooped it into her arms, cuddling it to her breast as though it were a real child.

'You can get up.' Her voice was defiant. 'I have the painting now and you will not take it. Not even you could be such a blaggard you would fight me for it.'

But Spencer Wayland was in no mood for fighting. No mood for living, in fact. When he made no answer she tiptoed a little nearer. His body was splayed across the hall at an awkward angle and his head seemed to be looking the wrong way. Then she saw it. The blood. A gash of red slowly spooling across the unforgiving stone.

'Spencer?' she said uncertainly. 'Spencer?'

But there was no answer and never would be.

Chapter Thirty

Panic, pain. The cold, cold chill of the hall. Frozen claws sunk deep, holding me prisoner. Sobs in my ears, tears on my cheeks. What was happening to me? What was I doing here, crouched in foetal position, my hands over my eyes? Tea, I remembered, a boiler that wouldn't work, wallpaper... A tragedy, but not mine. Sophia's tragedy. I staggered to my feet and there was Deepna. She must have grown tired of waiting and come in search of me. Her face told me how strange I must look.

'I couldn't get the boiler to work.' My voice was so weak it barely sounded.

'Is that all? I thought something really bad had happened.' Something had, but I couldn't speak of it.

She walked up to me and stroked my arm in sympathy. 'It's okay. Let's forget the tea. I should get to my uncle's in any case and say hallo. I'll stay over with him and come back tomorrow. We might have come up with some idea then of how best to deal with this. Unless you want company tonight...'

'No,' I was quick to say. 'Go and see Das. If you want, you can tell him what's happened to the shop. You never know, he may have a brilliant suggestion – he's a good businessman. And could you mention the boiler?'

She gave me a warm smile. 'I'll do that, certainly. And I'll be back in the morning.'

As soon as I had seen her to the door, I stumbled into the sitting room and threw myself into a chair. Now that I was alone, I could let my feelings go. But where to start? I'd had no time to recover from Deepna's devastating news before I'd been plunged into something far worse. And I'd felt every minute of it: the sexual betrayal, the theft of savings, the dashing of every hope and dream. Sophia and I were centuries apart, but I had lived through it all. Betrayal is timeless after all, the stealing of trust and treasure knows no boundaries, nor, too, the destruction of a life.

I hadn't lived through that last scene, though, and I hoped I never would. Her husband was dead. The handsome young man, who had carried her laughingly over every threshold of the cottage, was now a lifeless body sprawled across a bloodsoaked hallway. I knew now why that part of the house had always felt so malevolent. Evil had found a home there, but it wasn't Sophia's evil.

She would have to make that clear, I thought, explain to the authorities that Spencer's death was an accident, otherwise accusing fingers could point in her direction. Her husband had not died by her hand, but if it were known Spencer was leaving her for another life, for another woman … she might be judged a scorned wife who had taken her revenge.

I shivered. Surely not. But she was vulnerable, a woman alone and heavily pregnant, and I was worried for her. What would she do? How would she live? How would *I* live? The question was as pertinent now as it had been a hundred and fifty years ago. Deepna would consult her uncle, but how realistic was it to expect any kind of resolution?

The tickets to Buenos Aires hadn't been the final scene of a bad play, after all. There had been an epilogue, one more scene, and the most savage yet. I should have foreseen it. Would have foreseen it, if a small part of me hadn't still believed in Julia's essential goodness. But even about that, I had been wrong. She had stripped me of my livelihood without a second thought.

If I were lucky, I might manage to sell the business as it stood, and with whatever profit emerged, pay off my creditors. I would never pay the outstanding mortgage, though, and the building was sure to be repossessed. There would be nothing left: no stock, no goodwill, no home. My stomach heaved at the thought. I was homeless. Gil had offered me shelter but I'd shrunk from making the commitment – and how unfair on him if I ignored the hesitation I still felt. Other than that, I was wholly dependent on Das's good nature.

I sat in that chair for hours while the sun gradually sank beneath the cottage roofs opposite. It was the sound of Gil coming through the front door that eventually roused me from my state of paralysis. I was cold and stiff.

'Bare arms, the evening air – could you be thinking you're in the Caribbean?' He loitered on the threshold, a half smile on his lips. 'You do know the door to the garden is wide open? I'll close it before you freeze in your seat.'

He walked into the room and then stopped. 'What … what is it, Megan?'

My resolve to stay strong evaporated and tears began to dribble down my cheeks. Then I broke down completely, and it was only after he'd held me tight for minutes on end that I forced myself to tell him the news Deepna had brought from London.

'There's still a huge mortgage on the shop. Not to mention outstanding bills – rates, utilities, suppliers I owe money to. By the time I've paid it all, there'll be nothing left.' I snuffled to a halt.

'Moneywise, that's true. But you're left. And in all this miserable mess, that's what's important. You'll be your own solution.'

I was feeling nothing but despair and his words jarred. I wriggled out of his arms and sat rigidly beside him. 'I hope you're not going to be positive.'

'Yep. That's what I'm going to be. You've suffered a severe blow, I get that. It's a blow that could destroy your future, but you're not going to let it. You're going to start over.'

'So easy,' I murmured sourly. 'But how exactly?'

'Stay here and get a job, and in your spare time keep painting.'

'There are no jobs in Hastings, or at least nothing I can turn my hand to. And no one will buy my paintings.' My dejection was complete.

'Listen to you – you can do better than that. You'll do whatever job will earn money, I know, and yes, there will be a market for your work. We'll pull out all the stops, make sure we broadcast your name across Sussex. I've noticed you're painting more easily these days, and maybe in time you'll have sufficient work for an exhibition.'

'Such grand schemes,' I mocked. I couldn't believe in any of them.

'But not impossible. It will be hard, very hard, but you can do it.'

'And my shop?' I mourned. 'How hard will that be?'

He put his arms around me again and, ignoring my

resistance, dragged me into another embrace. 'I know. A complete bugger.'

I gave in then and laid my head on his shoulder. 'If I can come out of it not owing anything...' His energy was having some effect, it seemed.

'And you should. The shop is a thriving concern with a large amount of goodwill. There'll be someone who is willing to take it on, and hopefully for the right price. In the meantime, Julia's theft needs reporting to the police. Their jurisdiction won't reach Argentina, but there could well be an extradition treaty. It's worth a try – at the least, it makes sure she can't set foot in this country without risking arrest.'

Julia's behaviour had been so shocking I was still struggling to believe it. I uncurled myself a little and searched his face. 'I don't know how she could do this to me.'

'Don't you? She did it because she could. Because she envied your good fortune, or what she saw as your good fortune.'

'If that's true, it's quite mad. I agree that in some ways I've been lucky, but in others definitely not.'

'See it from her angle. It's a twisted viewpoint, but not implausible. You had a famous father when she hadn't even a name for hers. You inherited money and that gave you the power to dispense favours, while she was forced into the role of grateful recipient. You had a steady boyfriend and a settled life. I know nothing of Julia's personal affairs, but I imagine they verge on the chaotic. I guess she was jealous – she wanted what you had. All of it.'

I thought for a while, turning over in my mind the years I'd spent with her. 'I did sometimes wonder if she was jealous,' I admitted.

'I never doubted it from the moment I met her.'

'Really?' I'd always considered him a perceptive man, but the blunt statement shocked me.

'When she came to Hastings and we went walking on that miserable Sunday, I caught her several times just staring at you. You didn't notice, maybe you were used to it, but I thought then she was a funny kind of friend. She looked at you as though she disliked you.'

'I don't think she's always disliked me.' I couldn't bear to think our friendship had been a complete sham. 'It was Julia who helped me break out of a depression that was getting a grip. And she had no ulterior motive – she genuinely wanted to help, to see me get back to myself. How could she have changed so much?'

'People do. The dynamics of a relationship change all the time. Think about it – when you first met, she was in charge. You were wretched, you were suffering, and she was the one who could reach down and lend a helping hand. But once you bought the business, your positions were reversed and you were the one calling the shots. I know you made her an equal partner, but she probably never felt she was.'

The ideas that Julia had wanted to push flitted through my mind. I'd back-pedalled on all of them, and she must have felt frustrated to a degree I had never imagined.

'I expect you're right.' I couldn't stop a heavy sigh from escaping. 'I just never noticed she'd changed towards me.'

He kissed the top of my head and I snuggled back into him. 'You're a dear girl. You tend to think the best of everyone and you would have kept thinking the best of Julia, no matter what.'

For a while I was silent, thinking over the years I'd shared with her: the laughter, the fun, the daily ups and downs of running the business, the sheer hard work of it. And felt immensely sad. But it had gone and Gil was right, I had to plan a new future.

'I didn't know you were coming this evening,' I said dreamily into his chest. The stress had taken its toll and I was half asleep.

'I can't keep away, haven't you noticed, though I did have a good reason for calling. I brought you news, but I don't think now is the right time. You've had enough shock for one day.'

'What's it about?'

He gave a small regretful murmur. 'Okay. I heard from Will again this morning. I didn't expect him to carry on digging, but he seems to have got hooked by the Waylands' story. He's discovered the reason Sophia and her beau didn't stay here for long.'

'I know the reason. Or at least I can guess.

'You can?'

'Spencer died.'

'How do you know that?' He disentangled himself and stared at me.

'How do you think?'

Concern was writ large on his face. 'You saw them? Do you know *how* he died?' He was being cautious, unwilling to add to my unhappiness.

'I do. Violently.' The calm I had been curating deserted me and my voice began to shake. The splayed limbs, the twisted head, the pool of blood, were there in my head, vivid and indestructible.

'Poor Megan, to have seen it happen. What a day you've endured.'

'I left Sophia bent over his body,' I said in a small voice. 'I've no idea what happened next. No idea how she fared afterwards.'

'You might be happier not knowing.'

For a moment I thought of ignoring what was evidently bad news, but Sophia hadn't been a coward and neither would I. 'Tell me the worst. Let me get it over with.'

He reached into his pocket and brought out a photocopy. 'This is a page from an 1851 newspaper. Will found it quite by chance. It's a report of a court case, not much more than a snippet stuffed in among all the hoohah over the opening of the Great Exhibition.'

'A court case?' I was aghast. My worst fears were coming true.

'Spencer Wayland's death was treated as manslaughter.'

'But how can that be?'

'His wife had cause to get rid of him – at least that was what the prosecution maintained and the jury believed them. His new amour testified to the fact he was about to leave the family home and take his money with him. In the jury's mind it must have added up to a very good reason for Sophia to ensure he never went anywhere.'

'But it was an accident. I saw it happen.'

'Unfortunately the jury didn't,' he said wryly.

I sat staring blankly at the wall in front of me. Sophia accused of manslaughter and found guilty. How could that have happened? 'Did she go to prison?' I was fearful of asking, but I had to know.

He nodded and handed me the slip of paper. 'I'm afraid so. Look.' His finger pointed out a line printed in bold type. *Mrs Spencer Wayland was today sentenced for the manslaughter of her husband, Mr Spencer Wayland, at Lewes Crown Court. She will serve a total of eight years in prison.'*

'Eight years!'

'It may not seem it, but she was fortunate. Manslaughter means the prosecution accepted she hadn't contrived a deliberate plan to kill her husband, that it was an irrational act when her mind was overset. Otherwise, she could have faced a charge of murder. It was lucky for her the Victorians considered a woman's mind to be delicate, especially in pregnancy. But even for manslaughter, hanging was the punishment, or if you were lucky, transportation. The fact she was about to give birth must have worked in her favour.'

'But eight years when the sentence must have meant exactly that.'

'There was no remission certainly.'

'And what of the baby?'

'Sophia would have given birth in prison and been allowed to keep her daughter – at least until she was weaned, I think. Maybe longer, I'm not sure. But the child wouldn't have stayed with her for ever. Children were usually taken away by the time they were two years old.'

I was horrified. 'And then what?'

'I don't know,' he said sadly. 'I hope someone took pity on the girl and gave her a home.'

'And if they didn't?'

'If they didn't, there was the workhouse. But you're not to think of it. Whatever happened, it's history and can't be changed. And right now, you've sufficient problems of your own to cope with.'

But it wasn't history for me and I couldn't stop thinking.

Chapter Thirty-One

Long after Gil had fallen asleep, I lay fretting. I couldn't get from my mind that Sophia had gone to prison for eight long years and no doubt endured the harshest of treatment. The child she had borne had been her only possible comfort, the little girl allowed to stay with her mother long enough to form a deep bond, but then wrenched from Sophia's side and abandoned to a merciless world. She was a blameless woman – her husband's death had clearly been an accident – and to punish her so pitilessly for an act she had not committed filled me with outrage.

There was something else, too, that was almost as upsetting. I had felt that terrible moment happen, really felt it. It had been as though I was inhabiting Sophia's body. I'd felt fear when Spencer had toppled past me, almost knocking me from my feet, fear for the safety of the unborn child I carried. Then horror at the thwack of his body hitting the cold, unyielding stone. And sick dread as the realisation dawned that he would never move again.

It had been an extraordinary feeling, a horrible feeling, but one I should have expected. Ever since I'd walked through the thin veil separating Sophia's time from my own, I had been heading for this moment. Over the weeks,

I'd fallen deeper and deeper into the past, until today I'd been pulled so thoroughly into that other world that for an instant I had become Sophia. I couldn't tell Gil. I couldn't expect him to understand when I didn't understand it myself. He had been unswerving in his support, a true friend and a true lover, and I was close to believing he'd be my future. But tonight I must pass the worrisome hours alone.

How swiftly would news of the court case travel to London? Would it have travelled? Did Sophia's parents know what had befallen her? Would she or someone on her behalf have written to them? They might have stayed ignorant of their daughter's fate, or if they knew, indifferent to it. And indifferent to the child she carried. Spencer's parents would know, of course. I could imagine their reaction. He had been the longed for son and heir and now, according to a jury, he was dead by his wife's hand. They would have nothing but hostility for their unwanted daughter-in-law. And nothing, I guessed, to do with the grandchild they would be too proud and too heartbroken to acknowledge.

That poor little darling, Sophia's dream child, would be consigned to the workhouse and a life of servitude and misery. And for what? For a painting that her mother had been determined to protect. But at what cost! A painting that was lost forever, with only an embroidery left to tell the story.

The embroidery. Suddenly, I had to see it – it was, after all, the image that had begun this whole chain of events. I had to see it now and study it closely. The impulse was so keen it would give me no peace until I'd crept down the stairs and into the sitting room. By the light of the street lamp, the girl's gown was as blue as ever, her hair as richly auburn, her eyes blue and grey and every shade in between. They still searched my face, were still asking something of me, but what, I had no idea. Tired and frustrated, I climbed wearily back to bed, cuddling up to Gil's warm body and longing for sleep to obliterate this day from my mind.

* * *

I must have slept, I suppose, but I wasn't sure. I was back in the hall and the cold was all around, stark, icy, forcing me to clasp the shawl around my shoulders. My foot slipped and I looked down. It was blood. I had slipped on blood. I tried to bend down to Spencer, but my great bulge made it impossible. I cradled my belly with one hand and very carefully lowered myself to the floor, first on one knee and then the other. Spencer's face was turned away from me and I gently eased it from the ghastly angle it had assumed. He was looking at me, looking into my face, but he didn't see me. He saw nothing. His eyes were blank, clouded, and when I felt for the pulse at his neck, the skin was limp and cooling rapidly.

'Spencer! Spencer!'

I cried his name over and over again, as though somehow I could reclaim him from the place he had gone. But I knew my hope was forlorn. He was dead and I was alone. I was filled with dread, with foreboding. What did I do? Who must I tell? A neighbour, perhaps. Yes, my neighbour. He would fetch a doctor, though no doctor could breathe life into this poor man at my knees. My love for Spencer had long ago withered, but he was my husband and once my true sweetheart. He did not deserve to die so young and so mundanely. He was grander than that.

I would go to my neighbour. With difficulty, I hauled

myself to my feet, gathered the shawl around my shoulders again and made for the door. Please God, he was in. It was early evening, a time when he might still be drinking at the Cutter, but I would wait for him. His wife was always friendly to me. She would let me stay. I couldn't stay here, couldn't keep company with this mangled body.

I had unlatched the front door when a thought came, sudden and sharp. The picture. Would it be safe? Maybe the police would come and the coroner, and I would have to tell them what had happened, that Spencer had fallen down the stairs while hurrying to take the canvas away. I could lose the picture. They might impound it as evidence and I would never see my darling girl again.

I walked back along the hall, averting my glance from Spencer's staring eyes, and loosened the painting from his grasp. I would hide it. When the authorities came, I would say that Spencer was hurrying to catch a train to London – that was true enough – and had tripped and fallen in his rush. There would be no need to mention the portrait. I tucked the canvas beneath my arm and made a stumbling start up the stairs.

It was hard, very hard. Panting and bent nearly double, I reached the half way landing where the staircase twisted in its climb. For several minutes I had to cling to the wall for support. I could feel the baby pressing down and I was fearful I might go into labour at any moment, before I'd had the chance to hide my precious burden. When I could wait no longer, I started up the final flight and almost fell through the doorway into the studio. It had taken me too long to get here and I felt a ripple of panic. I should report the death without delay, but I had no choice but to rest again.

When I was able, I padded across the wooden floor. Several of the boards were loose. Spencer had long ago promised to take a hammer to them, since whenever we walked in the attic their squeak and grind sounded throughout the house. But he had never done so. He had been far too busy in London, making false friends, spending money, finding women. But now I was grateful for it. It took me a few seconds to locate the worst offender and raise its edge with the tip of my slipper. The floorboard I'd chosen was six feet from the wall, almost directly beneath the skylight. That was important to remember. When all the fuss and bother was over, I would retrieve the painting and, if I were able to earn money from my sewing, would have it framed and hung where it belonged – alongside the embroidery.

I found some waxed paper in the drawer of the chest and rolled the canvas into it, then wound the neat tube I had made into a sheet of linen. The package was the right size and shape for the hiding place I'd devised. It took a fair while to get down on my knees again, but the satisfaction of tucking the painting into its aperture and closing the cover to keep it snug and safe, made up for the discomfort. When I'd regained my feet, and that took more time, I walked back and forth over the floorboard to ensure it was fixed into place. No one but me would know the treasure that lay inches below the surface. Slowly down the staircase again, sliding past the body – for that is how I now thought of Spencer – and out into the street to look for help.

* * *

A kick against my ankle jumped me awake. I opened my eyes, but saw nothing. Where was I? Who was I? I lay stiff and tense, scrabbling for sense. Then I heard it: calm, mea-

271

sured breathing. Gil. It was he who'd inadvertently woken me. And I was Megan and back in my own century.

'Gil,' I whispered urgently. 'Something's happened.'

He shuffled to the other side of the bed. 'Gil,' I said again, shaking him very gently. He yawned and turned over then grabbed the bedside clock and brought it close to his eyes.

'It's four in the morning,' he protested.

'I know, but I have something important to tell you. I had this dream.' Had it been a dream? I didn't think so, but I couldn't burden him with what I really believed, that for a short time I had become Sophia.

'That's good, a dream's good.' His voice tailed off lazily and he yawned again.

'This dream was. I know where the painting is.'

There was a long silence. 'What painting?' He propped himself on his elbow, and even in the half light I could see his forehead creased in puzzlement.

'Sophia's. The portrait she did of her daughter.'

He groaned. 'Shall I throttle you now or when it's fully light?'

'I'm serious. I know where it is.'

'Let me get this right. You're saying you know where to find the portrait that a dead woman painted of a child who wasn't even born?'

'I do. It's a Wayland painting, Gil. A rare find – you should be tempted.'

He should have been, but he wasn't. 'There *are* no more Waylands. If there ever were, they've gone missing. Now go back to sleep.'

'This one isn't – missing, that is. In my dream I saw where it was hidden.'

'Megan,' he groaned again.

'I know it sounds weird, but it's true. Really, it is.'

'Weird? It's more than weird. Where is it then? Stuffed up the chimney? Under the third rose bush from the left?'

'It's in the studio at the top of this house.'

'There is no studio.'

'There was and there still may be. We just need to find a way in.'

'Oh, is that all?' He flopped back onto the bed. 'Go to sleep.'

'I mean it. I'll have to ask Das if we can break through the wall in the hall, the blank bit opposite the kitchen. That's where the staircase went up to the studio. It must have been boarded up before he bought the cottage.'

'And I'm pretty sure he'd like it to stay boarded up.'

'Not if there's a valuable picture to find.'

'That's a big if. And if you managed to persuade the poor bloke to take the wall down, what's the betting the staircase is no longer there? Or if it is, that it's unsafe and completely unusable.'

'Then I won't be able to recover the painting.'

'But Das will be left with a hefty bill for knocking the wall down and putting it back again.'

In my excitement I hadn't thought of that. In fact, I hadn't thought it through at all. It was a real risk, as Gil said, and if there were no crock of gold beyond, I couldn't afford to repay my landlord whatever expenses he incurred. The thought kept me quiet for a while, but the dream or whatever it was, hadn't merely been vivid, it had been a part of me. I was so certain the portrait was there. And Das was a risk taker, wasn't he? Only a man inured to gambling would have moved from London to open an antique shop in a faded seaside town. Surely he would take a risk on this?

'I'll ask him,' I decided.

Gil thumped back on to the bed and hunched his pillows. 'You do that. Now can we go to sleep?'

Chapter Thirty-Two

For the rest of the night I managed only a doze, and the shrill of the alarm came as a welcome sound. Long before opening time, I was waiting for Das outside his shop, but it was Lucy rather than her boss I saw, making her way along the road from the station and dragging a small suitcase behind her.

She hurried towards me. 'You're an early bird! I caught the first train from Rye, but you've beaten me to it. Are you escaping Gil? Send him back if he's getting on your nerves. He can be a pain, I know.'

'It's nothing like that.'

I felt my cheeks flush an unbecoming pink. Lucy took it for granted we were a couple, but I was still getting used to the idea. It made me awkward, though it shouldn't have. Life was too short to dither and last night's events had somehow tipped the balance.

'I've some news for Das. Are you expecting him this morning?' Excitement was taking hold of me again.

'He'll be along soon. Let me find the key... I told him I'd open up today – a special treat for giving me a break I didn't expect.'

'Did you have a good time?'

'We always have a good time. We talked about the job and Mum is fine about my taking it. Delighted, in fact. And delighted about you and Gil.'

I was keen to change the subject. 'So how about the job? Any second thoughts?'

She led the way into the shop, picking up a pile of mail spread maze-like across the floor. 'Das has been shirking while I've been away,' she tutted. 'It looks as though he's not collected his post for days.' She dumped the pile of paper on the counter before she answered. 'I've accepted their offer, so I can't complain about leaving Hastings, can I?'

'You don't sound too enthusiastic.'

I must have looked as concerned as I sounded because she patted my hand and smiled. 'Don't worry, I'll get there. It's a big change for me, but I know it's one I need. Do you fancy a coffee? There was nothing open on the station and I'm parched.'

'I'd love one.' I was certainly in need of caffeine, if only to prop my eyes open. Excitement can only do so much.

By the time Das bowled through the door, I'd drunk two large mugs and was feeling ready for anything, but after I had explained my mission, a creeping uncertainty began to take hold. He had allowed me to talk on without saying a word and now stood scratching his head, clearly perplexed. Lucy stood beside him, staring in disbelief.

'You had a dream,' he kept saying.

'I know it sounds ridiculous, but I believe it's the truth. It was so powerful, Das. You said yourself you'd heard there was once a staircase from that part of the hall, and the painting in the Driftwood makes it clear the cottage must have had an upper floor. Also, there's a step down in one of the bedrooms. At some stage, its floor level has been lowered to accommodate a room above.'

'Maybe you are right – I'm not sure. The staircase was a rumour I heard, no more. And a painting? It was a dream you had, Megan, and dreams can mislead. Particularly if you are feeling confused. And you've had much to confuse you.'

'I'm not mad if that's what you're suggesting.'

'No, not mad, not at all,' he said soothingly, 'but perhaps a little…'

'Unbalanced?'

'Thanks, Lucy.' It was evidently what Das was thinking, but was too polite to say.

'Only joking. *I* think it's a great idea. Wow, a valuable painting hidden in a secret room. Better than the da Vinci Code.'

'I know the work will cost money, but I promise it will be worth it.' His face told me he thought it far from likely. 'I'll get a loan.' I was desperate. 'As long as you'll agree to my knocking down the wall.'

'A loan? Is that wise? Deepna has told me of your difficulties.'

As though on cue, Deepna appeared in the doorway, frowzy-headed and blinking wildly. She had spent the night in one of the rooms above the shop, and it seemed to have been a restless one. I whisked through the explanations again and saw with relief that she was excited by the idea of finding the studio. Maybe it was a distraction from her worries over Palette and Paint, but whatever prompted her she began urging her uncle to agree, and in the end he did.

'I'll phone a builder,' he promised.

'When?' I was almost hopping. I think the double dose of caffeine may have been partly responsible.

'Builders are busy men.' He had begun to prevaricate.

'I mean when will you phone?'

'He'll do it now,' Lucy said, 'won't you, Das?' And she whipped the receiver from its rest and handed it to him.

As it turned out, Das's favoured builder couldn't come that day and couldn't come the next, but he promised to call at All Saints Street on Thursday, complete with van and tools. How was I to contain myself until then? I'd already begun to fidget.

Lucy had been watching me and her voice was decided. 'You must go and see Mum. She'll want to know about your dream… the studio … everything.'

And she'll keep you out of everyone's hair was the subtext. But I didn't mind. I liked Rose enormously and I had things to talk to her about other than paintings and staircases and secret rooms. I wanted to talk about Gil.

* * *

'You are sure, Megan?'

I was sitting in Rose's front room looking out onto Church Square and she was perched on the sofa opposite, her head inclined towards me, listening eagerly.

'I am. It's taken me a while, but I know I want to be with Gil.'

She jumped up from her seat and was across the room in a few strides, pulling me into a motherly hug. 'I can't tell you how happy I am. I've known for weeks you were right for him. And Gil has known it for weeks, too.'

'The thing is,' and my voice wobbled a little, 'I'm not so sure Gil does know, not any longer.'

Her arms dropped and she looked uncertain. Perhaps I shouldn't have confessed my fears, but I needed reassurance.

'It's this business with the studio. When I told him about the dream, I thought he'd be as excited as I was, but he was lukewarm – even dismissive.'

'And when you mentioned you were opening the staircase?'

'He tried to persuade me not to go ahead, and was annoyed when I said I must. He thinks I've inveigled Das into wasting money.'

Annoyed was a mild description. After leaving Das's shop, I'd called at the Driftwood to share my news and Gil had come as close to anger as I'd ever seen him. In the short time since, he had not once mentioned the portrait. I'd always felt secure with him, even from our first meeting on the steps at East Hill, and this new lack of trust hurt me deeply. It was stoking old fears of abandonment.

'Could it be that he's worried for you? You have had a difficult summer and he might be concerned this search will end in disappointment.'

I thought it unlikely and said so, but Rose was determined to be positive. 'Once the wall is down and the studio found, you'll both forget any small squabble. And then we can celebrate. Why don't we celebrate now? Elderflower wine? My neighbour dropped a bottle off only yesterday. I wouldn't drink it myself, but –'

'Tea is fine. A pot of Darjeeling? But celebrating doesn't feel right, not now. Gil hasn't said so, but I'm pretty sure he thinks I'm unhinged.'

'Your dream must have been tremendously vivid,' she said diplomatically. If she thought I'd gone haywire, she wasn't saying so.

'It *was* vivid. I really believe there's something there.'

'Then you must find out what it is.' Very little disturbed

279

Rose and I envied her the ability to let life flow and accept whatever came her way. 'Think what fun it will be for Das, too!'

I wasn't at all certain Das would see it that way; he had been more or less coerced into funding the project. But I knew I had to get behind that wall and I was taking no prisoners.

'Come into the kitchen while I make the tea and talk to me. *I'm* going to toast you both even if you won't. I've been waiting for this moment.'

'No more waiting then.'

My voice turned husky. I had grown immensely fond of Gil's mother and her evident joy at adding me to her family was making me tearful. It was making me troubled, too. What if my compulsion to discover what lay behind the wall meant I'd burned my boats? What if Gil took the view that in ignoring his advice, I was saying he didn't matter. It could mean the end before we had really begun and Rose would be back to waiting again.

I followed her into the small room at the back of the cottage while she busied herself with kettle and pot and cups. 'You and Gil will sort this problem out,' she said comfortably. 'And then you must tell your mother your news – she'll want to meet him. I hope she'll be pleased with your choice.' She said this casually, but I heard a smidgen of anxiety in her voice.

I would have liked to reassure her, but I couldn't. My mother's attitude to any man who had dared come into my life had been unwelcoming, and in Dan's case, positively hostile. What would Ruth Lacey make of Gil? I had no idea for the simple reason that she was highly unlikely ever to meet him. Rose, of course, had no idea how bad things were between my mother and myself.

'I don't honestly know.' I prevaricated. 'But I'm sure she'll like him. Why wouldn't she?'

'You must give me her telephone number and I'll ring and invite her to stay. Then she can meet Gil and Lucy and see Hastings for herself.'

I felt the carpet being pulled from beneath my feet and tried to regain lost ground. 'I'll talk to her. As soon as I know what's happening at the cottage.'

It was a false promise and I felt bad, but at the moment I couldn't cope with more complication, not when my mind was filled so entirely with a studio twelve miles away.

'That's good. And in the meantime, you must paint. It will make you feel better. Take the itch out of your fingers.'

She was right. My brain might be fizzing too loudly, but my fingers were longing to paint. I needed to take my thoughts elsewhere, away from Sophia and her child and her painting, and into something over which I had some control.

I stayed two nights in Rye. Rose left early each morning for her secretarial job, and for the rest of the day I had the house to myself. It was blissfully quiet. I set up the easel in the sitting room bay where the light was excellent, and began work on the view from St Mary's church. Every evening, Rose cooked me a wonderful meal and looked over the work I had done, making the odd suggestion but mostly nodding her approval. Those few days in Rye passed peacefully enough, but hovering over my shoulder always was the coming storm, as likely to bring misfortune as elation.

* * *

On Thursday morning, I woke to limbs tense with expectation and a stomach trawled by a thousand butterflies. This was the day I would prove I was right, either that or a sad fantasist. Far more importantly, it was the day Sophia's child might be rescued from her long sleep.

Rose had secured a day off from work and planned to travel to Hastings with me. 'I have to be in at the kill,' she said. It was an unfortunate expression, but then she wasn't to know what had happened all those years ago.

Mike, the builder Das had phoned, was as good as his word, and by the time we reached the cottage he had let himself in and unloaded his tools. We found him at the end of the hall, contemplating the blank wall.

'Morning ladies,' he said cheerfully. 'I'm not sure where best to start. Can either of you give me a clue?'

'I can.'

I stepped forward and almost immediately, I felt ice. The cold had been conspicuously absent from my dream, and I understood why. Death had struck only minutes before, and the evil surrounding it was still young; it lacked the centuries in which to fester and expand into the force I knew today. It was evident neither of my companions had felt the change in temperature, but I couldn't have been more certain of where Mike should begin.

'Here,' I said, indicating an oblong of wall opposite the kitchen door.

'Fine. Here it is.' He picked up a sledge hammer from his pile of tools and heaved it at the wall. 'Time to stand back, ladies. It's likely to get messy.'

'We'll be outside,' Rose said, ushering me out of the way. I think she was worried I'd want to wield the sledgehammer myself.

The sky was grey and tumbling with clouds. Rain was

clearly in the offing, but we took a metal chair each and sat around the table as though we had been invited for an *al fresco* lunch and were only waiting for our hostess to arrive with a tray. Rose tried to engage me in conversation and I tried to respond, but it was impossible. I couldn't concentrate and I couldn't sit still.

I turned my head to look longingly at the kitchen door. 'Better leave him to it, my dear,' Rose said placidly.

I was so on edge that when finally I could sit no longer, I almost toppled the chair in my haste to get up. There was only the small square of garden to walk in – or rather, march in – and I set off like some clockwork doll wound to breaking point. Once, twice, three times round, until my companion walked over to me and led me gently back to my seat.

We had been sitting in the garden for an hour and the waiting had become intolerable, when a figure erupted through the doorway and onto the small terrace. It was Lucy.

'Megan, Mum, come quickly. There's a staircase!'

I gave what sounded like a strangled cry. 'I can't have missed the moment!' But there was no time to feel regret.

'Not really,' Lucy comforted, as we poured into the hall. 'You've still got the staircase to explore.'

'We'll have to see about that,' Mike said grumpily.

He was sweaty and begrimed and standing amid a pile of broken masonry. I looked beyond him and saw the staircase, following it with my eyes as it disappeared into the void above. The wood was dark and worn, but somehow venerable. I wanted to bend down and touch it, kiss it even, it had been in my mind and my heart for so long.

'These stairs are old, very old,' Mike was saying. 'I've no idea how safe they are – or what's at the top.'

'Then we'll have to find out.' If he thought I was stopping

now, he had a surprise coming.

'I must phone Das.' Lucy was jumping with excitement. 'And Gil. They need to come. Meg was right, wasn't she about the staircase? And she'll be right about the painting, too.'

I loved her belief in me. Rose, though, was looking doubtful. 'Will you go up, Mike?'

He looked unhappy at the suggestion, but he need not have. I had no intention of letting him be the first up those stairs. 'I'll go.'

'You can't. It could be dangerous,' Rose said.

'I can.' My voice held a new firmness. 'I have to.'

And before anyone could put a hand out to stop me, I had launched myself up the staircase that Sophia had climbed on her last day in the cottage.

Chapter Thirty-Three

It was the smell that hit me first. Heavy and stale and clinging. A thick must that filled my lungs until I could hardly breathe. The staircase and the studio above had remained sealed for a hundred and fifty years, truly a Victorian burial chamber.

'Here, you'll need this.'

I looked back and saw Mike waving a torch at me. What was I thinking climbing these dangerous stairs without a light? It was that compulsion again, the one I'd felt so often since I'd lived in this cottage. I leant down and took the torch from him. By its small circle of light, I could see dense cobwebs hanging from the ceiling and a multitude of dead spiders crowded into every crevice. Several, though, were very much alive – luckily, I'd never suffered from a phobia.

I crept up the stairs, one by one, the dust lying deep on every tread but flying upwards as I climbed, to float above me in an ever increasing cloud. Where I'd disturbed it, I could see that at the centre of each stair there was a distinct hollow, a reminder of all the feet that over the years had travelled up and down this staircase to the attic above. It was only one pair of feet, though, that interested me.

I could hear footsteps from behind. Mike must have

decided he couldn't stand by while a female led the way, but when I looked back again I saw the others were following, too. Rose held a flashlight the builder had dug from his tool box and was circling it wildly up and down the plastered walls. At the top of the stairs was a wooden door with a large iron circle of a handle. The handle seemed out of place somehow, too heavy, too forbidding, for what had once been an artist's studio. Very gingerly, I pushed the door open.

'Be careful when you get inside. There may be floor-boards missing.'

Mike was only a step behind me now and breathing hard. He looked an averagely fit man, but the staircase was extremely steep and I wondered how Sophia, heavily pregnant, had managed it day after day. But I didn't have to wonder, did I? Several nights ago, I had made the same journey myself, and in the same ungainly state.

I flashed the torch around the first few feet of the studio, then stepped cautiously forward, allowing my foot very gradually to take my full weight. It seemed fine, and in a few seconds I had found my way to the middle of the room and the others were crowding through the doorway.

'The floor appears intact,' I said.

Mike nodded. 'We're lucky. Often places boarded up for years have termites in charge and the floor crumbles with the first step.'

I waved the torch into each of the four corners. 'The whole studio is intact.'

I marvelled at what I saw. A pile of canvases were stacked against one wall, a chest, its surface covered by drawing implements, against another. On the floor lay several aban-doned palettes and a holder made of tin and full of brushes. Immediately behind me, an easel lurched to one side, but had stayed upright. The room must have been sealed straight after Spencer's death and never visited again. I was standing in the space that had last held Sophia in her frantic rush to hide the portrait of her child.

'Well, we're here,' Mike said a trifle unnecessarily. 'What next?'

'Next we prize up the floorboards.' It was Gil's voice, and Das was at his shoulder. 'I've pillaged your tools, Mike, and brought the crowbar.'

I knew Lucy had danced off to tell him the news, but I hadn't expected to see him. I walked across and held out my hand. 'You've come.'

He ignored the hand and put his free arm around me. 'How could I resist?'

I thought it very likely he could. But he was here, beside me – and wielding a heavy implement. That showed faith.

'We may have a crowbar, but where the hell do we start?' Good builder he might be but Mike, I decided, was a bit of a curmudgeon.

I walked over to the dilapidated easel and looked up. 'The skylight must have been above here. Yes, look. There's the faintest outline where it's been blocked and new material grafted on to the old.' Everyone obediently flashed torches at the sloping ceiling and grunted agreement.

'So?' This was Mike again.

'So we count six feet from the wall, stop beneath the sky-light, and jump up and down.' It was a good job it was too dark for me to see his face.

'Perhaps you'd like me to translate that into centime-tres?' he asked sourly. 'That way, we'll be sure to find the place.'

I was ready with a tart response, but Gil interposed. 'The

Victorians measured in feet, and that's what we should do.' It seemed he had decided to throw himself behind the endeavour after all.

I paced out the steps I thought I'd taken that night and gave a small bounce. Not a squeak. Had it been further to the right? I tried to remember, but I was beginning to feel confused. By torchlight it was impossible to see the whole of the studio, and without the window that had once been there, the attic looked much less familiar. I sensed an uneasy shuffle around me, as though I was confirming everyone's fears that this was a wild goose chase and they'd already indulged me too much.

I shut my eyes tight and tried desperately to remember the room I'd seen, but it was impossible. My experience had been dreamlike and dreams gain the power they do because by their very nature – fleeting and evanescent – they are impossible to reclaim. The effort to retrieve that night was just too hard, and I was about to shame myself by confessing as much when Sophia took over. It's the only way I can describe the sudden illumination that propelled me a few inches to the right. I bounced again and this time there was a decided groan. With Sophia still at my elbow, I walked a straight line to the end of the floorboard. The creaking was audible to everyone.

'This is it.'

Mike sighed. 'Okay, here goes.'

He fitted the crowbar beneath a corner edge and yanked, but in the event he had no need of a tool. The board came up in one easy movement. I could have lifted it myself. And then I remembered why: Spencer had never nailed it down. Several torches flashed their light into the cavity. I got down on my knees and, bent nearly double, delved into the black space, wafting my hands backwards, forwards, across, down, until they touched what I searched for. I heard a cry of triumph – it must have been mine – and pulled from the space a linen-wrapped package.

* * *

We made the trip down the stairs a good deal more swiftly than we'd climbed up – the steps had turned out far safer than Mike had anticipated. And the studio above was in reasonably good shape, too, so much so that Das wondered aloud if it might be worth his while to widen the staircase and open up the skylight.

'What do you think, Mike? The renovations wouldn't be too costly and with the studio converted, I'd have a three bedroom cottage to rent. I could charge more.'

'You should leave the studio untouched,' Lucy put in. 'Someone died on those stairs.'

'Pff. That was years ago. Who cares about that now?'

He was right. Not many people would, but I did. When Mike had departed for another job and we had made cups of tea all round, I spread the rescued canvas across the kitchen table. The waxed paper in which the painting had been wrapped had prevented it from cracking, that and the fact the studio had been sealed off from the world, its environment protected. Das and Lucy were still discussing possible building works, while Gil dived into cupboards looking for heavy bowls to weight each corner of the canvas. Then he took his mother to one side and I was left alone, to stand and look.

I spent a long time looking; the portrait was so beautiful I could have cried. I did cry a little. The painting was a replica of the embroidery hanging in the sitting room, its colours as pure and bright as those Sophia had sewn. The child's dress, her skin, her hair, all the same. It was her gaze that was very slightly different, though it might have been what I wanted to see. Something, though, made me sure it wasn't. Her eyes radiated contentment now, no longer questing, no longer demanding. I had done what she wanted.

Gil carried the portrait into the sitting room and held it up beside its sister embroidery. The two shimmered with an almost unworldly glow.

'They belong together,' I said, wiping away another burst of tears. 'Look, I think I can read a title. It's written very small, but it's to the left of the Wayland signature.' I peered intently into the picture. 'What do you think that word is, Gil? Does it look like Rowena?'

It was his turn to peer. 'Rowena it is,' he confirmed.

'A beautiful name for a beautiful child.'

Das had followed us into the sitting room. 'Gil tells me the painting is valuable. I know the Pre-Raphaelites are very popular – at auction they fetch large sums of money.'

'The painting has a connection to the group, certainly,' Gil said, 'but I reckon it will be its rarity value that will make the money. Art historians know of very few Waylands.' His face gave nothing away.

'You must sell it then, Megan. You could make much money.'

'It's not mine to sell. It's yours, Das. It was found on your property.'

'Finders keepers, isn't that the English saying? And you could do a lot of things with the cash.' He nodded at me meaningfully. 'Anyway, what do I want with two pictures exactly the same?'

'I couldn't take it.' I was adamant. I couldn't take what

was legally his, nor could I sell the painting. I wasn't sure which option felt worst.

'There might be a solution.' Gil's calm voice broke the stalemate. 'The gallery still has the money we raised to purchase the Jepson. I've been searching for a painting to replace it, and this ticks every box. Why shouldn't I use those funds to buy a newly discovered Wayland? We could give the work pride of place, alongside the one we already own. Its rarity would be sure to bring in the visitors, build a new audience perhaps. *And* it would stay in Hastings.'

Trust Gil to get it right: Das would get his money, and Hastings would keep the portrait. But Das wasn't going to let the matter go. 'I know the gallery has a very big sum for its new purchase – Lucy has told me. But Deepna has also told me things.' He walked up to me and took my hands in his. 'Forgive me if this is rude, Megan, but you are in a bad situation, I think. You have lost your business and your home. It is right you have the money. It is the perfect solution.'

'The perfect solution would be for Megan to move in with me – permanently.' Gil's comment was wholly unexpected and stunned his audience. Lucy was the first to gather her wits.

'A proposal,' she crowed.

'Don't rush the girl.' Her brother was smiling across the room at me. 'One thing at a time.'

Chapter Thirty-Four

After Lucy and Das had returned to the shop and Rose hurried off to catch her train to Rye, we sat down together on the old velvet couch.

'I'm sorry I jumped the gun back there,' Gil said. 'The last thing I want to do is hustle you. You've a lot of decisions to make, and you'll need time.'

I'd already made the most important one, I knew, but I kissed him on the cheek, grateful for his understanding.

'Perhaps the first thing to decide is what to do with the painting. I'm not sure you've realised quite how much it's worth. I'll have to get it independently valued, but I'm fairly sure the entire Jepson fund will be needed. If you did decide to accept a share of the money, you'd be able to buy a new shop – a Palette and Paint for Hastings – or simply take the money and run. Back to London.'

'I'm staying here. I decided that weeks ago, even before I knew the worst Julia could do.'

'I suppose she hasn't been in touch?'

'I've heard nothing. But I have finally got my act together and instructed the solicitors to find an agent. Between them they can arrange the sale of the business and negotiate with the mortgage company. If there's any money left when everything's done, she'll get her half – minus what she stole. That's if she ever dares return home. Best of all, I need never have contact with her again – it's amazing how good that feels – and after all those years of being in awe of her, of wanting, of needing her friendship.'

'Does that mean she's forgiven?'

I pulled a face. 'I suppose you could say so, though forgiveness sounds as though she matters to me and she doesn't. This is what matters.' I pointed to the canvas resting on the sitting room table. 'I've uncovered a secret I knew was there all the time. And brought a beautiful image out of darkness. It was a wonderful idea of yours to buy it for the Driftwood.'

'It makes sense. The only difficulty I can see is that the painting will be viewed as a Spencer Wayland and that's something you won't like.'

'No, I won't, but I can't see a way out of it. We can't prove that Sophia was the artist. All we have is my testimony, the testimony of a crazy woman!'

'Not so crazy, as it turns out. You found the painting.'

'But who will believe me? You didn't when I told you where it was hidden.'

He fixed me with those greeny grey eyes, his expression troubled. 'It's not true to say I didn't believe you. I believed what you had seen in the dream. What I found difficult was believing the dream was reality, though in retrospect I don't know why. Everything else you've seen has happened.'

'I thought you'd dismissed what I told you – thought it a nonsense. You wouldn't talk about that night and it hurt.'

'I'm sorry, Megan, but I honestly thought it was your reaction to knowing the worst about Sophia, and I didn't want you even more upset. If you'd had Das knock that wall down and found nothing, think how devastated you'd have been.'

Rose knew her son, it seemed; it was precisely what she'd suggested. I cuddled a little closer. 'Okay, you're forgiven.'

'I should earn my forgiveness.' He dropped a light kiss on the top of my head. 'I'm thinking of trying to prove it was Sophia who painted the Wayland pictures. I can dig around, do more research. These days the gallery runs like clockwork and I could spare a few hours. I'm sure if I worked hard enough, I could find evidence that at the time Sophia was painting, Spencer was in London or elsewhere and living the high life. In which case, he couldn't possibly have devoted the necessary time. And if I could turn up any work he actually finished, I could draw a comparison between their styles. It might be worth a punt.'

'More than anyone I want to see Sophia properly valued, but it would be an enormous undertaking.'

'It would take time, sure, but think how my stock would rise when I published my ground-breaking research in *Art History*.' He gave me the familiar half smile. 'I could laud it over academia and enjoy every minute.'

'It would be amazing if you could rehabilitate Sophia, but for the moment it's enough to have her close. She'll be only half a mile away.'

'It's a happy thought. And I've something here that should keep you feeling happy.' He pulled a folded sheet of paper from his pocket and placed it in my hands. 'See, I've already started researching.'

It was a photocopy of another newspaper cutting, this time a blurred photograph.

'What do you think?' I wasn't sure what I was supposed to think.

'Look really closely.'

I did as he instructed. It was the image of a young woman and there was the faintest familiarity about her face. When I still looked puzzled, he gestured towards the wall opposite. Towards the embroidery.

'Well?'

I gasped. 'It can't be.' I looked again. It might be. There was a definite similarity.

'But who is she? The woman in the photograph?'

'Her name is Rowena Fairchild. She was a much admired artist in the latter part of the nineteenth century. The accompanying article heaps praise on her.'

'Rowena.' I rolled the sound on my tongue. 'The name on the painting.'

'And the name of Sophia Wayland's mother, too. I managed to check that.'

'So this Rowena could be her granddaughter? Could be Sophia's daughter – if the artist chose to use her mother's family name rather than her father's.'

'As no doubt she did. Yes, the photograph could well be of Sophia's daughter, but we'll never know for sure.'

'But if it were, then she didn't end in the workhouse as we feared.'

'Let's believe that.'

I twisted in my seat and flung my arms around his neck. 'Gil, you are the most amazing person.'

'I like to think so.'

I kissed him long and hard and he was about to roll me off the sofa on to the floor, when he stopped. 'I wonder… have you given any thought to moving in with me?'

'I have. And it's a yes.'

In the past few days, we had come close to drifting apart and I was overjoyed it hadn't happened. Rose had been right again when she had called it a small squabble. There would be times ahead when I'd feel vulnerable and hurt – my past made sure of that – but Gil wasn't without his uncertainties either. I'd never told him truly how I felt and I needed to.

'I love you, Gil,' I said, 'and I can't wait to share your life, so…' He raised his eyebrows and waited. 'How about this proposal?'

'It's on its way. There's something we should talk about first.'

'More important than a proposal?' I teased

'Not that. But still important.'

I disentangled myself and sat back on the couch. 'What?' I wasn't sure I liked the sound of this something.

'Your mother. I'd like to meet her and maybe clear the air a little. Not if you're totally opposed, of course. I know the way she kept you from your father hurts deeply, and probably always will. And then there's the whole business of your accident. It will be difficult to build bridges, but I'd like it if we could try.'

I gave a long sigh. Ruth Lacey had come between us before, and now she was doing it again. A long time ago, I'd accepted my father was lost to me and there seemed little point in continuing to grieve, but the accident…

'I will admit my hand is doing much better these days.' I stretched out my fingers, and whether or not it was an optical illusion they looked straighter than they had for years. 'I'm beginning to think in time I'll be able to paint almost normally. I've no idea why – it must be the Hastings effect.'

He took my right hand in his and kissed the fingers, one by one. 'So what do you think – about your mother?'

I sighed again. 'I've been trying to think positively.

296

Knowing Rose has helped a little.'

'Maybe we could go up to London for the day and call on her. For an hour, no more.'

He was trying so hard to make it work I knew I had to do the same. 'I may have a better idea. I've been thinking… once I'm settled, I might invite her down to take a look at the town.' I said it as airily as I could.

'That's a great idea.' His voice was as casual as mine. 'And you never know, if you find the right shop, she could be helpful – she's seen you build a business before.'

Having my mother back in my life wouldn't be easy, but not having her wasn't easy either. There was a small hope in me that over the years she might have mellowed, and a stronger hope that I'd be more able now to deal with her moods.

I knew I'd have to take it slowly, very gradually get used to the idea, but I knew, too, that I had to try. These last few months had taught me a tough lesson. I'd been betrayed – once again – this time by Dan and even more so, by Julia. Betrayal seemed an inevitable part of human life, but it was not one to determine my future. What mattered was how I dealt with it, and forgiveness was the key. I had forgiven Dan and in a way I'd forgiven Julia. Now it was Ruth's turn.

'My mother might be useful,' I agreed. 'And it would be fun to plan a new shop with Deepna as manager – as long as she'd be willing to move to Hastings and I think she would. But Das must have a share of the spoils, otherwise I can't accept the money.'

'There will be enough for you both, I promise.'

A different future was unfolding and it looked good. So good it couldn't come quickly enough. 'I want to see my new home, Gil.' I hadn't realised the words were already in my heart before I spoke them.

'Now?' His grasp on my hand tightened

'Now. No hustling required.'

'And we're making it permanent?'

'I shall expect to be an honest woman within the year.'

'Nothing easier! Now shush.' And beneath the interested gaze of Sophia's daughter, he kissed me into silence.

Chapter Thirty-Five

Lewes, Sussex, October 1859

Rowena Fairchild held the young girl's hand in a tight grasp. They stood at the bottom of a steep incline, looking upwards at two immense square towers, granite-faced and crenellated, as though part of a mediaeval fortress, as in some ways they were. Pairs of arched windows, barred and grilled, punctured forbidding walls to form a symmetrical pattern, the windows growing smaller and narrower with each ascending floor, until at the very top of the building only the smallest sliver of light would be visible to its unfortunate inmates.

A double door made of sturdy oak and dividing the towers was equally immense, the summit of its arch almost delicately latticed but its central panels brutish and blank, staring grimly out into the world. The eyes of the elderly woman were fixed unwaveringly on the door.

'Will Mama come through there?' The small girl raised a trusting face and pointed ahead.

'She will, my dear. Now smooth the creases from your dress – you must look your very best. Don't forget that today is the first time your mother will see you.'

The child took a while before she replied, twisting her hand this way and that in the woman's clasp. 'It's not really the first time though, is it, grandmama?'

'No, not really. But the last time Mama saw you, you were in baby clothes. She will love the pretty dress you are wearing.'

The girl looked down at her skirt and smoothed its blue silk, then adjusted the silver butterfly brooch on the frilled bodice. Satisfied with her arrangements, she began to question again.

'When will I see her? When will she come?'

'I cannot tell you, child. We must be patient.'

'But the hansom might go without us.' The small figure began jigging up and down.

'Be still, Rowena. There is no need for you to worry. I have paid the driver to stay for as long as necessary. He will wait by the roadside for us. Now have you the picture to give Mama?'

With her free hand, the child waved a large sheet of thick paper. 'I have it here, but I think I may have creased it a little. Like my skirt.' Her beautiful eyes clouded for a moment.

'It is unimportant. Your mother will love that you have drawn it for her.'

But the child's eyes remained shadowed and she shuffled her feet in the chalky ground, sending up clouds of white dust. 'Do you really think she will know me?'

Rowena Fairchild looked down at her granddaughter and caressed the auburn hair that flowed loosely onto the girl's shoulders. 'She will know you, my darling, she would know you anywhere. Have I not told you she embroidered your image at the very age you are now?'

'I know you told me, but how could she do that? She couldn't know what I would look like. She has not seen me since I came to live with you, since grandfather died.'

'That is where you are wrong, my dear.' Her grandmother glanced down at the rosebud mouth, the creamy complexion and the dreamy blue, grey eyes. 'She knew just what you would look like. Now hush, the gates are opening.'

Together they stared at the wooden barricade slowly swinging open to reveal a cobbled courtyard within, hedged on every side by tall, granite walls. An old man, bent by age and dressed in tattered black, was silhouetted in the doorway. He heaved a bag onto his shoulders and limped towards them, passing by without a glance in their direction. Then a younger man, jaunty and unrepentant, seemingly without a worldly good to his name, whistled his way towards the road below.

The child looked up at her grandmother seeking reassurance, but the woman's eyes never left the open doorway. Together they stood and stared. A minute ticked by, another minute, and then another. Their two figures had stiffened and the child's grip on her grandmother's hand become painful. It appeared that no one else was to be released that day. Would the gates close and they be forced to return without the one they had waited so long to see?

They had almost given up hope when a frail figure emerged between the two huge towers and began, uncertainly at first, to walk towards them.

'Is that Mama?' the child asked, her voice a whisper.

'It is.'

The grandmother stood for a moment, as though hardly daring to believe her daughter stood before her. Then still holding tightly to the child's hand, she walked to meet the

301

stumbling woman.

It seemed to give Sophia courage and she steadied herself. Then, picking up her pace, she fairly flew across the final few yards.

'Rowena! Rowena, my own dear child!' For a moment she could not speak, and her cheeks were wet from tears that fell fast. She reached out a hand to trace the child's cheek, her chin, the dainty ears, then caressed the tumbling hair as though she would never stop.

'And Mama. At last.' She turned to the grey-haired figure still holding the child's hand.

'At last, my dear.' The two women embraced while the younger Rowena jumped up and down, half delighted, half impatient. 'See, Mama, what I have done for you.' She held out the sheet of paper.

Sophia took it in both hands and looked long. 'But this is beautiful, my darling. You have drawn yourself. Another portrait of my dream child, and so true to life.'

'Grandmama says you made the same painting. Where is it, Mama? Do you have it still?

Sophia's hands shook. She thought of Hastings, of that hidden canvas, the floorboards, the stairs, and blenched. She must not think of it. It had gone for ever.

'It is in its secret hiding place,' she managed.

'Can we find it?' the child asked eagerly.

'No, my darling. We will leave it for someone else to find.'

'And they will, I am sure,' her mother said quickly. 'This,' and she pointed to the younger Rowena's artwork, 'will be the final portrait.'

Sophia smiled. 'There will be no need for others. I have my child with me, now and for ever.'

She felt her heart soar and the years of sadness dissolve.

It was over, and these two beloved people were her reward: the child she cared for more than breath itself and her mother, her dear, kind mother, whose love had been every bit as strong as her own.

She held the picture at a distance and looked again. 'How talented she is, Mama.'

The older woman nodded, but there was a wistfulness to her expression. 'Her drawing master tells me she has an amazing skill and, with the right teaching, will go far. I have done my best, but he is expensive and I have been able to afford only the minimum of lessons. But even with meagre instruction, you can see that one day she will be an artist.'

'She must have more than meagre instruction.'

'But it will take money.'

'I will find the money, Mama, I promise. I am a free woman now and my life is my own. I will work as hard as I am able. I will sew, I will embroider.' For so long, she had planned this new world, and her determination to succeed had grown fiercer with every year. 'Together, we will make sure our child is safe, that her future is hers and hers alone.'

'It is what I hoped for you.' Rowena Fairchild could not keep the sadness from her voice.

Sophia reached out and hugged her mother close. 'I am so very sorry for all you have suffered.' How could she ever atone? Sorry did not erase the years and it broke her heart to think of the pain her mother had endured. 'I was a foolhardy girl, refusing your advice, bringing disgrace on the family.' She rested her face against the soft creases of her mother's cheek.

'Hush, Sophia. The disgrace is not yours. Your fault was to be young and heedless, no more. And if I have suffered, you have suffered far more.'

'You believe me innocent of the charge against me?'

'My dear, how could I believe otherwise?' Her mother lowered her voice, looking sideways at the child who had wandered over to a rare patch of grass and was picking a small posy of wild flowers. 'Your husband did not love you as he should. He was a selfish and greedy man. But how could it be otherwise with such an upbringing?'

She could feel the anger that still haunted her mother and wanted it gone. 'He is dead, Mama, and it is all in the past. The future will be different. This time, I will make it right – for you and for my girl.'

'Rowena, come here,' she called, and when the child came running, she gathered the three of them into a family embrace. Then with a small laugh, she asked, 'Are we to walk to Brighton?'

'Grandmama has ordered a hansom cab,' the child said grandly. 'Especially for you.'

'How honoured I am! Then we must make sure to enjoy our ride together.'

Out of nowhere a loud clang filled the air, reverberating through every stone and wall and tower, and rippling slowly towards the road below. The prison gates had swung shut. At the sound, the small trio turned for an instant but then, without another glance, joined hands and together walked towards the waiting cab.

Before you go ...

I hope you enjoyed reading *House of Lies*. If so, I'd love it if you could leave a review on your favourite site. Authors rely on good reviews – even just a few words – and readers depend on them to find interesting books to read.

If you'd like a sneak preview of another timeslip novel, *House of Glass*, just flip to the next page for a taster.

In the meantime, Happy Reading!

House of Glass

Appearances don't always reveal the truth. Grace Latimer knows that better than most. A troubled past has trapped her in illusions of commitment and comfort – until Nick Heysham charms his way into her world. Commissioned to recover a prestigious architect's missing designs for the Great Exhibition, he persuades her to assist in his research.

The mystery of the Crystal Palace seduces Grace, and once she discovers clues about a forbidden Victorian love affair, she is lured into the deep secrets of the past… secrets that resemble her own.

As Grace digs into the elusive architect's untold story, the ghosts of guilt and forbidden passion slip free. And history is bound to repeat itself, unless Grace finds the courage to break through the glass …

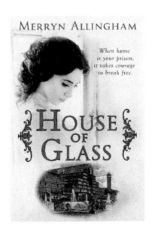

Chapter One

'Grace Latimer?' The voice was a little too energetic for this early in the morning. I held the receiver at a distance and took a gulp of strong coffee. 'Speaking.'

'Hi! This is Nick Heysham. You probably don't remember me.' There was a pause while I struggled to recall the name. 'We met last month at the Papillon — at the Gorski retrospective.'

Another pause, and then he added, 'I gate-crashed.'

A vision of a startlingly yellow shirt and suede trousers swam to mind. The trousers had clearly seen better days. He had come alone, I remembered, and was evidently not part of any of the noisy groups sipping their champagne. I'd suspected then that he hadn't been invited — for one thing, he'd been far more interested in the paintings than the people.

'Yes, I remember you.' I was cautious. 'How did you get my number?'

'A little amateur sleuthing.'

It wouldn't be that difficult; the staff at the gallery would be unsuspicious. Most of them existed in worlds of their own. They would have given my number to the Yorkshire Ripper if he'd called.

'How can I help?' I tried to keep my voice polite while hoping he'd called me in error. I had a mountain of work and this was a conversation I didn't need.

There was a deep intake of breath at the other end of the line. 'It's like this… I've been asked to do a project, a research job, and I've run into problems. I think you'd be able to sort it for me.'

'And why would that be?'

I could hear frost feathering my voice. A man, who gate-crashed Oliver's party and spoke to me for all of ten seconds, seemed now to be expecting I'd ride to his rescue.

'You're a pretty impressive woman, Grace, amazing qualifications and so on. In historical research — and that's what I need.' He sounded pleased he'd explained everything to my satisfaction.

'So can I be clear, Mr Heysham? You want me to do the research that you will then get paid for?'

'Nick. And it's not exactly like that.' He sounded sheepish. 'The job is paying very little as it is — but I can buy you a drink.'

'I believe I can do that for myself, but thank you for the kind thought.'

'I thought you might be interested. It's the Great Exhibition.'

'What about the Great Exhibition?' I knew I should put the phone down, but I couldn't prevent a small surge of interest. More than a small surge since I had written extensively on the subject. Before, that is, I settled for an easier life.

'Missing plans,' he said hopefully. 'Lucas Royde?'

Royde, I knew, had been the darling of Victorian architecture, but I'd never before heard of his connection to the

Great Exhibition.

'Can you be more precise?'

'Royde is supposed to have designed some kind of pavilion for the Exhibition, his very first commission, but I haven't been able to track the plans down. I was hoping you might know something.'

I didn't, but his words had got me thinking. Was there really anything in this, or was I just willing there to be? I was debating with myself whether or not I should simply bid Nick Heysham farewell when he seized on my silence.

'Can we meet? There's a wine bar just around from the Papillon.'

'I'm in Hampstead, not Hoxton.' That was something I shouldn't have divulged. I could have him knocking on my door in the time it took to hop on a Northern line train.

'Not today then. But tomorrow perhaps?'

My sigh was audible. 'I'm at the gallery tomorrow. I can give you a few minutes after work.' The faintest hint of a mystery was sufficient, it seemed, to ensure my surrender. My life must be more of a wasteland than I'd realised.

'Early evening?'

'Six o'clock at the wine bar.' I was unusually brusque, but I doubted it would have any effect, and it didn't.

'Great. Thanks, Grace. See you there.'

'Dr Latimer —' I began, but the phone went dead.

I sat holding the receiver for some time. Nick Heysham might be perfectly harmless, a little eccentric perhaps and overly enthusiastic. On the other hand, he might be a clever manipulator and turn out to be the stalker from hell. I shouldn't have agreed to meet him. Perhaps I should run it by Oliver first. No, I wouldn't do that. Too much of my life was already run by Oliver.

The sudden thought had me feeling guilty. I was grateful to Oliver. He had been immensely generous, kind, too, but over time I'd discovered he was a man who liked to control — events, people — and it had begun to grate. The phone call had come out of nowhere, and that was probably its appeal. That and the smallest possibility of uncovering something new. The researcher in me had risen to the bait and a small voice had whispered that, even at this late stage, I might take the art world by storm. If nothing else, finding a missing piece of Victorian art might help to bolster my spirits. They were worryingly dismal these days, and they shouldn't be. For the first time in my life I had security and the love of a good man. That should be enough, and yet somehow it wasn't.

I turned back to the papers on my desk and the letter from Marigold Carmichael surfaced from the pile where I'd hidden it two days ago. There was no escape from the latest in a long line of complaints from this most demanding of clients. It seemed Mrs Carmichael had become newly enraged by my suggestion that the 'original features' of White Heather Cottage had been added some time in the 1950s. Naturally she was gathering expert opinion to disprove my theory.

No wonder I felt low. It wasn't just Marigold Carmichael and her ilk, it was the work itself. What kind of a job was it researching the history of other people's houses, most of them vastly uninteresting except to their owners? No kind of job was the answer. Not, at least, for a woman facing the watershed of thirty. A stop-gap, a dead end, until the next foreign buying trip, the next gallery event, when for a short time I would blossom at the head of Professor Oliver Brooke's entourage. I wasn't sure how I had walked into this life. I used to have plans, ambitious plans, but then Oliver had come along and somehow they had been put on hold. I hadn't struggled. After years of turmoil, I had settled for an easier life, a simple life. But simple had gradually metamorphosed into dreary, and I had only myself to blame.

Chapter Two

By ten minutes past six the following evening, Nick Heysham had not made an appearance. The wine bar was humming, excited chatter almost drowning the wail from the stereo system. I was hoping that none of the Papillon staff would decide they needed a drink before they left for home, but just in case I'd found a seat in one of the bar's darker enclaves. I'd spent a frustrating afternoon at the gallery and had no wish to encounter any of Oliver's colleagues again. I'm sure they saw me as an interloper whose visits interrupted their pleasant routines. I was still trying to tidy up paperwork from the Gorski show, but getting their co-operation was painful and I'd managed to do almost nothing.

I craned my neck around a gargantuan palm that obscured my view of the door, but there was still no sign of Nick. Five more minutes, I thought, then time is up and I can leave with a clear conscience. I should never have agreed to meet him, but when he phoned I'd been working against a deadline and wanted to lose him as quickly as possible. If I were honest, though, I'd only said yes because for an instant an implausible search had sent a ripple of colour through my life. And it was implausible: what possible excitement could the Great Exhibition provide? It was a terrain that had been so thoroughly sifted by generations of researchers that it was now barren. I gathered up my bag and took my coat from the nearby rack.

'Sorry I'm late.' Nick Heysham emerged from behind the palm, breathing heavily. 'I lost a wheel on the corner of Gosset Street.'

'Lost a wheel! Your car lost its wheel?'

'Bike. Remember I work for a pittance.'

'What's happened to the bike?'

'I abandoned it. It has no one to blame but itself. The brakes have been faulty for weeks, but losing the wheel was the last straw.'

His nonchalance in the face of potential death made me blink, but he appeared wholly unperturbed. He was dressed in frayed jeans and a tee shirt that proclaimed Same Shirt, Different Day. At least it looked clean. He glanced briefly at my empty glass and ordered two large glasses of white wine. I was about to quarrel with this high-handed behaviour when I took a sip. It was surprisingly mellow. He might be short of money, very short by the look of him, but somewhere in the past he had acquired a knowledge of good wine.

'Thanks for coming.' He smiled engagingly and I found myself drawn into studying his face.

He was eminently paintable. A strong jawline, dark hair and very blue eyes. He could have sat for a study of any Romantic poet, except for the expression. That was as far from soulful as you could get.

'Thanks for coming,' he repeated, and I realised just how hard I'd been staring. I flushed with annoyance.

'I've only got half an hour — you better fill me in on

313

details.' It wasn't like me to sound so ungracious.

He grinned, rightly gauging my embarrassment. 'I take it you've heard of Lucas Royde?'

'Of course I've heard of him. He was probably the most influential of all Victorian architects.'

'Right, well this is the thing. The Royde Society is putting on a celebration to mark the centenary of his death. They want to do a life-size mock-up of one of his designs and use that as the venue.'

'So where's the problem?'

'They've decided to focus on Royde's beginning rather than his final years. So the design has to be his earliest project — that's the problem.'

'I can't see why. It must be well documented. You said something about a pavilion for the Great Exhibition, but I think you'll find it was a chapel — 1852?'

'Hey, you're pretty good.' He smiled his approval. 'Royde designed an Italianate chapel for the Earl of Carlyon.'

'A very individual take on an Italianate chapel,' I corrected him, recalling shreds of my past studies. 'His design got rave reviews and was copied any number of times over the next few years.'

'Really?'

'Forgive me, Mr Heysham.'

'Nick.'

'Forgive me, Nick,' I steepled my fingertips together in deliberation, 'but you seem to have only the haziest idea about Royde. Why would the Royde Society ask you to research his plans?'

He looked a little self-conscious. 'My sister works in events management. They asked her to come up with the goods. And she asked me.'

'Your sister? So this job…'

'Pure nepotism, I'm afraid. But I need the money. And I *am* a freelance writer with plenty of research under my belt. Lucy thought I could manage it. I thought so, too, but it turns out I can't. And that's a shame — I've just about got through the nice, fat cheque from *Art Matters* and I'm almost penniless.'

'What were you doing for *Art Matters*?' I found it difficult to imagine the man, who sat opposite me, writing with any sensitivity on art.

'I did a series of profiles on significant Eastern European artists. Gorski was the last.'

'Hence the gate-crashing.'

'Sorry about that.' He didn't sound too sorry. 'I needed to see his paintings before they went on general display. It worked, too. The magazine paid me well, but now their bounty is gone.' His tone was mournful, but almost immediately he recovered his bounce. 'That's where you come in.'

'Me?'

'Yes, I need to find those plans for the pavilion — if they exist.'

'The Victoria and Albert has the archive for the 1851 Exhibition and probably the Royde papers, too.'

'So I gathered from the net, but not all of them, it seems. That's the difficulty. They have the stuff on the Carlyon chapel, but nothing earlier.'

'Are you certain there was anything earlier?'

'The Society is convinced there was. They reckon Royde spent a couple of years in Italy, Lombardy I think it was then, came back to England around 1850 and then got involved in some way with the Great Exhibition. They imagine he was engaged to design one of the hundreds of display spaces.

But I can't find a trace.'

'So what do you want from me?'

'Could you discover whether there's anything earlier than 1852? You've probably got a lot more sources available than I can tap into.'

He exuded a confidence I didn't feel. I sipped my wine slowly while I thought it over. Did I really want to get involved? All I could do was conduct the same search in which Nick had already failed. It was unlikely to yield a different result, although it was possible a specialist's eye might alight on something he'd missed. I knew I was probably fooling myself, but even so I couldn't prevent a slight frisson of anticipation.

'I don't have other sources, as you call them, but I'm willing to look through the papers at the V and A. There may be something you've overlooked, although it's doubtful.'

His face smiled pure pleasure. 'You're a pal,' he said breezily. 'And if you do come up with anything, I'll stand you another drink.'

'That goes without saying.'

And for the first time I allowed myself to smile back at him. I could see he was momentarily stunned by the difference. I've been told I look ten years younger when I smile and a great deal more fun. And my eyes, which often seem misty and indeterminate, become an electrifying green. I watched his stupefaction with some amusement.

'How long have you been a freelance writer?' I asked. It was time to lighten the atmosphere.

'Too long!'

My eyebrows must have risen and his voice became defensive. 'Four years, maybe a bit more. I've never had what you'd call a 'proper' job.'

'Nor me,' I confessed.

'How come? You look pretty well set up.'

'Looks can be deceptive. I spent years as a student and now I fritter my time away investigating the history, if there is any, behind people's houses. It's mostly a vanity project for them — and for me, I guess.'

'But what about the gallery? Don't you work there?'

'Odds and ends when I'm needed. My main role is hostess at events like the Gorski. Oliver Brooke owns and runs the gallery. Actually he runs three galleries, the one here in London, one in Bristol and one he's just opened in Newcastle.'

'Busy man.'

'Successful man.'

'So why, if it's not an indelicate question, aren't you involved in running any of these galleries multiplying across the face of England?'

I took my time to answer. 'Oliver prefers me to take a background role. I manage my own small business, but I need to be on hand to accompany him on buying trips or trade fairs, new exhibitions, that kind of thing.'

Nick finished his wine before he said flatly, 'He's your partner.'

'Yes, he's my partner.' My response didn't sound hugely enthusiastic even to my ears, and he was encouraged to probe.

'How did you meet?'

'Oliver visited my uni when I was an undergraduate. He gave a lecture on gallery management. I got talking to him afterwards and the upshot was that he took me on for work experience at the Papillon during the summer. He even paid me.'

'Generous!'

'He is very generous.' I was suddenly serious. 'He funded me through my postgraduate studies. I couldn't have made it without him.'

I wished I hadn't told him that. He was a stranger, and here I was spilling personal information all over the place. I tried to change the subject.

'Have you had much published, apart from the series you mentioned?'

'Bits and pieces. It doesn't amount to much.'

I must have frowned because his protest was instant. 'You don't know how difficult it is to get published.'

'That's where you're wrong. I know very well. You must have to take on other jobs— unless you have a wealthy family supporting you.'

'Wealthy family, yes. Supporting me, no. My father washed his hands of me when I refused to follow him into the law.'

'And your sister? She hasn't followed in his footsteps either, it seems.'

'Lucy? No. But that's okay with Dad because she's a girl, would you believe? He set her up in business — events management. Did I mention that?'

I nodded.

'I don't think he ever expected to see a penny of his money back, but amazingly she's turned out to be businesswoman of the decade. My brother is the most successful barrister in his chambers, which leaves me as the family failure.'

'Hardly. *Art Matters* is a prestigious journal. If they thought you were good enough to publish, you should get other offers.'

'That's what I thought, but it hasn't happened. I've been

hanging around on the off chance that some eager editor will get in touch — I've written a corker on art fraud in Romania — but no one's interested. So it will soon be back to waiting tables.'

'And that's presumably why you contacted me?'

'I've worked really hard on the papers from the Exhibition,' he assured me. 'It's not that I want you to do my work for me.'

I allowed myself a slight smile since that was precisely what I did think. In response, he leaned across the table, his body tense. 'I figured that if you looked through the stuff at the V and A and came to the same conclusion, then I'd be justified in telling the Royde Society that earlier plans simply don't exist.'

'And you can happily advise them to use the Carlyon chapel for their nostalgia fest, meanwhile collecting your fee en route?' I finished for him.

'If they do pay out when they get the news — I'm not convinced, these cultural societies are often tightwads. Anyway, if they do pay, I'll stand you dinner.'

'My reward is rising all the time. How can I refuse?' It was a very slight mystery, but any mystery was an event in my present limbo, and there was always a chance I might strike gold. 'I'll have a look through the V and A archive once I've settled Mrs Carmichael,' I found myself saying.

'Who's she?'

'She is my current burden — sorry, client. I'll give you a ring when I know more.'

He got up to go, pulling down the tee shirt that had ridden up to reveal a neatly compact body. 'Thanks, Grace, you're about to save a dying man,' he said, and started off at a sprint.

'Hadn't you better leave me your number? Do you have a card?'

'*Please*. Do I have a card?!'

He grabbed the menu and looked hopefully around for a pen, as if one might materialise out of the air.

'Here.' I handed him my silver ballpoint and he scribbled on the menu. 'And I'll have it back.' He was half way to the door again.

'Sorry, but there's a pawnbroker around the corner,' he joked, and handed me back the pen.

Perhaps not such a joke. Nick Heysham appeared to live on the edge of respectability. Oliver would not approve. He would see him as a liability and wonder why I'd taken it into my head to befriend him. But when I broached the subject over dinner that evening, he seemed relaxed about the idea of my undertaking research for someone I hardly knew and without any likely recompense. His mind was on other things.

'I've an idea to move the Gorski up to Newcastle next month.' He absently stroked the small, spiky beard he'd managed to grow in recent weeks. 'The exhibition worked brilliantly at the Papillon, and we did a good deal of extra business from it.'

'Do you think Gorski is well-known enough in Newcastle?'

It was a foolish thing to say. Oliver was very strong on the notion of 'art for the people.' But at the same time he was good at spotting the next big thing, which is why he lived in a large house in Hampstead and drove a top-of-the-range Mercedes.

'Don't be snobbish, darling. The art world there is

buzzing. Think of the Baltic, the Laing, the Shipley.'

I thought about them while he began to clear the table.

'We might take a trip together.'

'To Newcastle?'

'Yes, of course to Newcastle.' He sounded a trifle impatient at my obtuseness. 'If the exhibition is as successful as I expect, we must celebrate.'

He was loading the dishwasher in a distracted fashion, imperilling some very expensive china. He always performed household chores in a kind of disassociated way, as if they were being done by someone else. He straightened up with the last rattle of cutlery and allowed a smile to lighten his customarily austere expression.

'We could travel on from Newcastle. We haven't had a real holiday for a long time and we'd enjoy a few days in the Highlands.'

I tried to smile back convincingly, but wondered why Oliver always talked about 'we.' He made the decisions and I went along with them. It was feeble and a small part of me felt ashamed at taking this road, but the past was still writ large in my mind, and that was my excuse.

As it seemed I would shortly be hoisted northwards, I decided I should make a start on Nick's research as soon as possible. I knew for a fact there were volumes of papers involved in the Great Exhibition, and they would all need to be checked. Once Mrs Carmichael was placated. And she would be. Tomorrow.

Other books by Merryn Allingham:

The Buttonmaker's Daughter (2017)
The Secret of Summerhayes (2017)

The Girl from Cobb Street (2015)
The Nurse's War (2015)
Daisy's Long Road Home (2015)

About The Author

Merryn Allingham was born into an army family and spent her childhood moving around the UK and abroad. Unsurprisingly it gave her itchy feet, and in her twenties she escaped an unloved secretarial career to work as cabin crew and see the world. The arrival of marriage, children and cats meant a more settled life in the south of England, where she's lived ever since. It also gave her the opportunity to go back to 'school' and eventually teach at university.

Merryn has always loved books that bring the past to life , so when she began writing herself the novels had to be historical. She finds the nineteenth and early twentieth centuries fascinating to research and has written extensively on these periods in the Daisy's War trilogy and the Summerhayes novels.

House of Lies and its companion volume, *House of Glass*, move between the modern day and the mid-Victorian era.

For more information on Merryn and her books visit http://www.merrynallingham.com/

You'll find regular news and updates on Merryn's Facebook page:
https://www.facebook.com/MerrynWrites
and you can keep in touch with her on Twitter
@MerrynWrites

Sign up for her newsletter at www.merrynallingham.com and receive *Through a Dark Glass*, a FREE volume of short stories.

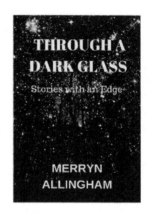

Printed in Great Britain
by Amazon